VENUS

NICOLE MELLO

DEDICATION

I would like to dedicate this book to my parents, who taught me how to read and write and who believed in me from birth; to my friends, who have supported me on my journey to publishing; and to Backpack Digital, without whom none of this would have been possible.

CONTENTS

ACKNOWLEDGMENTS

My special acknowledgements go out to my father, first and foremost, who had me reading and writing as soon as I could conceivably manage it, and encouraged me every step of the way. Next, my mother, who always reminded me it was most important to be happy with myself, and everything else came second. To my partner, Renan, who has pushed me through this entire process and served as an amazing editor. To my best friend, Sarah, who is one of the greatest people of my life and without whom this book never would have existed. And, lastly, to Hayden, who believed in me when he had no reason to and is the reason this book exists.

Chapter One

Juliet Alva had lived in Big Bay, Michigan since the day she was born until that very January when she decided to change everything. She attended Redbreast State University, briefly, for her bachelor's degree, but that had been the furthest outside of her northern town she had ever gone. She liked to think she had bigger aspirations, dreams that could only flourish outside of Big Bay - but, when one hit twenty-four years old and one had never left their home state before, one began to wonder about their own aspirations and dreams.

Juliet - from a family of two brothers, two parents, and herself - attended the same school system from the age of four, had held three jobs total (a high school job, a college job, and a post-college job, none of which were in her field), and had never seen the ocean. She was still learning what it meant to be her. She barely knew what anyone else was meant to be, let alone herself. She was afraid that, maybe, there was nothing out there for her.

Juliet was also going to be late for work if she kept laying in bed, holding the covers tight over her head, wishing she were anyplace else but home.

"Yo, Jules, are you gonna go to work, or what?" Lorenzo shouted through the door after pounding on it with his fist. Juliet groaned and threw her pillow to the floor.

"I'm almost ready," she called back, and she heard a sigh before her brother's footsteps retreated down the hallway. She hauled herself up out of bed, dragged herself into her work uniform, tied on her shoes as tightly as her tired fingers could manage, and, somewhat

3

triumphantly, left her bedroom. When she got to the bottom of the stairs, Lorenzo was nowhere to be seen, but the clattering of dishes in the kitchen suggested he had found something else to do besides bother his sister. Angelo was stretched out on his back on the living room floor, playing some sort of game on his phone, which he held high above his head.

"If you don't leave soon, you're going to be late," her father said, coming around the corner. Abraham Alva, partial to 'Abe' from his friends but more partial to 'Dad' when it came from his kids, never called Juliet by her name. "Don't want to lose your job, do you?"

"No, Dad," Juliet answered. He skimmed by without touching her, but doubled back and kissed her cheek before disappearing up the stairs.

"Be nice to your father, he's just looking out for you," her mother called, in the misshapen vowels of her heavy Michigan accent, from the kitchen, presumably where she and Lorenzo were washing and drying dishes, or maybe just throwing them at the ground.

"But I didn't-"

"It was your *tone*," her mother interrupted, an old familiar argument that Juliet had anticipated ending when she was eighteen, but showed no signs of death just yet. Her mother, Beatrice, preferred 'Bea' most of the time, 'Beatrice' some of the time, 'Mom' from her children, and 'Mama' if it suited any of the four of them involved. She appeared in the doorway into the living room. "Don't you have work, Juliet?"

"Yes, Mama," Juliet answered. Bea was more willing to call her by her name, but Juliet could feel the cringe that hid behind it every time. She grabbed her phone and wallet, shoved them in her pockets, and kissed her mother on the cheek before allowing her mother to kiss her back. "I'll see you later, love you."

"I love you, too, sugar," Bea replied before turning back around the corner and disappearing to the linoleum haven of the kitchen. Juliet turned around just as Angelo dropped his phone on his face.

"Good work, idiot," Juliet shot off at him, grinning, and Angelo pulled off his hat and flicked it at her. She tossed it back like a frisbee, and he sat up to catch it, smiling.

"Have a good day at work, Jules," Angelo said, dropping back down to the shag carpet her mother refused to get rid of. Juliet blew him a kiss and left. Her bicycle, slowly dying and probably praying that Juliet might soon put it out of its misery, leaned against the side of the house where she had left it the night before. She hopped on and spun off down the road, a route she had taken a thousand times and had gotten sick of nine-hundred-and-ninety-nine times ago.

Juliet had worked at the Laurens Tavern for two years. Every shift had the same routine - come in, sign off next to your name in the book in Dwight's office, tie on your apron, and find where you need to be. The only other step was to be there until clock-out, which Juliet always was. She had never come late, she had never left early, she had rarely ever missed a shift. She was, she told herself, a fundamentally good worker, and probably a fine person overall.

"Juliet!" Dwight called from his office, and Juliet narrowly avoided colliding with a customer with their head down when she turned to look at him. He motioned to her, and she ducked between tables and snuck behind customers' backs to get to his office door. For the manager of the place, his office was the size of a fairly dinky closet. Probably because Paige - the owner of the bar and a real hardass, not that Juliet would ever say anything, being a fine person and all - had a big office in the back that she refused to share.

"What's up?" Juliet asked, rifling through the pockets of her apron for a washcloth to wipe her hands off on. Dwight jerked his chin in the direction of the front door.

"There's been a girl standing outside the door for a few minutes," he informed her. "Just leaning there. Will you tell her to scram or sit, please? I don't need anyone scaring off customers by spitting at them or something."

"Yeah, sure," Juliet agreed. She stuffed her washcloth back in her apron pocket and weaved through the throngs of customers to the front door. She shivered in the January air; the sun had fallen out of the sky only a couple of minutes ago. The woman almost seemed to be waiting for her, standing in the streetlight outside the restaurant.

"Hey, there," Juliet called, and the woman turned towards her with a slow tilt and turn of her head. Juliet stared at her for a second, at her square jaw, her black hair thrown half-up in a bun, otherwise rolling down her back in waves. The woman grinned lazily at her, cigarette between her full lips, smoke curling upwards from her mouth and around her long nose like it had nothing better to do. She had heavy eyebrows above her dark brown eyes, irises laughing, pupils staring, and dark freckles scattered underneath her eyelashes. Her skin was dark, lighter than Juliet's but shaded like sepia, rich like ochre.

"You gonna invite me in?" the woman asked. Her thick body was shorter than Juliet's, her head coming up to Juliet's shoulder. Juliet beckoned her over, and she came, the mole under her right eye becoming visible the closer she got. Her left ear was pierced several times, Juliet could see, with shining silver studs, a couple of bars, and one glimmering red jewel.

Juliet stammered, a little thrown off. She was a fine person overall. She was fundamentally good. She was a good worker, she did her job well. "You either gotta come in or leave, I'm sorry."

The woman raised an eyebrow at her, looking her up and down, dragging those brown eyes over her from ankle to hairline. "So, that's a yes, then?"

"To what?" Juliet asked, before she could think the question through. Both of the woman's eyebrows raised and she smiled, pulling the cigarette from her mouth.

"Inviting me in," she repeated, leaning in, pulling at Juliet's apron. She snapped at her nametag. "Juliet." Her eyes darted up, still smiling. "You gonna invite me in, Jules? Or am I gonna have to stand out here all night?"

"You can come in," Juliet assured her. "My boss said-"

"I'm sure they did," the woman interrupted. She dropped her cigarette to the dirt and crushed the lit end under her boot heel. She took the door from Juliet and motioned for her to go inside. "After you, Jules."

"It's Juliet," Juliet corrected, but the woman ignored her protest in favor of nudging her through the door. She followed Juliet in, all the way to a table that may have been in Juliet's section, and, really, so what if it was. Nobody cared. Sadie would probably thank her for taking on another customer, since it gave her more time to hide in the handicapped stall in the employee bathroom and read erotica on her phone.

"Like I told you, my name is Juliet," she said, handing over the menu she snagged from the hostess stand on their way by. "Here's your menu. Are you over twenty-one?"

"Would I be at a bar if I wasn't?" she asked. Juliet stopped herself from raising an eyebrow at her and her ratty brown leather jacket, at her psychedelic shirt underneath, at her torn jeans and her choker necklace, at her messy hair and her roguish grin, cocked and at the ready.

"Yes," Juliet answered, and the woman's smile widened a bit, twinkling up into her eyes.

"You're right, I would be," the woman agreed. "But I am over twenty-one. In fact, I'm twenty-three."

"Fantastic." Juliet held out her hand. "ID?"

The woman stared up at her, incredulous, before sighing and digging through her jacket pockets for the battered license she forked over. Juliet scanned it. Daksha Sonali Paracha, originally from New York, had no business being in Big Bay, Michigan, let alone in Laurens' Tavern, let *alone* in Juliet's booth. And she was, it seemed, twenty-three, and had just celebrated her birthday the week before.

"Thank you," Juliet said, passing the license back. Daksha took it with a grin.

"Dax is fine, now that you know my name," Dax informed her. Juliet did not smile or raise an eyebrow at her. She was beautiful; Juliet was a good employee.

"Daksha, let me know what you want to drink and if you want anything to eat," Juliet told her. She shoved her hands in her apron pockets and forced herself to walk away from Dax's table. Diana waved at her from behind the bar, summoning her, three beers lined up and ready to be served, and Juliet was only half-thankful that she had somewhere else to be. She tried to ignore Dax's eyes burning holes in her back while she actually did her job, but it was hard when every time she turned, all she could see was a gorgeous chin in a smooth palm, her elbow on the tabletop, holding her eyes up as she watched her work.

"Are you ready to order?" Juliet asked Dax when she inevitably caved and returned to her table. Dax tipped her head back to look at her, hair spilling over her shoulders and down her back as she moved.

"Do you know why I'm here?" Dax inquired, sounding almost polite. Juliet could tell it was an accident that she did.

"No," Juliet answered. "Of course not."

"Well," Dax said, "if you bring me a beer or two, I'll tell you."

"They're not free."

Dax flashed a grin at her. Her teeth were white enough. "Nothing ever is."

Juliet considered her for a second, then left to get the house tap from Diana. She brought the mug to Dax, who took a long swallow, throat pulled back handsomely, before she leveled a grin at Juliet.

"I'm running," Dax told her, and Juliet frowned.

"Where?" she asked, and Dax shrugged, leaning back in her booth bench.

"I'd say that the question is more 'from what' than 'to where,'" Dax offered in lieu of an answer. She set her mug down and traced the rim with her fingertip. "I'm trying to find aliens."

Juliet hesitated, sure she heard her wrong. "Aliens?"

"Yup," Dax replied, popping on the 'p'. "Aliens. I'm not from around here."

"I saw," Juliet interrupted, and Dax raised an eyebrow at her. Juliet pointed towards her pocket, where her license was resting. "New York."

"Attentive." Dax took a sip from her drink. "I like it. Anyways, no, I'm not from around here. I just came from Sault Ste. Marie. Did you know an Air Force pilot disappeared over Lake Superior? My guess is aliens took him."

"What evidence do you have for that?" Juliet asked, and Dax shrugged. She picked a spot off her jacket and flicked it to the ground.

"I don't," Dax said. "Just something to run to. I know there's something else out there, you know? So, I'm gonna find it. Just boppin' from place to place until I do."

"And what brings you to Big Bay?" Juliet asked. "I don't think we've had any abductions here, to be honest with you."

Dax looked her up and down for a moment before eventually answering, "Dinner brought me here. Does this place have food?"

"Burgers and wings, stuff like that," Juliet told her, and Dax smiled.

"Never been a vegetarian." She picked up her menu again and flipped it over. "Can I have this burger with the fried egg on it? And onion rings?"

"Sure thing," Juliet said. They stared at each other for a second before Juliet remembered herself and stepped back. *Good employee,* she reminded herself. *Be good at your job.* "I'll be right back with that, then."

"If you're quick, I've got more stories where that came from," Dax promised, and Juliet resolutely did not trip over her feet on her way back to Geoffrey in the kitchen. He frowned at her when she gave him the order.

"You didn't take down a slip?" he asked, and Juliet tore her attention away from watching Dax through the kitchen window as she took off her leather jacket. She frowned at him, taking an extra second to process what he had asked of her.

"What? No, sorry." She fumbled in her apron for her notepad and ripped it out, scribbling down the order for Geoff to pin up. "Hey, did you ever hear about an Air Force pilot going missing over Lake Superior?"

"Why the hell would you wanna know about that?" Geoff asked grumpily, more in the direction of his chili than in the direction of Juliet's face. She stuffed her notepad and pen back into her apron, sparing another glance over her shoulder.

"Just curious, I guess," Juliet answered. She checked up on her other tables, bringing a couple checks and refreshing a couple drinks before Geoff called up Dax's order. She tried not to seem too hasty grabbing the basket and bringing it over, but the look on Dax's face when she set it down in front of her told her she may have failed at that.

"So, in Bloomer, Wisconsin, some lady once said these aliens abducted her and made her feel all weird and burned her backyard, right?" Dax began, shoving a handful of onion rings into her mouth and motioning for Juliet to sit down. Juliet glanced over her shoulder; she could see neither Dwight nor Geoff, and Diana was paying her no attention, so she slid into the booth opposite Dax.

"Did you go to her house?" Juliet asked, and Dax snorted, sliding her onion rings into the middle distance between them. Juliet hesitantly took one.

"I went to the woods outside of her house, and I'll be fucked if I wasn't lying there in the dirt and all of a sudden it got cold, right? And there was a mist that came around me, I swear to it. No little grey dudes came and abducted me, but clearly something was going on. It happened three nights in a row." She shoved the burger in her mouth, sesame seeds wriggling loose and dropping down past her wrists. "And before that, I was in Elmwood, at the top of Tuttle Hill, and, hand to God, I saw a UFO. It was bright orange." She swallowed her mouthful. "Shitty paintjob, if you ask me."

Juliet was smart. She was educated. She was also intrigued, and very attracted to the young woman sitting across from her.

"And where are you going next?" Juliet asked. Dax picked up an onion ring and shrugged.

"Wherever the space race takes me," she said, fairly dramatically, waving the onion ring before cramming it into her mouth. "Why?" She chewed, swallowed, raised an eyebrow. "Thinking you might care to join me?"

She said it flirtatiously, tauntingly, and rejecting her obvious joke was on Juliet's lips - but she could hardly bring herself to actually say it. She stared at Dax, thinking it through. If she - well, if they - *Hmm.* She had been looking for a new job and a new place to live, somewhere rather than her family home with her two brothers and her parents. Going to grad school had been an option, but returning to Redbreast State University was not entirely appealing. An unwise patchwork decision to take a major in hospitality, plus one minor in Native American Studies and another in Astronomy, could only take her so far, regardless. Maybe time off could be beneficial. Her advisor had told her a few times to take a year off, when she was done getting her bachelor's, but she never had - jumped straight back into work, never thought of a year off as an option.

Maybe it was something she needed to do, she wondered, still silent as Dax gave up on getting an answer to her (probably rhetorical) question and started eating again, letting Juliet stew in her own head. Maybe she did need that year off; maybe (and it was a big maybe) she should just… *leave.* Just pack up and go. People must do that, right? Just go?

Well. People must. But not people who are fine overall, who are good employees, and good daughters, and good… goodness.

Well… Well.

"You're looking for something?" Juliet asked, eventually. Dax nodded, not looking up from her burger. She licked up a trail of juices and grease that was tracking down her wrist, towards the vibrant silk shirt rolled up to her elbows.

"I saw a UFO when I was a kid," Dax told her, the yolk leaking out of her burger. "I know I did. And I'm gonna find it again."

Well, Juliet thought, they had that in common. Searching for something long-lost from childhood, that was. A sense of purpose; a place to belong. A friend, maybe. Something you believed in, at least, rather than something you have to be told to believe in, or to find purpose in, or to exist as. Feeling suffocated was not conducive to figuring out who one wants to be for the rest of their life. She just wanted air.

Maybe, Juliet thought, what she needed was some space.

"You let me know if you want to tag along, beautiful," Dax told her, wiping her hands on a couple of napkins yanked from the tabletop dispenser. She flipped the menu over and skimmed the prices before tossing a twenty on the table. "Keep the change as a tip. You've earned it."

"That's a six dollar tip," Juliet pointed out, and Dax raised an eyebrow.

"It was an expensive burger," she retorted, picking up the mug and tossing back the foamy dregs of her beer. She slammed the mug back down, boisterous, and winked. "Keep it real, kid. Have a good one."

Dax shrugged her jacket back on and gave Juliet a half-hearted salute before leaving the bar with an attitude that Juliet had only ever really seen in movies, and was either an act or an indicator of an extremely dramatic and possibly excessive attention-seeking personality. She pocketed the twenty and brought it to the register to chime in.

Chapter Two

"Hey, Juliet? Can you focus, please?" Geoff called from the kitchen. Juliet paused, hand on the register, watching Dax's retreating back through the window in the front door. She shut the register and steeled herself.

"You know what?" she said, heart pounding in her chest, hands going numb with fear. "No."

"What'd you say?" Geoff asked. Diana looked around a patron's shoulder to watch them. Juliet gripped the edge of the register for a moment before turning to face Geoff.

"I said no," Juliet repeated, louder this time, louder than ever before. She picked up a stack of menus for something to do with her hands, then instantly regretted it, not sure what to do now. "I am- I am sick of- I just-" Juliet slammed the menus down on the hostess stand next to the register, thankful for both the dramatic effect and being rid of the menus. "I'm leaving!"

"Why?" Dwight asked, appearing in the doorway of his shoebox office. "Did someone say something to you?"

"Yeah," Juliet answered. She glanced back through the door again. "But it wasn't that bad." She looked to Dwight, to Geoff, to Diana. "I'm leaving. I'm not coming back."

"Why-"

"Because what the hell am I going to do with a hospitality degree?" Juliet exploded. Sadie stuck her head out through the bathroom door, looking bewildered. "We don't have hotels. We barely have *motels*. I never moved to Lansing, I never went to grad school. I never did anything and I'm never going to do anything if I don't... If I don't just *do* something!"

"What the hell?" Geoff muttered, and Juliet wished she could slam the menus down again.

"I have to go," she told them, leaving the dropped menus and the surprised customers and the whole of Laurens' Tavern behind her as she burst through the front door and approached the van.

"Wait up!" she called, and Dax looked up from where she was leaning against the side door, fiddling with an ancient flip phone. She raised an eyebrow at her. Juliet was in serious trouble if that tic kept up.

"Did I forget something?" Dax asked, shoving her phone in her pocket and patting herself down, searching for what could be missing. "Did *you* forget something?"

"Yes, yes, I want to come with you," Juliet told her, a little out of breath from her tirade and subsequent jaunt outside. She could feel eyes on her back through the windows of the bar. Not many - she was hardly that interesting - but still a few. "I accept. I care to join you. Let's go."

Dax looked genuinely surprised for a moment, eyes flicking over Juliet's face, seeking out the joke. Finding none there, she looked Juliet up and down. Juliet could see her considering laughing her off, not bringing her along, *oh, what, that was just a joke* somewhere in the back of her mind, somewhere in her mouth. Juliet braced herself for the embarrassment.

"Alright, yeah," is what *actually* came out of Dax's mouth. Juliet's muscles relaxed from their coils in shock.

"Fantastic," Juliet said, without thinking. She and Dax stared at each other. "Can we- Should I get my things?"

"Sure thing, sweetcheeks," Dax answered. "Hop in and we'll-"

"I rode my bike here this morning," Juliet interrupted, turning to point to the rotting bicycle chained pathetically to a pole, as though it were safe there, or even worth stealing. "Can we- Maybe-"

"I'm sure it'll fit in the back of the van," Dax told her, looking over her shoulder at the bicycle.

"Just to my house," Juliet assured her. "I'll leave it for one of my brothers, and I'll take my things, and we can go."

"Go where?" Dax asked, reaching up to tug her bun down and start pulling all of her hair back up, rather than only half of it. Juliet shrugged, heart still pounding, adrenaline coursing, hands trembling.

"Wherever's next," Juliet answered. "Anywhere. Everywhere." She jogged back to her bike, unlocked the chains, and wheeled it back to the beat-up clunker of a van Dax was opening up the back doors of. The old van was wide and long, blue and rusted. The back doors creaked when they opened, and she helped Juliet load the bicycle up on top of a heap of blankets. Juliet stood back as Dax slammed the doors four times to get them to close properly.

"Shall we?" Dax asked, and Juliet almost said yes before she remembered. She held up a finger and ran back to pick up the cigarette butt Dax had flicked into the dirt earlier. She tossed it in the trash can by the door and jogged back to the van. "Seriously?"

"I would've just been thinking about it the whole time if I hadn't," Juliet told her, mostly to make her smile, partly because it was true. Dax did smile, if only until Juliet headed for the driver's side.

"Okay, where the hell do you think you're going now?" Dax asked, moving quickly and protectively to stand in front of the driver's side door.

"You had a drink," Juliet reminded her. "You can't drive like that."

"I've driven like worse," Dax argued, and Juliet put her hands on her hips, hoping she looked authoritative and not like a child with an attitude.

"Not with me," Juliet said, firmly. Dax stared at her, then looked down at the keys dangling from a keyring on her pointer finger. She handed them over with more trepidation than Juliet had ever experienced from another human being.

"Only to your house, and so help you *God* if you hit anything," Dax said through her teeth, a little smile tugging at the corner of her beautiful mouth, and Juliet gingerly accepted the keys.

"So help us both," Juliet agreed, opening the door for herself. Dax sighed heavily enough that it was audible over the door slamming shut, but she retreated to the passenger side. Being seated there, however, did not at all hinder her ability to watch Juliet like a hawk as she fumbled for the ignition, slid the keys home, and threw the van into drive.

"So," Juliet said, after a long beat of silence as they left the parking lot of Laurens' Tavern. Juliet wished, a little vindictively and a lot dramatically, that it would be the last time she ever saw it. "Aliens?"

"Aliens," Dax agreed, leaning back in her seat, still watching Juliet's hands with an impressive amount of focus. "Definitely aliens. I *know* there's something out there. It's just a matter of finding it. It's like one big game of hide-and-seek." Dax took her eyes off of the road for long enough to glance out the window, watching Big Bay flick by.

"Do you usually drive drunk?" Juliet asked, for lack of anything else to say. Dax glanced at her, looking a little annoyed. Juliet resolutely kept her eyes on the road.

"I'm not *drunk*, and, no, I don't," Dax answered. "Don't be so quick to judge. You know, don't judge a book by its cover, and all that junk?"

"I don't judge a book by its cover," Juliet argued. "I'm black. I have enough of it happening to me without worrying about doing it to other people."

"You can still judge and be judged at the same time when you're black," Dax shot back.

"And trans." Juliet glanced at her out of the corner of her eye. Dax looked back, clearly a little surprised. She looked her over again, then leaned back in her seat.

"Like I said," Dax said, a smile playing on her lips, "you can still judge and be judged, you epitome-of-what-old-white-people-think-is-wrong-with-America, you."

Juliet smiled, just a little bit. She tightened her grip on the wheel and kept driving. "I guess that's true. But you'd think I wouldn't."

"Yeah, you'd think," Dax said back, and Juliet thought it just might have been teasing. It felt… weirdly nice, actually. Juliet slowed down in front of her house, and Dax leaned into the window and whistled low. "Nice place."

"On the outside," Juliet answered, parking out front of her house. "It's not so bad. I guess I just…"

"Don't fit in?" Dax offered, when Juliet ran out of words. She nodded, letting the car settle and allowing the engine to start to cool down.

"That's a good way to put it." Juliet stared up at the house and wondered when the next time she was going to see it would be. Surely she would see it again. Surely this was never going to be the *last* time. She still loved her parents, and her brothers, whether she felt she belonged there or not.

"Your shit's not gonna pack itself," Dax eventually said, interrupting the silence. Juliet sighed, softly, only to herself, and had to kick the driver's side door open to get herself out of the van. She pulled her bicycle from the back, waving off Dax's offers to help.

"I'll just be in and out," Juliet told her, more than a little concerned of the excessive reaction whoever was home might have to Dax, who is a virtual stranger, a woman, and who has no sense of boundaries. She hauled the bicycle up the lawn and propped it next to the front door before letting herself in.

"Hey," Lorenzo called from the kitchen. Juliet weaved through the short distance from the front door through to the back of the house and found both her brothers sitting at the kitchen table, two plates of pizza rolls between them.

"You're home early from your shift, aren't you?" Angelo asked, licking sauce and cheese off his thumb. Juliet rocked back on her heels, leaning in the doorway.

"Yeah, kind of." She glanced down at her hands. "I think I'm gonna go on a trip."

"Where the hell to?" Lorenzo demanded, leaning back in his chair. Angelo looked a little less concerned, focused more directly on his pizza rolls, watching his siblings from the corners of his eyes.

"I actually don't really know," Juliet answered, trying to be as honest as possible. She avoided looking at her watch. "I just came to grab some stuff. I'm leaving my bike, so, you can use it while I'm gone, Angelo."

"Thanks, Jules," Angelo said, smiling up at her. "Have a nice trip."

"I don't know when I'll be back," Juliet informed them both. Angelo shrugged with one shoulder; Lorenzo just kept staring at her, brow furrowed. "I'm going with a friend. I'll keep my phone on me. You wanna let Mom and Dad know?"

"Sure thing," Angelo agreed, throwing another pizza roll in his mouth.

"What the hell are you doing, man?" Lorenzo asked, leaning back in his chair and scrubbing at his face with his hands. "Do you even have any money?"

"All I ever do is work and save the money, Lorrie," Juliet reminded him, trying to stay gentle. No need for a blowout before leaving indefinitely, just in case she died in Dax's less-than-capable hands. "I just need to get away for a while. That's all. I'll have my phone, you can call whenever. Just tell Mom and Dad?"

"You can't just ditch Mom and Dad," Lorenzo argued. Angelo rolled his eyes.

"Man, she's twenty-four years old, just let her cut loose and run for a while," Angelo said. "Go for it, Jules. I'll tell Mom and Dad you scooted out for a little while or something. Just keep us posted on where you're at, all right? You know how they get."

"Yeah, I do." Juliet crossed the few steps on the linoleum to kiss the top of Angelo's head, then Lorenzo's, reluctant as he seemed. "I love you guys. I'll call you, okay?"

"Okay, whatever," Lorenzo muttered, grabbing another pizza roll. Juliet took one, and Angelo offered her a wave.

"See you soon, sis," Angelo said cheerfully. She thumbed away the sauce in the corner of his mouth, Angelo playfully shoving her away. "Have a good one."

"You, too," Juliet replied, ducking out of the kitchen before either Lorenzo tried to snag her into staying or Angelo started rambling on with a story that had no definite ending or any route to a climax or a conclusion. She darted up the stairs to her bedroom, a room she could fairly call smaller than Dwight's office but larger than the back of Dax's van. She grabbed two of her duffle bags and packed her hormones, her medications, anything she could think of that she used on a daily basis; then, her favorite choices of clothes, of books, of jewelry - all went in the bags. She took a quick scan of her room, her eyes landing on an old school notebook tucked into her bookshelf.

Juliet ripped a page out of the notebook and a ballpoint pen and scratched out a message to her parents. She explained what she was doing, where she wanted to go, what she wanted to do, why she was doing it at all. She asked them not to get rid of her things; to box them up, if they were going to do anything. She promised to call. She told them she loved them. She pretended her whole family was not going to feel relieved at her absence. She left the torn paper on her bed with the pillows she was leaving behind, hitched up her chosen belongings, and jogged back down the stairs and out the front door to the van.

"Took you long enough, kid," Dax called out to her, leaning against the side of the van by the back door. She popped the doors open when Juliet got close enough. "Jesus. Got enough shit?"

"I'd say this is a conservative amount of shit, thanks," Juliet retorted, tossing it in the back next to what appeared to be Dax's own clothes and belongings. She threw the pillow and blankets she had grabbed down next to some dingier bedding and snagged her car charger from one of her bags.

"Well, fine," Dax mumbled to herself. She kept losing her smile and getting it back, like she was unsure whether or not she was meant to keep it. Juliet thought she looked better with it, but she looked fantastic either way, if she was being honest with herself. "Get in the van, then."

"Where to?" Juliet asked, heading for the driver's seat. Dax grabbed her shoulder.

"Whatever campground's closest to here, because I am not letting you drive my van anymore, and if you're not gonna let me drive I'm just gonna sleep off what you're calling *drunk* and then we'll hit the road in the morning." Dax clapped her shoulder and gave her the keys back. "Sound good, Jules?"

Juliet's fingers closed around the warm metal of the keys. "Yeah. That sounds fine." She looked up at the house she had lived in since birth and waved to Angelo in the front window. He waved back, grinning, Lorenzo drifting by like a ghost behind him. He offered a short wave. Juliet hauled herself up the step into the van, and they were off again, heading for a campground in the next town over, Juliet hoping - possibly in vain - not to be recognized.

"I've got Bank of America," Juliet commented as they pulled in to park. "They're everywhere, right? I just…"

"I really don't think I'm scamming you, man, since you're the one who wanted to come along," Dax said, putting her hands up in a mock-surrender. "I didn't even ask."

"Technically, you *did* ask," Juliet countered, parking the car next to an unassuming-looking camper surrounded by kids, a mom at the grill in the front and a dad laying in the pine needles and dirt while children crawled all over him. "You just expected it to be more rhetorical than it was."

"You're a real stickler for particulars, aren't you, kid?" Dax asked. She turned to her in her seat. "I'd say that once we leave tomorrow there's no going back, but you can really go back any time you want. I'd just say, you know. Be ready to head out. I'm thinking my next stop might be back in Wisconsin. A bunch of people in Merrimac saw UFOs in the late '90s, so I'm thinking there's something to that."

"*Our* next stop," Juliet corrected. Dax did not roll her eyes, but it seemed like she had to try pretty hard not to. Juliet glanced back at the mattress in the back of the van, their pillows side-by-side, their blankets a mess on the old bedspread. "So. Where do I sleep?"

Dax raised an eyebrow, looking between the mattress and Juliet before pointing at the pillows. "Um. There?"

"Don't you sleep there?" Juliet asked. Dax did roll her eyes this time, a Herculean roll that Juliet suspected could have killed her had she suppressed it.

"Do you see a guest bedroom?" Dax retorted, hauling herself up out of her seat and kicking the passenger door open. She leapt from her van and stretched her short body, arms reaching as high above her head as they could, joints popping with sickening cracks. Juliet slipped out her side and slammed the door shut behind her.

"Now what?" Juliet asked, and thought for a moment how that question might apply to the broader range of her life and experiences as they stood right in that moment.

"Now, we do whatever we want," Dax told her. She banged the passenger door shut behind her. "*Right* now, though, I'm gonna go pay for our spot and piss. You stay with the van and I'll be right back."

"Alright," Juliet agreed. She leaned back against the van, watching the kids at the camper next to them chase each other in circles before the smallest one grabbed the largest one by the ankles and tackled them to the ground. She saw them all pile up on that biggest one and smiled. She pulled her phone out of her pocket and shot a text off to Angelo, letting him know that she was still alive and staying at the campground. He sent back an emoji of a dancing little boy, and she smiled, locked her phone, and put it away.

Tipping her head back, watching all the trees that had not yet begun to turn into green, still twitching from the crimson and brown of dying things, she felt fairly affirmed by her decision to leave. The branches waved back at her in the light of the setting sun, dead emeralds and weakened rubies sparkling against the fading sapphires of the sky. She shut her eyes and felt the breeze tickle across her face, smelling a lake not too far away. Her fingertips chilled, all the way down to the knuckles that stuck out against the backs of her hands. Closing her eyes made her feel tired, in a way she had never felt tired before, in a way that made her feel like waking up would actually make her feel rested, rather than exhausted.

"You look like you're thinking something annoying," Dax said, breaking Juliet's train of thought and feeling. Juliet opened her eyes to look at her, waning sunlight backlighting Dax as she stood, one hand on one cocked hip. "Knock it off. We've got an early start tomorrow. You tired?"

"Yeah," Juliet answered. "Yeah, I'm exhausted."

Dax cracked open the back of the van and climbed in first, adjusting the pillows so she got the left side and Juliet took the right. She spread out her own blankets on her side, Juliet's on the other, neither of them sharing. She pocketed her car keys and offered Juliet a hand up into the van, which Juliet took, gracious. Her hands were smooth, steering-wheel-calloused, scarred in a couple places, knuckles round, fingernails bitten down. Dax kicked off her shoes, stripped off her jeans and her jacket, leaving her in the silk shirt that looked like it might have been pajamas to start out with. Juliet unlaced her shoes more gingerly, lining them up in the window when she finished. She changed underneath her covers into a pair of pajamas she had brought in one of her bags, discarding her work uniform neatly back in the bag when she was done.

"Get some rest," Dax instructed, reaching above them to flick off the van light and tug the curtains stapled and rolled up above the windows down, blocking out the last of the dwindling sunlight at the campground. Juliet could feel a couple pine needles in their bed from the ground outside. She pulled her glasses off, folded them up, and tucked them inside her shoe. "We're gonna leave when we both wake up."

"Should I set an alarm?" Juliet asked, and Dax looked half-bewildered, quarter-humored, quarter-confused.

"Why would we?" Dax pulled her covers up tight around her

shoulders and smiled at Juliet in the darkness, a flash of teeth between pink lips. "G'night, Jules."

"Goodnight, Daksha," Juliet said back, softly, out of deference to Dax's closing eyes and to the nighttime. Dax fell asleep fairly quickly, a small smile fading as she dropped off. Juliet had enough time to panic briefly about her choice and calm herself down before she shut her eyes, practiced her deep breathing, and followed Dax.

Chapter Three

The next morning, Juliet woke up before Dax, and found herself looking at her face, studying the square build of her jaw and the curved softness of her cheekbones as she slept. That got boring after not too long, so she fished her glasses out of her shoe, turned her phone on, and started reading while she waited for Dax to wake up. It was already light out - she could tell by the way light was creeping under the edge of the homemade curtains - but Juliet was in no rush for them to hit the road. She was, remarkably, calm for the first time since she stormed out of work the day before.

She had read twenty-six pages of her book but absorbed almost none of it, lost in her own thoughts and imaginations of the life she had just thrown herself into, when Dax's face scrunched up. Her eyes squinted tight, nose wrinkled, lips pursed, she peeked out at Juliet with one eyelid opened to a slit.

"Are you awake?" Dax asked, and Juliet smiled a little, unable to keep it from coming out.

"No," Juliet answered, and Dax reached out and pushed Juliet's face back into her pillow. Juliet laughed, feeling lighthearted for the first time a long time. Dax groaned for a while longer, covering her head with her covers, stretching out, pulling the curtains back and glaring at the sunlight. Juliet watched her go through what she could only assume was a daily routine. Eventually, Dax kicked her blankets off, stared up at the roof of the van, and sighed heavily.

"You ready to go?" Dax inquired, throwing her head to the side to look at Juliet where she was still tucked under her own covers, watching Dax have her mini-meltdown.

"If you're driving, I'm not so sure," Juliet replied, and Dax shoved at her face absently. She sat up, starting to comb through her hair with her fingers.

"We can use the bathrooms and the showers and then head out?" Dax suggested. Juliet agreed and started putting her belongings into one small tote bag she brought along. Dax just hauled a gallon-sized plastic bag out of her side of the van, the clear plastic filled with various toiletries of different colors and patterns. She yanked a towel from another pile and turned to Juliet. "You remember a towel?" Juliet shook her head. Dax tugged a second towel from the pile and handed it over; Juliet took it, three feet of cotton that looked like it had a hand-painted drawing of some little alien cartoon repeated on it over a dozen times, nearly faded into oblivion. Dax wrenched a pair of flip flops from the floor and kicked the van doors open.

By the time they both had showered, Juliet had self-administered her hormones, and the two of them were dried and dressed, the sun was at a sideways angle in the sky. The light glinted off Juliet's glasses as they locked up the back of the van and climbed back into the front.

"Now, you'll learn how a *real* driver does it," Dax told her, proud, as she threw her beloved van into drive and peeled out of the campground. Juliet was disappointed to see Laurens' Tavern again, since her dramatic "I'll never see that again!" moment from the day before was ruined a little when they had to drive past it, but they were on the road and on the way to their first stop before long. They drove past Lake Independence, Juliet's nose against the window until Dax leaned over and cranked it down for her. Juliet stuck her head out the window, smelling the water and the trees and listening to the last sounds her town had to give her, the last memories it had to dredge up for her, begging her to stay and make more. Juliet cranked the window back up when the lake was out of view and tried her best to forget. She focused instead on the fact that Dax had a map spread out all along the dashboard and kept fidgeting, sitting up on her knees to better see the map as she drove.

"Why don't you just get a satellite map?" Juliet questioned, pulling the map down and snapping it out so it held up at a crisper angle. "Or a phone that works in this century?"

"Because the map works just fine, thanks," Dax answered, snatching the map back and laying it out on the dashboard again.

After their next missed exit, though, Juliet just picked up her phone from where it was plugged into the car charger and tapped *Merrimac* into her search browser.

"If you listen to my phone's directions, we should get there in five-and-a-half hours," Juliet pointed out to her, and Dax huffed and grumbled but ultimately let Juliet fold up the horribly distracting map and hide it in the glove box. Juliet ended up muting the voice giving directions and narrated it herself, doing impressions just to make Dax smile as they drove.

When Juliet pointed it out, Dax drove down the scenic roads that tracked through Ottawa National Forest, the two of them stopping every half an hour because the view was just so overwhelming. Juliet took an absurd amount of pictures on her phone, including a selfie of the two of them, their first one, Dax grinning, pointing up at the camera, caught in a half-laugh, while Juliet tried to fit into a pose around her, in front of a hell of a lot of turning trees and a big wooden sign that welcomed them to the forest.

"Can we camp in here?" Juliet asked, and Dax tipped her head to check Juliet's watch.

"We haven't been driving that long, really," Dax told her, the two of them sitting on a rocky outcropping masquerading as a short cliff's edge, watching a waterfall cascade over jagged stones and into a pool shrouded by leaves. "We can still make it to Merrimac today if we wanted."

"But we don't have to, right?" Juliet turned to Dax, who shrugged.

"We can do whatever we want," Dax reminded her. "We don't *have* to do anything."

They found a campsite in the forest, but ended up falling asleep in a frigid cave on accident. They found it hiking, late at night; it seemed to glow almost purple in the moonlight, the opening covered by a heavy branch. Juliet fell asleep first, but Dax must not have had the heart to wake her up, or, at least, not the will. When Juliet woke up, head pillowed on her jacket, back aching from sleeping on the ground, Dax curled up on her side next to her, she felt even better than she had when she woke up the day before.

"We have to get to Merrimac today," Dax informed her, after they had both woken up and Dax had, rather boldly, washed her hair out in a river. She was combing through the tangled wet tentacles of her hair with her fingers as they walked. "Goals are what keeps us going, remember. We're not total barbarians, we're doing something here. We're in the business of UFO catchin', Alva. Don't forget that."

"Gotcha," Juliet agreed, watching the sun break through a cloud, then hide, then emerge again. Dax managed to find them a path through the trees back to their campground. They brought the crisp, earthy smell of the cave and the river and the bark and the dirt into the van with them. Leaning back, closing her eyes, Juliet could almost see the waterfall through the windshield in her imagination.

"How far are we from Merrimac?" Dax asked, once they were on the road again. Juliet stopped flipping through the pictures she had taken in her gallery and went back to her search browser.

"Got a little under four hours to go," Juliet answered, and Dax laid heavy on the gas, aiming for a reaction from Juliet. What Juliet gave was a smile, a little exhilarated by the whole thing, but Dax's answering grin and coloring of her cheeks suggested she might have wanted the outcome she got.

Dax was a semi-chatty person when she relaxed and felt like she could turn off, even if it was only a little bit. She told Juliet about her sister, a twin named Fahira, and her father, Sunny. Her mother was hardly mentioned; Mariam, who seemed to have left when Dax was younger and who Dax skimmed over in her stories. Fahira and her father took a more prominent role in her memories, though, as she regaled Juliet with them.

"They're still back in Queens," Dax told her, leaning back in the driver's seat, her grip relaxed on the steering well, her shoulders loose. The late morning sun was warm when the windows were rolled up in the van. "I know fuck-all about my mom's life anymore. She's off God-knows-where while my dad actually sticks with Fahira, since, you know, he's her *parent*." Dax rubbed at her face with one hand. "Your parents sound like good people, though."

Juliet shrugged. "I love both of them, and my brothers. My dad had a hard time with me when I came out as trans, though. He had his three sons, he had been happy with that. I don't think he really gets the whole thing. He probably still thinks it's just a phase or something like that, even though I started my hormones and had my reassignment surgery before I even hit puberty." Juliet watched the trees flick by outside the window, the lines of the road vanishing under them before she could count them. "He never wanted to call me 'Juliet.' He didn't think it felt right."

"Doesn't matter what feels right to him," Dax said, tapping a cigarette out of her pack and rolling down her window with one strong arm. Juliet resisted the urge to reach out and pull the cigarette from her mouth. "Only matters what feels right to you."

"I don't disagree," Juliet replied. She glanced at Dax, leaning back against the headrest. "Why do you smoke?"

"I was stupid enough to start in high school because I made some friends I shouldn't've," Dax answered, seemingly honestly. She lit up her cigarette and made sure to keep the smoke out the window. "I'm working on it."

"We'll work on it," Juliet amended, turning her attention back out her own window instead, missing the look Dax gave her as she moved. "nicotine patches. Snapping rubber bands on your wrist. Something like that."

"Yeah, something like that," Dax allowed, tapping her cigarette against the edge of the open window, smoke and ash spiraling off down the highway.

Reaching Merrimac took about as long as her phone had predicted. The drive was filled with the odd anecdote, a rogue detail of one story leading to another, and to another, until they reached Merrimac, which seemed to have twice, maybe even three times as many people as Big Bay. Juliet thought that might not mean much, though, since Big Bay had just under three hundred people living in it. She cranked her window down again and let her hand rest on the outside of the van, the wind whipping against her fingers, the smell of Lake Wisconsin in the air. Juliet could not identify exactly why, but it smelled different than Lake Independence.

"Where's this UFO sighting, anyway?" Juliet asked, pulling up her phone to put in their specific destination. She put in her hormone prescription at the pharmacy in town to pick up after they found their campground.

"I don't remember where, exactly," Dax answered, taking a smooth left, aimless. "Like, I don't have a street address, if that's what you're asking." She tipped her head forward to look up at the sky through the windshield. "If a UFO comes, I'm assuming we'd see it through the whole town, wouldn't we? If we-"

"Found it," Juliet interrupted, pulling up the article talking about the sighting on her phone. The website had a hectic, starry background and flashing blue bars all over it, but the words were legible. She tapped the address into her phone, and they managed to find a clearing near the trees down the road. Dax maneuvered fairly skillfully through the trees, weaving under branches and between trunks with the van until they got to the spot in the clearing with the clearest view to the sky.

"Now what?" Dax asked, sliding out of the van and looking up into the sun twinkling down at them through wispy clouds. Juliet checked her watch.

"Maybe… We get dinner?" Juliet suggested. Dax snapped her fingers at her excitedly, pushing away from the van.

"Can you find us a place to eat in your phone?" Dax requested, reaching for Juliet's phone in the pocket of her jeans. Juliet twitched away without thinking about it, pulling her phone out herself.

"I don't think we can eat in my phone, Daksha," Juliet joked dryly, searching for restaurants in their area. They ended up walking down a ways to a little greasy spoon place, right near Lake Wisconsin, the watery air blowing their hair back as they read the sign outside the diner. It looked just like the kind of rustic wood cabin Juliet might expect from her mind's eye if she had tried to predict this place. The grass outside was greener than any grass she had ever seen before, she thought, and probably fake, as the two of them walked over it to the door.

"I'm gonna eat an omelette," Dax announced, the very second she set foot inside the cafe. Juliet smiled, actively trying not to laugh, as the hostess brought them to the counter. Dax checked Juliet's watch and apparently decided it was too early to drink, or at least not the right moment for it, because she ordered herself a coffee instead. Juliet followed her example and skimmed the menu while they waited.

"So," Juliet asked, looking at the omelette stuffing options, "what kind of UFOs are we looking for, here?"

"Hm?" Dax looked up from where she was adding enough milk and sugar to make the coffee into a cake instead. She stirred absently with her spoon. "Oh, I don't remember. Something with red and white strobes, maybe some green, looked like spheres, zigzagging around at night. Definitely not a helicopter, they said. We'll get 'em. Nothing stays hidden from me for very long." Dax sipped her coffee and frowned instantly, her nose wrinkling. She reached for the sugar again.

The two of them did order omelettes, which took a while to actually arrive. Juliet spent that time with her chin in one hand, watching Dax make her coffee whiter than either of them could ever dream of being. Juliet sipped at hers - dash of milk, one spoon of sugar - and observed Dax trying to be a chemist and balance the elements.

"Would you have preferred a glass of milk?" Juliet asked, eventually. Dax raised one eyebrow, still focused on stirring in sugar as it poured.

"I'm an adult," Dax informed her, not raising her eyes. "Adults drink coffee."

Juliet kept watching as Dax finally got her coffee to the right balance, then pulled her hair down and combed through it with her fingers. She yanked it up into a half-bun at the back of her skull and let the rest of it hang, still thick from drying after the river water.

"Who puts spinach and avocado in an omelette, anyways?" Dax muttered, smiling a little bit. Juliet shrugged.

"I'm sure adults do," Juliet answered, and Dax did look up at her this time, loose hair falling in her face. "I'm an adult."

Dax laughed. "You don't have many jokes, man, but when you do, I'm into it."

Juliet almost frowned, but decided on being amused. She thought she was almost always joking. Whatever. Dax would get to know her, and wasn't *that* frightening to consider.

"So, tonight, we'll watch for the UFO," Dax informed her, using her omelette as the van in her example, putting two home fries on top of it to stand in for them. "Usually, I just stay until I see the UFOs, then I head out."

"Don't you want to find the actual aliens?" Juliet asked, and Dax shrugged.

"They know when you've seen 'em," Dax told her. "I don't think they want to see me, anyways. I'm the predator, and they're the prey."

"How sure are you about that?" Juliet picked up the home fry that stood in for her and ate it. Dax raised an eyebrow.

"Pretty sure." She ate her own home fry and started eating her omelette-van, stuffed with sausage and peppers. "Besides, if they were gonna abduct me, they would've done it by now. I just want to chase them. I live for that chase, man. One state after another, just me and the UFOs." Dax swallowed the omelette in her mouth and waved her fork at Juliet. "And now you, I guess."

"Thanks," Juliet said dryly, taking a sip from her coffee and starting in on her own omelette. She pulled out her phone when she finished, since Dax was only halfway through hers. Besides being a phenomenally slow eater, Dax was also incapable of being quiet long enough during a meal to actually chew and swallow her food.

Juliet started searching the Internet for a potential next stop after Merrimac was through, showing Dax ones she found in states nearby when she found them. Dax would only make a little humming noise at her to acknowledge them before barreling on with whatever other topic she had been previously occupied with. Juliet bookmarked a couple of tabs and created a folder to save them in as Dax was, at last, taking the last bites of her omelette. As Juliet started stacking up their dishes to make it easier for the waitress, she saw a 'Help Wanted' sign reflected from the window behind her.

"Hey," Juliet said, snatching up Dax's attention from the silverware she was attempting to stack. Juliet twisted around on her swivel chair and pointed out the sign. "What do you think?"

"About windows?" Dax asked, tipping her head back to get the last dregs of her coffee. "Not much. Why?"

"No, the sign." Juliet hopped off her stool and went to grab the sign before bringing it back to Dax. "I could work here for a little bit, make us a little cash. How long do we usually stay?"

"I usually stick around until I see the UFO, man," Dax informed her, listing from side to side on the swivel chair. She took the sign from her and picked at one of the frayed edges. "Or until I get sick of the place. It doesn't take very long."

"I can be upfront with them," Juliet replied, taking the sign back. She craned her neck, searching for a manager or anyone who might work there. "They seem understaffed. They could pay me minimum wage in cash for a few days, doesn't hurt anyone, helps us out a little bit, you know?"

"Never really thought of getting a real job anywhere I went," Dax said. She started fiddling with the silverware tower again. Juliet wanted to ask what kind of jobs she *did* get, but it was then that their server returned and Juliet grabbed their attention, asking what kind of help they were looking for.

"Well, what kind of help are you good at?" Fiona (as so her name badge declared her to be) asked. Juliet handed over the sign and shrugged a little bit.

"I just finished working in a restaurant bar for two years," Juliet offered. "I worked as an office assistant before that for four years, and a grocery store clerk before *that* for-"

"So, yeah, you're not terrible, you worked in a bar," Fiona interrupted, looking Juliet over. "You quick?"

"Quick enough."

Fiona eyed Juliet.

"I can only work for about a week, if you pay me in cash," Juliet added on. Fiona pulled a phone out of her pocket and started flipping through her calendar.

"Our usual girl has been on maternity leave and won't be back until next Tuesday," Fiona informed her, putting her phone away. "Can you work until then?"

Juliet turned to Dax, who had been watching the whole exchange in almost-silence, save for the light clattering of her silverware construction project. Dax raised an eyebrow at her, still indecipherable, and turned to Fiona.

"She'll get paid in cash?" Dax clarified, and Fiona nodded.

"Yeah, that's fine with me," Fiona answered, and Dax leaned back against the counter, shrugging at Juliet.

"Up to you, then, kid," Dax told her, and, after a little bit of staring with Dax that failed to actually communicate anything, Juliet confirmed with Fiona that she could work until the next Tuesday. Fiona pulled up her calendar again and scheduled Juliet in, asking to see her license as an afterthought. When all was set and done, and the two of them had paid for their breakfasts, they headed out. They made a pit stop at the pharmacy to pick up Juliet's hormones before they started back on their path.

"You're a real go-getter, aren't you, man?" Dax commented as they began their aimless walk towards Lake Wisconsin, the ferry looming tiny in the distance, getting larger as they walked. "First place we stop at in this town, and you've got a job there."

"Only until next Tuesday," Juliet replied defensively. "It's not a real job. It's just a way for us to make some cash. How else are we supposed to do it?"

"We're nomads," Dax said, knowingly cryptic. It annoyed Juliet enough to make her nose scrunch up a little bit, but she kept her eyes ahead instead of looking at Dax. "It figures itself out, you know?"

"I don't," Juliet said, and Dax shrugged, the two of them lapsing into an almost-silence. Dax seemed to be going out of her way to step on crispy brown grass and particularly crunchy-looking fallen leaves, dead things cracking under her feet as she walked. They reached a wall of trees, eventually, and Dax kept going, ducking under branches, weaving between stumps and trunks. Juliet followed at a close distance, lighter on her feet but more susceptible to catching her sweater on a snapped branch end.

"Can you hear that?" Dax asked, softly, as they walked. Juliet listened, but heard only the pops of twigs and leaves under their feet. She shook her head, and Dax grinned. "That's silence."

Juliet shoved at Dax, unable to keep from grinning herself as they continued to trudge. Patches of mud sucked at her boots, but she kept pulling out and moving through until they hit water's edge. Looking out over Lake Wisconsin, sharing a look with Dax before the latter hopped down to the first dock she saw and continued walking, Juliet felt an overwhelming sense of having made the right decision.

Strolling to the end of the dock, as at ease as though she were any of the animals who inhabited those woods or that lake, Dax was the picture of nomadic impulse and rebellious actions. Juliet pulled out her phone and snapped a quiet picture as they continued on to the very end of the long dock. Despite the bite in the air, Dax sat herself down at the edge of the dock, pulled off her socks and shoes, rolled up the cuffs of her jeans, and let her legs swing over the side, toes grazing the water. Juliet sat cross-legged beside her.

"Live a little, Big Bay," Dax teased, trailing her foot through the water. Juliet leaned over the side, peering at her own watery reflection, wondering if the cold and the inevitable post-water struggle to get socks and shoes back on would be worth it. "Just do it. Don't think."

"How are you not dead by now?" Juliet asked, but she still followed Dax's lead, peeling off her own socks and shoes and hesitantly joining Juliet by the edge. She lowered her feet into the water rather gingerly. It *was* cold, she knew it would be, but had hoped against hope it might embrace her with warmth as a surprise. *Alas, it was not to be,* Juliet thought, lowering her feet in inch by inch until they were submerged to the ankle. She leaned back on her hands and let her body adjust to the chill.

"See? Not so bad, is it?" Dax commented, dry, observing Juliet when she turned to look at her. Juliet shrugged, focusing her eyes more on the ripples of the water than on anything else.

"Not so bad," Juliet agreed. After a long while, in which the sun started to fall out of the sky and Dax rambled on about the movements of the trees, the two of them got up and let their feet dry in the air. Once their shoes and socks were replaced, the two of them started back through the woods, pine needles sticking to the mud on the soles of their boots.

"It's nice here," Dax said, out of the blue, in the middle of a new train of thought. Juliet made a sound of agreement. "Not somewhere I could stay, though."

"No," Juliet agreed. "But then again, it is the woods."

Dax laughed, shoving at Juliet's shoulder, the both of them making it to the road at the same time, falling into step alongside one another as they retraced their path back past the diner, returning to the road to the van. It seemed to take a shorter amount of time to get back to the van than it had been to get to the diner the first time. Juliet plugged her phone in in the van when they arrived before grabbing a sweatshirt from her bag and tugging it on.

"Now what?" Juliet asked, watching as Dax climbed up into the back of the van to snatch up their blankets. She handed Juliet her pillow and blanket and clambered up onto the roof.

"Now," Dax informed her, "we wait."

Waiting was really only that, waiting. Dax lit up a cigarette once they were situated on the roof of the van, laying side-by-side like they did when they slept. The smoke trailed above their heads, disappearing against the grey of the clouds in the sky. They could barely see the blackness of the sky for how overcast it was. Juliet remembered drowsily checking her watch around 12:25, the two of them having laid up there for hours by then, watching for something that never seemed to come.

Chapter Four

The next thing Juliet knew, Dax was shaking her awake, one hand on her shoulder shoving roughly at her. Juliet blinked her eyes open and smacked Dax away before grumbling, "What?"

"I don't think it's coming," Dax informed her, starting to pack up her bedding. She slid down the windshield and hopped off the van, Juliet tiredly following. "We'll have to check again tomorrow."

"Sounds good," Juliet agreed easily, yawning and trying not to drag her covers in the dirt as she moved around to the back of the van. Dax cracked the back doors open and helped Juliet crawl up into the back of the van and fix her bedding. Juliet was asleep before Dax had even laid down.

She was awake long before her the next morning, though. Juliet slipped out of her covers, still dressed in her clothes from the day before - *Gonna have to start wearing my pajamas whenever she decides to get up on the roof,* she thought, pulling at her sweatshirt - and left the van. The door creaked a little bit (well, kind of a lot), but Dax seemed to be a fairly heavy sleeper and barely stirred.

Juliet shoved the door shut behind her as quietly as she could. The morning still had the night's wet chill in it, and a quick glance at her watch told Juliet that it was 8:23. She opened the front passenger door of the van to grab her phone before heading off into the woods a bit, poking around through the trees, enjoying the total silence afforded to her by a secluded morning. She could hear a woodpecker high above her head as she walked, slamming their head into the trees. She thought she understood what they meant by that.

She found herself a rock that seemed good enough to sit on, but ended up damp and uncomfortable. Pride and a lack of options kept her there, though. She tapped out a message to her family's group chat with her brothers and her parents, letting them know she was still safe. She tipped her head back against the top of her rock and let the rising sunlight wash over her. Sitting in the sun, the light warmed her skin up a little bit, enough to distract from the bite in the air and the seeping damp cold from the rock. She shut her eyes against the sun and let herself drift for a little while, feeling the breeze on her, just letting herself exist in the silence.

She was unsure of how long she drifted like that, but she awoke to her name being shouted from somewhere nearby. She rubbed at her eye under her glasses and hauled herself to her feet, having, at least, the presence of mind to grab her phone before setting off towards Dax.

"Hey, whoa, calm down," Juliet murmured when she caught Dax at the edge of the clearing. Dax steered her by the elbow back to the van and did a poor job of pretending she wasn't checking her over.

"I woke up and you were gone," Dax explained to her, still examining her for wounds of any sort as she sat on the back edge of the van. Finding none, she smacked her upside the head. "I thought you left or something. You could've been hurt, you dumbass."

"I'm not going anywhere," Juliet assured her. "I'm in this."

The two of them stared at each other without saying anything, Dax above Juliet, for once, since Juliet was sitting. Eventually, Dax looked away, rubbing at the back of her head.

"Well, we should find a place to shower," Dax suggested, attention more on the trees than anything else. Juliet hopped up.

"Sounds good," Juliet agreed. She and Dax gathered up their toiletries in one of their tote bags and headed off in search of some sort of bathroom to at least use the sink of. They ended up finding a gym and sneaking in to use their showers before the place opened for the day, which resulted in hiding behind the showers when the janitors made a sweep of the place. They escaped out the back, hair still wet, pulling on new clothes as they ran.

On the way back to the van, Dax borrowed Juliet's phone, skimming through her browsers for something; Juliet could barely see the words. She tried not to look over her shoulder, but ended up checking her search history anyways when she got her phone back. There was nothing in there at all. *So, she must have deleted it,* Juliet thought, glancing up at Dax, who was tapping a broken stick against the trunks of trees as they passed them.

"So, you've got work today, right?" Dax asked as she shoved her stuff into the back of the van and Juliet self-administered her hormones. "Back at it again?"

"Back at it again," Juliet agreed, searching for a second pair of socks, since her feet being kind of cold was her priority at that moment. She successfully found more socks and her gloves to tug on.

"I can drop you off at the diner," Dax offered, watching Juliet struggle to get her boot on over two pairs of socks. Juliet glanced up at her.

"I can walk, we walked yesterday," Juliet answered. She could feel a little frown on her face, but was helpless to stop it. She was struggling to understand. "Are you leaving this spot?"

"No, no, we'll come back here, there's nothing wrong with the spot," Dax reassured her. "I just want to look around the town, you know? See what's up. We have the van, we may as well be using it instead of walking everywhere."

"Yeah, that's fine, I wouldn't mind a ride." Juliet finally succeeded in getting her socks and shoes back on and stood, dusting herself off. She checked her watch. "Oh, Jesus. I'm gonna be late for my first day."

"Does it count when your last day is in a week?" Dax asked, and Juliet kicked a little bit of dirt at her in retaliation, making Dax laugh and drop the weird cryptic act. The two of them headed off in the van, weaving through the trunks the way they came to get back to the road. Dax left Juliet at the diner with a few sharp honks of the horn, a wave out the window, and a middle finger as she disappeared around the bend. Juliet waved until Dax was completely gone from her sight.

Falling back into the pattern of working as a server was easy. Juliet found the mindless work to be just that; it was fairly automatic, an old routine she couldn't break. The hours flew by in a blur of cleaning, serving, smiling at customers, taking their orders. By the time Dax showed up outside, honking her horn wildly and leaning out the window of the van to grin wildly at her, happy as a clam,

Juliet had almost forgotten what they were doing together. Fiona gave Juliet the cash from her hours and her tips and sent her off with hours for the next day.

"Hey, fucker," Dax shouted out the window. She reached out a hand for Juliet to high-five as she went around the van to climb in her passenger side. Juliet slid in, untying the apron she had been given as she went. "How was your day, dearest?"

"It was fine," Juliet told her, slamming the door shut. "Just work." She pulled the money out of her apron and dropped it on the dashboard. "Got some cash for us."

Dax shoved her hand in her jacket pocket and shuffled around for a moment before pulling out a fistful of cash and slapping it down next to Juliet's money. "Same here, sweetheart. Shall we paint the town red? Maybe go get some fast food? Maybe even Italian, if we're feeling fancy?"

Juliet glanced at her, unable to keep herself from smiling. Dax threw the van back into drive and the two of them set out in search of a place to get themselves dinner.

"Too bad we don't have a fridge so we could get groceries," Juliet commented as they passed a little market. Dax wagged her finger at her.

"Uh-uh-uh, don't be so quick to assume," Dax admonished her. "You know what they say about assuming." Dax pulled up the center armrest on top of the console between them. "Stick your hand in that bad boy."

Juliet glanced at her, then hesitantly slid her hand in. It was chilled to the touch, and she bent over it to look further into it. "What the hell is this?"

"That, my dear, is my fridge," Dax told her, "so we can get groceries." She took a u-turn and went back for the grocery store. "We can grab anything your little heart desires. What'll it be?"

Juliet met Dax's eyes, then lost the contact as Dax looked back to the road in time to take the turn into the grocery store parking lot and park the van. "Can we make pasta?"

"I have a hot plate in the back, so we can certainly try," Dax answered with a toothy grin.

Going to the grocery store with Dax was an interesting adventure, to say the least. As soon as Dax pulled up at the grocery store, Juliet was out the passenger door, making a grocery list for them between the van and the grocery store. It seemed Dax could not have cared less about it as she trailed her hand down chipped silver paint on her way towards the shopping carts. Juliet followed at a slower pace, watching Dax as she hopped up into one of the carts, folding her short legs under her and looking up at Juliet expectantly.

"I'm not gonna push you around," Juliet warned her, getting close enough to grab the handle of the cart. Dax jabbed her fingers against her temples and squinted at Juliet, trying hard not to crack a smile.

"You will push me around in the cart," Dax ordered in what seemed to be her best eerie voice, a grin twitching at the corners of her mouth. Juliet pretended to heave an annoyed sigh, but she took hold of the handle anyways, and Dax shot her finger guns and a click of the tongue before taking her seat in the bed of the cart. Juliet gave her a hard shove towards the doors. Dax spread her arms, turning to grin at Juliet when the automatic doors opened, looking proud like she had anything to do with it.

"You're six years old," Juliet pointed out, wheeling her over to the fruits. Dax leaned up to start picking through the tomatoes.

"Yeah, but you're still here, so I'm not very worried about it," Dax replied distractedly. She held up a little red tomato. "Yes or no? I think it's okay, so I feel bad that it has a bruise because-"

"Save the story," Juliet interrupted. She held out one of the plastic fruit bags. "Toss it in."

Dax saved that tomato and two others before Juliet stopped her and picked the rest out herself. She handed Dax the tied-off tomato bag and started pushing her again, letting Dax read the list of ingredients off her phone as they went. Dax would periodically stretch up out of the cart and snatch something off a shelf, tossing it into her lap or behind her back. Juliet grabbed things now and then, as well, but sometimes Dax would just frown at her and put it back.

"We have a list," Dax reminded her, determined. Juliet stuck a box of sugary cereal in the cart anyways. With a grin, Dax added a box of toaster pastries for good measure after a beat of silent staring.

The frozen food aisle was Dax's downfall, since she was self-proclaimed to be "shit at cooking" and believed she still might be able to properly convince Juliet that she was good at it, since she had the ability to serve her frozen food on a plate. Juliet knew she was a liar. She didn't call her out on it, because she looked so damn proud of herself this whole plan.

"I like the fried chicken," Dax mused quietly to herself, leaning half-out of the cart, her face and arms shoved in the cold freezer as she mulled over two different dinner options. She tapped at one of the boxes. "But you said you like the sliders."

"Just get both, they're only a dollar fifty each," Juliet offered, and Dax glanced up at her, then back at the boxes, then back at her, before hauling the boxes back up into the cart with her. The cart tipped precariously as her weight shifted, and Juliet's hand shot out to catch her. Dax laughed, twisting around to say something, an inch too close, breath unexpectedly warm on her face. Dax stopped short, caught off-guard.

"Thanks," Dax murmured near her mouth. They stared at each other for a moment before Dax lost the game of chicken, if that was even what it was, and turned back to their grocery list. Juliet bit back a groan and leaned back over the handle, shutting the freezer door before starting to push their cart again.

"What else do we need?" Juliet asked, looming over Dax to try and read the list. She gave a little push, enough to gain momentum so she could hop up onto the bar at the bottom of the cart and let them glide for a little bit. Dax hummed to herself.

"Parmesan cheese, pesto, cat food for you," Dax answered, holding up the phone so Juliet could see the real list better, nearly punching Juliet in the face in the process. Juliet grabbed her wrist and raised her eyebrows, smiling when Dax laughed, fingers twitching against Juliet's forehead. Juliet released her and started back on their path, guiding the cart down random aisles, comfortable moving slowly and aimlessly if only to enjoy her time spent here with Dax. The windows of the store looked black against the nighttime as it set in, the bright interior lighting illuminating them in a glow that seemed to exclude the rest of the world. Juliet felt *alive*.

Dax reached out of the cart, starting to have difficulty moving with the weight of the boxes and bags stacked up on her, and grabbed a cheap bottle of wine. She waved it at Juliet, one eyebrow cocked. She grinned, rakish and happy, dimples deep and joy etched into every pore of her face.

"We could have a real fun night ahead," she suggested, waving the bottle at her. Juliet pushed her to the end of the aisle and turned near the snack counter. Dax reached out blindly and chucked a bag of pretzels at her. Juliet laughed, grabbed a second bag of pretzels, ignored Dax's snorting laughter, and started towards the registers.

"Wait!" Dax exclaimed, and the cart screeched as Juliet tugged it to a sudden stop. "We forgot something."

"What could we have possibly forgotten?" Juliet asked, motioning at Dax. "We've got half the goddamn market in the cart with you."

Dax twisted her head back to grin up at Juliet, her face upside-down as she smiled. "I think I've got some coupons out in the van, if you wanna go grab 'em."

"Oh, man, I hate you right now," Juliet grumbled, and Dax reached up to pat at Juliet's cheek, grinning at her. She pulled away, tapping at Juliet's nose before releasing her and sitting normally again.

"I probably won't tip over while you're gone," Dax semi-promised, starting to organize the boxes and bags in the cart by color. Juliet impulsively flicked her ear and started off. She turned at her last moment in Dax's sightline.

"Don't you dare put any more candy in that goddamn cart, Paracha," Juliet threatened, and Dax tossed the bag of candy in her hand back at the shelf so hard that three more fell onto the floor. Dax laughed so hard she knocked the cart over, and Juliet left her there, laughing in her groceries, while she got her damn coupons. By the time Juliet got back, Dax had vanished; a cursory scan of the store turned her up pretty quickly, putting back the groceries they had grabbed jokingly and turned out to not actually need. The cart Dax was lazily drifting with had, primarily, Juliet's ingredients, plus a couple of nice little extras. She headed over in Juliet's direction once she caught her eye.

"I don't know if this is what you meant," Juliet told her, handing over the coupon section of the Merrimac newspaper she found crammed between the driver's seat and the floor in the van. Dax grabbed it and started flipping through the coupons, gingerly tearing out the ones that matched up with items in their cart.

"You gonna make us a fancy dinner, Jules?" Dax teased absent-mindedly as Juliet handed over some of the cash from their work that day. She kept forgetting to actually ask Dax what she had done that day to get money, but she felt the moment had passed and she would have to wait until - or if - it happened again to figure it out.

"I'll certainly try my best," Juliet answered, taking back the rest of the paper when Dax handed it over. Juliet tried - and failed - to successfully make them pasta on a hot plate in the back of the van, the end of the hot plate fucked up beyond recognition and Frankenstein'd with a car charger by Dax so it would work. Even then, it was simply not enough. The two of them ended up at an Italian restaurant in town, sharing one basket of breadsticks, one bowl of soup, and one pasta plate between them. That night found them out on the van's roof again, staring up at the sky, waiting for aliens that did not seem to want to come.

The thing was, logically, Juliet believed in aliens. The fact that the universe was basically endless and the belief that Earth had the only intelligent life in it was ridiculous and cocky as hell, she thought. There was way too much *something* to have so much *nothing* in it. The concept that aliens had not only visited Earth, but had frequently returned to random places only to abandon them, though? *That* concept, Juliet was having a harder time with.

Still. Better than nothing.

And the look on Dax's face as she stared up at the sky, smoke coming from between her lips, eyes bright in the darkness - that was pretty good, too.

Maybe Juliet should never be so quick to judge. Maybe there *are* aliens. If only to keep the two of them going.

"You really shouldn't smoke," Juliet pointed out, somewhere near 11:30. Dax blew out a puff of smoke and turned her head on her pillow to look at her.

"I definitely know that," Dax told her. She pulled the cigarette up to her lips and inhaled again. "Like I said. Shouldn't've started, but I did."

Juliet reached into her jacket pocket and fished out the nicotine patches she had grabbed at the grocery store. She dropped them on Dax's chest. Dax huffed a laugh, flicked her extinguished cigarette off the side of the van, and started reading the back of the box. Juliet picked up the butt and threw it in her little garbage bag in the front of the van before they went to bed that night, still without having seen a UFO.

The next few days continued in almost exactly the same way

each time: the two of them parted ways after grabbing something quick for breakfast, then Dax came to pick up Juliet by the evening rolled around, and the two of them either went out for a cheap dinner or attempted to make one themselves. Sometimes, they ended up having to do both, like their failed pasta night. Each night, same as before, they also saw zero aliens, despite staying up for quite a few hours in a desperate - and somewhat sleepy - attempt to catch them. It was during these little lookouts that Juliet typically fell asleep.

By Wednesday, the day after Juliet had to surrender her job back to the server who usually held the position, she was starting to wonder if maybe they should get a motel room. She voiced this to Dax, who furrowed her brow and shook her head.

"Well, then, maybe I should get a new job?" Juliet suggested. "We can't just keep existing this way if we're going to be staying here that long, you know. I can't imagine this'll be over quickly if we're not seeing anything now."

"No, you're right," Dax agreed, slumped in her driver's seat as they drove aimlessly, trying to decide on what to do for dinner. "Maybe we can start looking into motels tomorrow morning."

Juliet nodded; later, she had all but forgotten about their conversation, and fell asleep on the roof as usual, head dangerously close to Dax's shoulder as she drifted in and out of consciousness. Dax rambled as usual, telling stories that may or may not have been made up. The cadence of her voice was gentle, soothing, enough to lull Juliet away when the stories were less than engaging - which they ended up being, the later in the night it got.

"Jules!" Dax exclaimed, in the middle of one of these soft stories, the rhythm of her voice breaking off mid-story to shout at her. Juliet snapped into sitting up, hand reaching for her jacket pocket, even though all she had in there was two pens and her phone. She turned to Dax blearily, only to find she was staring straight up, one hand pointing just off-center of the moon, her other hand gripping Juliet's shoulder.

"Look," Dax breathed, and Jules looked, but nothing was there. "Ahh. Shit. You missed it."

"Missed what?" Juliet asked, rubbing at one of her eyes, her eyelashes sticking together. Dax squeezed her shoulder and let her go.

"The UFO," Dax told her, and Juliet was fully awake now, heart feeling like it might have actually skipped a beat, just like hearts did in books. "The real UFO, I did, I saw it! It was like, orbs of light, right up in the sky."

"Really?" Juliet peered up at the sky, frowning, making sure her glasses were still in place. "I don't see anything."

"They went away really quickly," Dax explained. She collapsed back against her bedding, turning her face towards Juliet, grinning widely. "We did it, Jules. We found 'em. Wisconsin can't hide *shit* from us, man, Merrimac's got our *backs*."

"I guess so," Juliet murmured, starting to get sleepy again now that the excitement was draining out of her and Dax was no longer screaming. "Can we go to bed?"

"To *bed*?" Dax repeated. "Man, we gotta start looking for our next stop! Merrimac is over, we've got new places to be, this place is stale."

"Stale?" Juliet shoved her face into her pillow and turned away. "Yeah, whatever. Did you take a picture?"

"Of what?" Dax asked, and Juliet forgot most of the experience on their voyage down into the back of the van. The tattoos on Dax's arm glistened in the sliver of moonlight through the van curtains that night; Juliet noticed she wasn't wearing a nicotine patch. They set out late the next day, driving without direction while Juliet flicked through her bookmarks, searching for a new destination for them.

"How about Waterloo?" Juliet asked, reading an article on a cheap website with an alien-patterned background about fifteen colorful spheres that spun around each other in Iowa. Dax turned to grin at her, sliding her sunglasses in place before she reached for the CD player. Classic disco filtered through the van's warped speakers, blaring at top volume, and Juliet laughed. She cranked her window down when Dax did the same, letting the wind hit them in the face as they drove down the highway.

Chapter Five

It took three-and-a-half hours driving southwest to get to Waterloo; by the time they got there, it was already starting to get dark. The bridge to downtown was lit in a heated orange, bright against the city and the darkening blue sky. There were no UFOs twirling around in the sky, but Juliet was hardly looking for them when Dax was in the driver's seat, backlit by downtown Waterloo.

"Where do we park?" Dax asked. "What's your website say?"

"Says the sighting was downtown," Juliet replied, flicking through the website before opening up her search browser and tapping in a search. "There's a campground by the lake, though. It's got good reviews. Take a left."

"Got it," Dax agreed, spinning to the left based on trust alone. The campground was, true to the reviews, right on the lake; Dax parked easily in the grass, the land sandy and threaded with reeds, flat for miles around. Juliet slipped her shoes off and rolled the cuffs of her jeans up to her knees before walking around the lake to the sand while Dax brought their money up to the front office. Juliet was standing ankle-deep in the biting cold lake water when Dax lightly splashed up beside her. When Juliet glanced down, the pant legs of Dax's overalls were rolled up a little bit, the small waves lapping gingerly at the edges.

"We're all set for the next few days," Dax told her, voice soft in deference to the silence of the lake. She pulled off her jacket and turned to chuck it towards the sand. It landed just out of reach of the water, Juliet noted with relief. Dax stuck her hands in the pockets of her overalls, the bare skin raised with goosebumps below the crop

43

top she had on underneath. She pulled the bun out of her hair and stood, watching the sun vanish over the edge of the flat Iowa horizon.

"I'm glad I came with you," Juliet admitted, the thought feeling as though it had been trapped and needed to be forced out. *Maybe it's time to work on expressing our emotions,* Juliet thought, as she saw Dax turn to look at her in her peripheral. Juliet hesitantly turned to look back, and Dax smiled at her. Her words felt less forced in the face of that smile, more like they should have come out before that moment anyways. Juliet smiled back.

"I am, too," Dax told her. She let herself stare for another moment before she turned her attention back to the horizon line. The water kept lapping at their ankles as they stood together in the quiet of the Iowa nighttime.

They laid down in the sand that night instead of on top of the van, abandoning their pillows and blankets for sand lumps and their jackets over them like makeshift covers to avoid getting sand all caught up in their bedding. Juliet could feel Dax's eyes boring holes in the side of her head every now and then, her attention hot on her face and obvious out of the corner of her eye, but she was, strangely, unable to look back. It felt weirdly like giving something up that she wasn't quite ready to surrender yet.

Same as before, they saw no aliens before Juliet fell asleep in the sand, getting it all caught up in her hair as she turned over onto her stomach in her sleep. Dax shook her awake, carefully, and led her back to the van to shake out her clothes and her hair and get her into their bed. Juliet watched her draw the curtains shut against the moonlight and wondered faintly what the most alien element of this whole thing was, exactly.

The next day, Juliet set out in search of a job. Dax dropped her off downtown and drove off to wherever it was Dax went when she vanished. Juliet thought she might have missed her window of opportunity where it was less weird to ask where Dax went; it had been about two weeks, and Juliet thought it might be too late or too weird now to ask what the hell she was up to.

Juliet strolled down the streets of downtown Waterloo, hands in her pockets to keep them safe from the wind that was growing sharper with each day heading into winter. She poked her head into a couple different restaurants, but none of them were hiring. She approached the one grocery store she found and told them she had experience as a clerk, but they didn't want her either. She let the wind whip her hair back in the streets, the sun blazing warm where her neck was uncovered by her scarf. She found a thrift store and went inside, and came out with a job for the next week and a half, starting the next day, until the kid who usually worked the counter came back from his family trip to New Hampshire.

With an entire afternoon left to kill until Dax came back, and no job to hold her over until then, she continued to wander the streets, peeking through windows when something caught her eye, distracted by the wind and the lights and the smells that wafted through open doors. Juliet ended up drifting further downtown than she expected, getting lost down alleys that seemed less familiar than she had hoped. She continued to stray, wandering down side streets, until she reached what appeared to be a soup kitchen of sorts. She pushed the door open and slipped to the inside wall, watching the organized chaos that was the lines of people both accepting food and eating it. She kept her hands in her pockets as she sidled up to a guy wearing a hairnet.

"Hey," Juliet offered, watching his hands instead of his face as he served mashed potatoes to the waiting line. The line never stopped moving; neither did he. "Need any help?"

"Did Rachel ever show up?" the guy called over his shoulder. A woman at the end of the line shook her head, serving chicken nuggets from a large metal bin.

"No, she's sick today," she shouted back over the din of the place, a natural result of that many bodies in a room that size. The guy paused in his scooping to duck under the counter the food was laid out on. He reemerged with a hairnet, gloves, and hand sanitizer, which he dropped into Juliet's waiting hands when she held them out.

"Clean up, suit up, go help make sandwiches," he instructed. Juliet thanked him and did what he said, scrubbing up to her elbows in hand sanitizer, tugging her hair back with an elastic from her wrist before tucking it up into the hairnet. The gloves slid on and stuck to her skin, tacky from the hand sanitizer. She joined an older woman, who introduced herself as Gracie, in making sandwiches at a table near the back corner, keeping her hands occupied with bread and peanut butter and knives, over and over and over again, whistling to herself as they worked. When she worked, hours passed like nothing, like minutes. It was familiar enough to distract her from time as it flew by her.

Handing out sandwiches came after making them, and cleaning up after that, then back around to making them again. She did as she was told, falling into routine, until her phone buzzed in her pocket. She ducked in the back to fish it out of the back of her pants. Dax's name and grinning face lit up her screen as she tugged her glove off to answer.

"Yeah, hi, Dax, what's up?" Juliet greeted her, clamping her other hand over her ear to block out the noise still filtering through the walls.

"Where the fuck are you?" Dax asked on the other end. "I'm at the bus stop and you… are not. Obviously."

"No, I got lost and I've been working in a soup kitchen," Juliet said, poking her head back through the doorway into the kitchen, watching Gracie as she started to scoop hot gravy at the counter. Dax laughed at her on the other line.

"Where the fuck did you hatch?" Dax sighed, lighthearted. "Do you want me to find you or do you wanna come back to the bus stop?"

"I'll start heading towards the bus stop," Juliet told her. "Meet me in the middle?"

"Where the fuck are you?" Dax asked, and Juliet went around the back to find a street sign.

"Rosebud Road," Juliet informed her. Dax told her she was heading her way and hung up. Juliet went to say her goodbyes to Gracie and the others - Max and Joanie, who clapped her on the back and sent her on her way - before she threw her gloves in the trash by the door and left. The sun had set at some point, and Juliet kept her hands in her pockets as she walked. Finding her way back was much more difficult than it was to find the soup kitchen in the first place. She tried to navigate towards the orange lights of the bridge leading into downtown, but the buildings kept blocking her view. She ducked down an alley only to find it had a dead end when she reached a wall. She sighed and turned, but the way back to the street was shadowed by three figures who had not been there before.

"Oh, sorry," Juliet murmured, head down, moving to duck between them and leave, ignoring them like her years of handling menacing strangers had taught her to do. One of them caught her by the arm.

"Sorry for what?" he asked. His grip was tight, bruising; Juliet's heart jumped up into her throat, her mind going blank.

"Uhm." Juliet pulled at her arm, not sure what to do, mind rushing with static. His fingers constricted, and she pulled again on instinct. A flash in the corner of her eye made her jump closer to the man holding her by the wrist, and he took her shoulder in his other hand to keep her still.

"Answer him when he talks to you," the owner of the flash said, voice surprisingly high, crisp, the kind of voice that read stories to kids in a library, not the kind that mugged strangers in alleyways. The third figure stood a ways away from them, watching the mouth of the alley.

"Sorry, I'll just be going," Juliet clarified. She cleared her throat when it clumped up, and the man holding her reached up to yank her head back by her long braids.

"Let's see your wallet, alright? Turn your pockets inside out," spat the one holding the flash - a knife, Juliet realized, when it gleamed in the streetlight. Juliet reached down with shaking hands and turned her jacket pockets inside out. The guy with the knife took her phone and dropped it from his own trembling hand to the cement, shattering the screen. Juliet instinctively moved to grab it, and the knife flashed out, slashing at her left cheek. She jumped back, clutching at her cheek, feeling somehow betrayed as the man behind her grabbed onto her again.

"Knock that shit off, man," the man behind her said gruffly, somewhere in the area of her ear. She heard a soft *click* behind her, and something cold touching the back of her neck. *Gun*, her brain helpfully supplied. *Fucking gun. Do not move. Fucking gun behind you.*

"You can have my wallet," Juliet whispered, voice cracking on the halfway point. "Please. Just let me go."

"I don't know," the man with the knife said, edging towards her. "You might just do us some good after all."

"*No*," Juliet snapped, fear starting to course through her veins, freezing cold like ice water. She went limp on instinct, dropping all her weight downwards, forcing the man with the gun to grapple for her. She jerked her head backwards, the back of her skull colliding with his chin and his nose. The man with the knife struck out at her, blind in the darkness of the alley and the tangle of her and his friend, but he only nicked the juncture where her neck met her shoulder. She threw herself forward, arms around his knees and tossing him back against the ground. A hand grabbed at her hair from behind, and she lashed out blindly, scratching at the face of the man who had been keeping watch.

Lights flashed in Juliet's eyes unexpectedly, the illumination jarring her out of her act-don't-think mindset. She scrambled her weight backwards until she hit the wall of one of the buildings, the bright lights still blinding her. She wondered wildly if it might be aliens, come to abduct her, or come to save her. A door slammed, and, bizarrely, she thought the alien was coming to pick her up and take her away. She lashed out in front of her with a fist, striking the face of the man with the knife, knocking his nose sideways. The lights were interrupted by a new figure, blocking them for a brief moment, and then there was a tight hand wrapped around Juliet's wrist without warning. She struck out at it, but Dax's voice shushed her.

"Come on, come on, let's go," Dax instructed her, urgent. Juliet scrambled to her feet, dimly aware that Dax had a gun in her other hand. She used it to smack the side of the watchman's head when he reached out to grab at Juliet's ankles, sending him sprawling sideways. Juliet kicked at the man with the gun when he stood up, Dax pulling her as they sprinted towards the mouth of the alley. The lights, as it turned out, belonged to Dax's van, the headlights blinding as they ran to it.

"Get in," Dax ordered, yanking open the passenger door. Juliet scrambled inside, hyper-aware of the pounding of her pulse, her heart thumping against her chest. She slammed the door shut, but Dax didn't climb up into the driver's seat. Instead, when Juliet looked up from buckling her seatbelt, Dax was headed back into the alley. Juliet yanked against the seatbelt, trying to free herself again with shaking hands. She threw the door back open and leaned out the side of the van.

"Daksha!" Juliet screamed. Dax turned back and held up one finger before she approached the guy with the gun, his nose bleeding down his busted chin. She pistol-whipped him, just once, knocking him against the ground. He blinked up at her, dazed, and Dax moved on to the watchman, who seemed to be the most wary. He skittered back to the wall, and Dax changed paths, instead approaching the man who had had the knife. His nose was broken sideways, smudged against his cheek, and Dax dropped her gun to hold him by the collar and punch him in the face once, then twice, aiming to go again before Juliet called to her. Dax dropped him, retrieved her gun and Juliet's dying, shattered phone, and jogged back to the van. She clambered up into the driver's seat and hit reverse before she was buckled, Juliet scrambling to shut the passenger door. She reached over to buckle Dax up before she snapped herself in, Dax flying more than driving as they sped through the dark, empty roads of deep downtown.

"We'll leave in the morning," Dax said, the first thing she had said since the alleyway. Juliet glanced up at her, heart still pounding, hands trembling against her thighs.

"What?" Juliet turned back over her shoulder, but the street through the back windshield was empty. The orange lights of downtown Waterloo were getting closer and closer. Everything felt like it was on the edge of absurd. "But we didn't see any UFOs-"

"Do you want to wait and see a fucking UFO, Jules?" Dax snapped, and Juliet shut her mouth. "You just got jumped, and I don't know why you'd want to fucking hang around, but I would much rather just leave-"

"But that's not the *point-*"

"It is the point, you fucking dumbass, we're not staying here after that-"

"But the whole reason we came is because-"

"*Juliet,*" Dax interrupted, hands tight enough on the steering wheel that her knuckles were getting pale. They passed the orange bridge and kept going, heading in the direction of their campground. The two of them were quiet; the only sounds that broke their silence were the pebbles that their tires kicked up and the wind whipping through the slightly-open windows. Juliet worried Dax might fly right past the campground, keep driving without a destination, too angry to think.

"Can we sleep?" Juliet asked, softly, into the silence. "Can we stop at the campground?"

Dax glanced at her, and Juliet wondered what she looked like, or at least what Dax saw in her. She found it hard to look back, but she made herself do it anyways. Dax broke away first, putting her attention back on the road. She took the left towards the campground without a word and pulled into the same spot they had been parked in the night before. The two of them sat in the car as the engine stopped and fell silent. Juliet listened for the soft lapping of the little waves on the lake's shoreline through the window.

"I'm sorry," Juliet offered eventually. Dax turned to her, her eyes hard, her face sharp.

"It's not your fault, don't you fucking apologize to me." Dax ran a hand through her hair, and Juliet remembered vividly her head being yanked back, fingers pulling at her braids. She took a deep breath and opened her eyes, hardly remembering when she closed them. Dax was a little closer when she looked at her. She reached out, touching Juliet's jaw, fingertips tracing up her cheek. Juliet was bewildered before she remembered she had been slashed there.

"I have a first aid kit," Dax told her, a little quieter. She glanced down at the knife cut between Juliet's neck and her shoulder before she squirmed between their seats into the back of the van. Juliet followed, more gracefully but with more difficulty, Dax's hand on her forearm guiding her through. They sat on their makeshift bed, Dax pulling out a little Tupperware box filled with miscellaneous first aid items. She unsnapped the lid and withdrew a few loose cotton balls, a brown bottle of hydrogen peroxide, and a box of bandages. She unearthed a bottle of water from under her blankets and had Juliet hold a towel under her face while Dax used the water to clean out the gash on her cheek.

"I don't think you need stitches," Dax murmured, careful with the water, hand shaking only a little as she moved down to her neck to rinse that slash. "I'll just clean them, and close them, and we'll go to sleep. Okay?"

"Okay," Juliet whispered back, keeping her eyes focused on the curtain above Dax's head to stay distracted from the sting of pain. Dax started to dab at the cuts with hydrogen peroxide on cotton balls with one hand, reaching out to hold tightly to Juliet's fingers with the other when Juliet flinched. "I'm sorry."

"Don't be." Dax moved gently, pushing only as much as she needed to. "Does it hurt?"

"A little." Juliet shifted, trying to get her legs out from under her.

"Are you okay?" Dax asked, close to her face to make sure

the wound was clean. Her dark eyes darted up to look into Juliet's, then returned to the wound. Juliet shut her eyes once Dax looked away, squeezing them shut tight, teeth sharp on her lip.

"No," she breathed. Dax finished cleaning out the wounds, unwrapped a few butterfly bandages, and taped them on tightly, pinching the sides of the cuts shut to even out the edges. She finished in record time before pulling Juliet into her arms, holding her firmly as Juliet started sobbing into her neck, heart pounding, muscles finally starting to relax.

"I'm so sorry," she hiccuped into Dax's throat, too loudly, and Dax stroked at her back, rubbing circles against the bumps of her spine.

"Shh," Dax offered, soft, and Juliet tucked her face into her shoulder and cried until Dax pushed the first aid box off to the side and laid them down on top of the covers, heads on the wrong pillows as Dax wrapped around her.

"I'm not going to let anything else happen to you," Dax whispered. "I promise."

"Okay," Juliet murmured, Dax's hair falling into her face, their shoes still on their feet. She felt like she was supposed to say more, but Dax was quiet, so she was, too. She fell asleep like that, still crying, drifting somewhere in the night.

Chapter Six

When she woke up, Dax was still folded around her, breathing softly in her ear. She pushed Dax's hair out of her eyes and mouth and reached up to tangle their fingers together before she shut her eyes and let herself sleep for a while longer.

The next time she woke up, it was because Dax was delicately trying to extricate herself from Juliet's grip. She froze when Juliet's eyes landed on her.

"I was gonna go get us some water," Dax said quietly. The sun coming through the window suggested it was nearing afternoon. Juliet sat up, blinking against the light, and Dax yanked the curtains shut tight. "How are you feeling?"

"Tired," Juliet answered, after a moment of reflection. She reached up and tentatively touched her cheek, rubbing at the edge of one of her butterfly bandages. Dax reached out, pulling her hand away and setting it in her lap gingerly.

"Don't poke at it," Dax murmured. "You'll just make it worse." She hesitated, then let go of Juliet, shoving her own hands into the jacket she must have slept in, since both she and the jacket looked a little rumpled. "Is there anything I can do for you?"

Juliet genuinely considered the question, her hand brushing over her cheek, her shoulder, her neck, feeling bruises and scratches and the edges of bandages. Her glasses, when she pulled them off to look at them, only had a small crack on one side of the frame. She reached up and felt along her hairline, into her braids. She pulled at her braids, one sharp tug, and remembered how long they took to grow to be the perfect length to be yanked back in an alleyway.

"Let's shave my head," Juliet suggested. Dax reached out hesitantly, touching one micro braid, letting it slip through her fingers.

"But you're beautiful," Dax murmured, letting another one slide past her fingertips.

"Then let's cut it," Juliet offered instead. "I don't know. Anything. I just don't want long hair anymore. I don't want these."

"Okay." Dax let her go and sat back, eyes skimming from Juliet's scalp down to the tips of her braids. "Can you take them out yourself?"

"We can both do it," Juliet told her. "I can show you how." Juliet leaned back and dug around in her bag, unearthing her conditioner and her combs. "Do you have any scissors?"

"Yeah, somewhere." Dax started rooting through her side of the van, pulling through the bags until she found a sharp pair of sewing scissors. Juliet showed her what to do, cutting the ends of her braids, running conditioner through them, working them loose with the wide-toothed combs Juliet had gotten years ago from her mother. It took them a few hours, the two of them working in relative silence until Dax got up and unearthed her book of CDs to play music. Her hair curled in every direction, black and frizzy, twining around Dax's fingertips when she ran her hands through it.

"Now what?" Dax asked, pulling out her last braid while Juliet twisted hair around her knuckle. She let it go, the strand softly springing back towards her head.

"Can you cut hair?" Juliet asked, picking up the scissors. She ran the pad of her finger along one edge, than the other, while Dax watched her.

"I've only ever cut mine," Dax answered, and Juliet handed the scissors to her.

"Close enough." Dax closed her fingers around the scissors and rubbed at them with the edge of her shirt to clean them off while Juliet watched. "I've never cut my own hair and I don't want a stranger to do it right now."

"Are you sure about this?" Dax inquired, holding up the scissors once they were shining again. "Doesn't grow back that quickly."

"It's just hair," Juliet said, but what she meant was *it's too much and I don't want it, it's just hair but it's scaring me right now and I need control over something in my life.* Dax seemed to understand anyways. She was getting pretty good at that, it seemed. She used her own shitty phone to track down some spotty WiFi and search for instructions on what to do. She moved carefully, *so* gingerly, like both she and Juliet were made of glass, liable to smash if she moved too fast. She took away large chunks at first, cutting them away from her head in fistfuls. She let Juliet scroll through the page and choose a style, then kept cutting, hacking away, taking years and years of weight from Juliet's scalp. It collected on the blue towel under her from the night before, stains from the hydrogen peroxide littered with pitch-black hair, ravens against a faraway sky.

"There," Dax said, eventually, when the slant of the sun through the edges of the curtains was turning down towards setting. She pulled out her razor and her frightening hot-wired extension cord and hooked it into the car charger before skimming over the sides and back of Juliet's head, carving her style from granite. She moved slowly, at first, then focused on the back and the sides, moving in an intricate, delicate way, patterning her, sculpting her. When Juliet reached up when it was over, she felt stubble on her skull; further up, soft, thick hair, standing off the top of her head, shorter than it had been since she was four and her parents cut her hair for her.

"Look in the mirror," Dax suggested, as Juliet traced a line on the back of her head. Juliet sat up to look in the rearview mirror at the front of the van, and saw a new person looking back at her. Half of her face was covered in white-beige, butterfly bandages holding her cheek closed, one of her eyes swollen under her glasses, her lips chewed up and raw, scratches on her forehead. Her hair pushed back and swept off her forehead and towards her crown. The shaved sides had intricate diamonds shaved into them, a pattern that had required a careful and well-intentioned hand to put it there.

"Thank you," Juliet whispered, following the outline of a diamond with her fingertip. Dax opened the back door of the van and shook out the towel, brushing as much hair as she could out onto the ground outside with her hands and a paper plate she had found under the front seat. "I missed work today."

"Fuck work," Dax said, louder than anything else she had said since yesterday morning, starting to sound like herself again. "We're leaving."

"But the UFOs-"

"And fuck the UFOs," Dax continued, like Juliet had only been giving her an idea, not trying to protest. "I don't want to stay here anymore. We're leaving."

"Okay," Juliet agreed, and Dax paused before turning back to look at her, squinting a little.

"Why 'okay'?" she asked, and Juliet shrugged, sitting back on her heels.

"Just okay. Let's find somewhere else to go." She picked up her shattered phone from Dax's side of the van, where it had ended up the night before after Dax snatched it up. "We both need new phones."

"I-"

"Your phone is a piece of shit and it's older than it is useful," Juliet argued, cutting her off. "Let's get new phones downtown and then go."

"Fine," Dax said. "As long as we leave afterwards."

"Fine."

"Fine."

Dax stared back at Juliet, her attention darting up to her hair after a moment, then to her cheek, before resting on her eyes again. "Fine. Let's go." She shut the back doors of the van and shoved Juliet through to the passenger seat. They drove back to the front office, Juliet watching the lake out the window while Dax went in and got their money back for the next week, and the two of them left. Downtown heralded few options to get new phones, and Juliet picked two devices out for them, sizable machines with a good weight and a sturdy connection to the Internet. Dax spent the whole time carefully weighing her options and selecting two new cases for them. The phones paid for with some of their money from Merrimac and some of Dax's money from her long-forgotten excursions the day before, the two of them set out, Dax driving while Juliet searched for directions on her phone to find their next stop.

The road spun by under the wheels of their van, Juliet mostly longing to have her feet on solid ground again as they drove and she searched. She turned up with Pierre, South Dakota, a cold capital city seven hours to the northwest. Juliet made a point of mentioning Pierre was the capital of South Dakota, which Dax only smiled at. From the pictures, it looked like it had more trees than it did people, the Capitol building standing proudly above the leaves and the Missouri River carelessly slicing through the city. There were reports of unidentified flying objects swirling above the city, zig-zag, serpentine, flashing red and blue at night when people were looking for something to do. Dax agreed, and Juliet put the directions into her phone, and the two of them set off.

Having slept so long the night before, Dax seemed content to drive through the night until they reached Pierre, but Juliet dozed in the passenger seat, slipping in and out of consciousness while Dax kept her attention half-on the road, half-on the radio, disco switched out roughly for familiar glam rock. Dax sang along in a low voice, probably thinking Juliet was too asleep to hear her. Juliet listened in silence, content to let the night pass her by with her eyes focused on the street lights flicking past them and the music filtering through the speakers.

Dax must have let Juliet sleep for a while, because when she woke up, they were parked just outside of Pierre, in a campground with a wintry-looking lake and a layer of frost on the ground and in the trees around them. She had her blanket draped over her, tucked around her shoulders, her hands, her thighs, and her head propped on her pillow, leaning against the window. Most notably, however, Dax was gone. Juliet breathed slowly, kept herself calm, and waited. The CD player in the van was turned off, but her phone was plugged in and playing quietly, R&B music filtering onto her thigh. She leaned over and swiped the music off, listening instead to the wind outside, watching the light dusting of snow drift down onto the van and the windshield.

"Hey," Dax greeted her from the driver's seat, and Juliet jumped, waking back up from her hazy half-sleep. Dax's hair was wet, frozen at the very ends. She pulled it all down her back and started French braiding at her hairline. "How'd you sleep?"

"All right," Juliet answered, stretching out her back. "Where'd you go?"

"You get three guesses," Dax replied sardonically, water dripping from her hair down her wrist. "How are you feeling today?"

"I'm okay," Juliet told her, rubbing at the back of her head, stubble patterns underneath her fingers. She tipped her head forwards, watching Dax's fingers as she deftly braided her hair using the driver's side mirror. Dax felt closer now than before; the weeks they had spent together built up to a fusion, forged by fire in that alleyway, tying them together in a seared-tight little knot. She felt… She was not sure how she felt about it. She felt like she wanted to settle down with Dax, just a little bit. Which, *whoa, feelings, what the hell?*

Feelings were their own problem that Juliet was trying - rather valiantly, she might add - to ignore, or at least save to process until they earned their space in her brain. At the moment, she was still attempting to process her time in Waterloo, the roller coaster of extreme emotions she had experienced and how she had felt coming out of it. Particularly, she thought, she was struggling with how she felt about Dax. Though emotionally and physically jarring, and definitely needing time to get over, getting beat up was not an unfamiliar experience for a trans girl in Michigan. That, she could process, she could handle. Dax, though. She had never been particularly close with anyone besides her brothers, acquiring only friends who she would hang out with now and then, a couple roommates in college. She was bad at keeping in touch. It was easier to just have a routine all to herself and stick to it. That seemed to be over, though, in the face of her budding relationship with Dax.

Dax was roguish and weird. She was a scoundrel, if those even still existed. She had no idea how to talk about her feelings, it seemed like she lied quite a bit about things that hardly mattered, and she disappeared and never told Juliet where she went. She was also intelligent, moreso than she let on. She was incredibly brave, a heart of melted steel, always ready to act out and speak up when she needed to. She was beautiful, and charming, and adventurous, and easygoing. There was so much to her that filled all the blank spaces in Juliet's life that she had never even noticed were empty. She was good company, a warm spot against her chest. Juliet ached, abruptly, because feeling vibes like these made sense when she spent this much time with one person, but, God, what didn't make sense was why someone as wild as Dax would be into someone as reserved and organized and weird-in-a-different-way as Juliet was.

"You gonna quit staring anytime soon or should I put on a show?" Dax asked, and Juliet jerked back against the pillow, the crown of her head smacking the window. She pushed her thoughts back, ignoring them as best she could. *Maybe*, she thought, *if these thoughts don't come back, I won't have to deal with them.* Besides, a crush is a crush; those go away. No point in ruining this trip just because Juliet was emotionally repressed and had never spent this much time with one person she actually cared about outside of her immediate family before.

"Sorry," Juliet murmured, remembering herself. She pulled up her phone and texted Angelo, letting him know she was in Pierre. He sent back a series of emojis that, Juliet thought, were supposed to add up to something equaling 'South Dakota'. She put in the address of the pharmacy down the road to pick up her hormone prescription later that day. "What are we doing today?"

"I've got a job tomorrow, but nothing today," Dax answered, finishing up her braid. Juliet offered an elastic off her own wrist for her to tie it off with.

"I should start looking for a job while we're here," Juliet said back, but Dax was already shaking her head before she had finished talking.

"Last time you went to get a job, I just- Nah, let's hold off on this one." Dax leaned back in the driver's seat and reached out to rub at the back of Juliet's neck.

"I'm going to have to get some work at some point," Juliet reminded her. She reached into the back of the van and pulled out her bag of toiletries. "Where's the showers?"

"I'll take you." Dax pushed open the driver's side door and hopped out of the van. Juliet shoved her pillow and blanket to the backseat and followed after her. She scrubbed her skin clean, every inch of it, scouring each bit of grime and dirt from her skin. She was careful around her bandages, but otherwise she rubbed her skin raw with soap and bubbles until she was red and aching, her skin hot, her body sore and tired. Dax knocked on the door and helped her get dressed once she was dry.

"How about we go and get some lunch?" Dax suggested, playfully fluffing up Juliet's hair with a towel. She had been slowly learning how to use her new phone, having never had anything beyond her shitty flip phone that now sat in one of the cup holders in the back of the van. She tried now to find them a restaurant on her search browser, and Juliet watched without commenting, letting her navigate and figure it out for herself. When she found one she thought was suitable, she bundled Juliet back up into the passenger seat, spent a few minutes switching out her bandages, then headed them off hopefully in the direction of some place she found online.

"We deserve to treat ourselves," Dax told her, winding through the frosty streets of Pierre. "You, especially, kid. You've had a rough couple days and now you deserve some wine and some carbs and to just chill out for a day, you know? Just relax." She took a soft left, curving down the road. Juliet turned her attention out the window, at the people walking through the city, at the shops, the restaurants, the planter boxes filled with icy, dying flowers and shrubs.

Lunch was as Dax promised; she drank two Shirley Temples and a Roy Rogers just so Juliet could drink wine, since Juliet had made it clear that neither of them was going to drive with even a drop of alcohol in their systems. Juliet ate her pasta and drank her wine slowly, talking with Dax easily once she realized they had no idea what the other's middle name was. Dax almost choked laughing on the cherry from her first Shirley Temple at the look on Juliet's face when she registered that.

"My middle name is actually my grandmother's first name," Dax told her, attempting to tie the cherry stem with her tongue even though she had already admitted that she had no idea how. "My father wanted to name one of us after his mother, but my mother hated the name. He agreed to give it to one of us as a middle name only. So, my middle name is Sonali." Dax pulled the cherry stem out of her mouth, untied and bitten almost in half. "What's yours?"

"Magnolia," Juliet answered, twirling her pasta around her fork. "I just liked it. I picked both of my names myself."

"What was your birth name?" Dax asked, stabbing at the chicken in her pasta, pulling them all off to the side. "If you don't mind my asking."

"I don't mind." Juliet kept her focus on her pasta, continuing to twirl it even after it was all wrapped around the fork. "My name was Romeo."

"Obviously," Dax laughed, trying not to snort with her laughter and failing. "Obviously you picked Juliet when your name was Romeo. You're such an asshole."

"That's me," Juliet said, smiling back. The only other person who had ever thought it was funny was Angelo. "Lorenzo's the oldest, so Abraham was his middle name, my dad's name. My middle name was just something my mother came up with, nothing that had any ties because neither of my parents liked their own dads."

"So?" Dax asked, when Juliet wasn't forthcoming with her name. She shrugged.

"Marquis," Juliet offered, eventually, before shoving her forkful of tightly-curled pasta into her mouth. Dax took a full minute to stop laughing so hard.

"I'm sorry, *Romeo Marquis?*" Dax asked, once she got her breathing back to normal. "Were your parents Edgar Allan Poe? Did they fuckin' hate you?" She took a sip of her drink, still laughing. "Jesus Christ, good on you for changing it. Juliet Magnolia is *way* better." She shoved four pieces of chicken into her mouth at once. "What's Angelo's middle name, then?"

The conversation continued comfortably from there. The itch from the past couple of days started to seep out of Juliet's muscles, to her skin, out through her pores as she finally relaxed. They shared tiramisu for dessert, which led to Juliet's realization that she did not like tiramisu very much. Dax pulled the whipped cream parts off to the side carefully for her to eat with the last of her wine. They dragged up some of Dax's money from her mystery excursion several days before to pay the bill and left. The van stayed in the parking lot while they walked through the city, Dax's arm wound through Juliet's as they navigated the sweet, cold streets of Pierre. Juliet had half an eye out for job openings as they went.

"I know what you're doing," Dax commented as Juliet peeked through the windows of a deli when she spotted a red sign. "Knock it off. We don't need cash that bad."

"We need to be making money," Juliet argued mildly, heading towards the door. Dax appeared to give up, going along with her like a tired dog being pulled along at the end of a walk. Juliet was able to get a job working for two weeks at the counter, a position the manager's wife seemed excited about. Juliet could hear her talking to her husband as she left about maybe getting out of town for a little bit, since she was taking her position for two weeks.

"See, I made her day," Juliet commented as they left, plucking a dying leaf off a shrub as they left the deli and kept walking. The sun was already starting to set. "We're doing pretty well for ourselves."

"Why aren't you more upset?" Dax asked abruptly, a hard edge to her voice. "I mean- *fuck*, Jules, come on. That wasn't a fun night we had the other night."

"No," Juliet agreed. "No, it wasn't. You're right." She

stopped walking and instead sat down on a bench they had been on the verge of passing. Dax hesitated before sitting down next to her, hands stuffed in the pockets of her jacket. Juliet fought the urge to reach out and fix the edge of her shirt's collar underneath her leather jacket. She was still learning the boundaries they kept up between them.

"I guess…" Juliet trailed off, thinking. Dax did not interrupt, for once, letting her work out her thoughts before she said them. "This isn't the first time this has happened, I guess. This happened back in high school a few times, a couple times in college. It hasn't happened in a little while, but it isn't new. And it wasn't for the same reasons. So, I just…" Juliet fiddled with the edge of her cuff for something to look at instead of Dax's face. She could feel her staring at her. "I just. It could have been worse, I guess. So, I'm focusing on that. I'm not thrilled about it. It's not like I'm happy it happened or that I'm ignoring it or anything. I'm just… I'm dealing with it."

"You can't bottle things up like that," Dax said, more quietly than she usually spoke. "You gotta talk things through. Pretending you're happy isn't helping either of us."

"Am I pretending I'm happy?" Juliet asked, turning up to look at Dax, abandoning her fraying jacket sleeve. Dax shrugged a little, reaching inside her pocket to pull out her cigarettes and lighter. She held the box out to Juliet, and Juliet took the entire box, shoving it into her own pocket.

"It feels like you are," Dax answered, putting her lighter away, a small frown creasing the space between her eyebrows. "I just want you to talk to me. That's it."

Juliet tipped her head to the side to watch her. How much had she been keeping inside? In the weeks they had spent together so far, Dax seemed content to just listen to what Juliet said and never push her for more.

She's a person, too, Juliet's mind supplied. Juliet frowned, her attention slipping down to the stuck collar of Dax's shirt. *She exists outside of you.* Juliet glanced back up at Dax's eyes, warm and nearly black, waiting for an answer that may or may not have come. Juliet had never pinned her for the type to talk about feelings. Maybe it was just *her* feelings Dax cared about.

"I'm sorry," Juliet apologized, and Dax paused before reaching out and slinging her arm around Juliet's shoulders, tugging her in. Juliet smiled, just a little bit, letting her head collide with Dax's collarbone.

"You don't have to apologize to me," Dax told her, voice muffled from her mouth pressing into Juliet's skull. She squeezed her once before releasing her, letting Juliet lean back into her own spot. "I just want you to be happy. You never talk about anything. I didn't want to push you, I just-"

"I understand," Juliet said. She turned her attention up to examine the street, reading the signs dangling over the sidewalk down the line of shops. "Do you want ice cream?"

"Fuck yeah." Dax sprang to her feet. She held one hand out, and Juliet gave her back her cigarettes. "I'm working on it, I swear."

"Sure you are," Juliet agreed, disbelieving, but Dax did pocket the cigarettes without lighting one up. "Your lungs will thank you."

"They might thank *you*," Dax said, reaching out to pull her arm through Juliet's again. "They're already pretty pissed at me for shaving a few years off their lives."

Dax got a banana walnut cone, after spending time scoffing at Juliet for playing it safe with a cup and a spoon. She also raised an eyebrow when Juliet was thinking about getting chocolate.

"What's wrong with that?" Juliet asked. Dax smiled, licking a drop of melting ice cream that was threatening to drip down her sleeve.

"Racism is dead, Jules," Dax joked before starting to laugh so hard she couldn't breathe, and Juliet ended up getting cherry vanilla just to stop her from laughing so much and potentially choking herself. Desserts in hand, Juliet and Dax headed back out into the streets of Pierre, Juliet marking down the address where the deli was located when they passed by it again, Dax flicking through what seemed to be emails on her phone, humming to herself tunelessly. They walked all the way back to the van, nonsense dominating their conversation, talking about anything that happened to logically follow the flow of topics. Dax bravely bit into the last of her cone so she could drive them back to the campground with both hands free while Juliet sat in the passenger seat and scooped the last vestiges of melted cherry vanilla out of the bottom of her cup.

"I've got to be at the deli pretty early tomorrow," Juliet mentioned, trying to get the last of the ice cream off her spoon without looking too desperate for it. *A battle lost before it has even begun.*

"If it's alright, I think I'm gonna go to bed earlier tonight. We'll have all night tomorrow to hang out."

"That's fine," Dax answered, pulling back into the campground and finding their spot again. She made sure to crank the windows shut as tightly as she could to keep the cold chill outside. The two of them changed rather quickly, Dax taking her hair down and combing the braid out with her fingers before she tucked herself up under her covers. Juliet fell asleep facing her.

Chapter Seven

Juliet had to shake Dax awake the next morning to get her to drive them to the deli, and that was where Dax left her, bleary and glaring at her through the window before she drove away to God-knows-where for the day. When Dax came back that evening, the sun still high enough to light the streets, Juliet joined her with a handful of cash.

"Where to?" Dax asked, already starting to drive without a destination. Juliet dropped the money on the dashboard and leaned back in her seat, wriggling to get comfortable before she tipped her head back to smile at Dax.

"I trust you," Juliet answered, and Dax fiddled with her search browser. "You're getting better at that."

"Thanks," Dax murmured, mostly focused on trying to find somewhere for them to get food and not running them off the road. Their dinner was at a moderately nice table, a booth where their ankles kept getting tangled, breadsticks hot on the small table between them. Juliet found them a karaoke bar to hang out in afterwards, where Dax proved just how many songs she knew from the top forty and Juliet slowly realized she was in over her head.

"Let's try and find a fuckin' UFO," Dax exclaimed, voice lifting out the open windows of the van as they left. "I can't believe you forgot last night. You let me go to bed at eight o'clock like we're a thousand years old-"

"It was eleven and you forgot, too-"

"So, now, we've got double the amount of UFOs to find tonight," Dax continued, ignoring any protest Juliet had to offer. Dax navigated like she had arrows on the road bringing her back to the campground; Juliet took a moment to appreciate her memory and natural sense of direction before the icy little snowflakes started to fall and whip into her face through the open window. She cranked down the window as fast as she could, but Dax still laughed when she turned to face her, brushing the snow out of her hair.

"Thanks, Jack Frost." Dax smacked snow out into her lap, where it melted almost instantly.

"Do you have a tent or anything we can set up?" Juliet asked, brushing off her arms. Dax kept letting the snow lash at her face without so much as putting up her collar. "Before you make us lay out on the roof and freeze to death?"

"First of all, I have bathrobes, so, nice try," Dax replied, pulling smoothly into their spot at the campground. "Second of all, I have a plan, so don't worry."

Fuck off, 'I have a plan,' Juliet thought bitterly an hour later, when she was still up on the roof, snow falling into her face. Dax had covered them both up with blankets and four bathrobes from one of her bags, tugged ski masks onto both of their faces, and gave them both sunglasses to cover their unprotected eyes. "This is not a plan," Juliet said out loud, letting Dax know she was feeling petulant. Dax probably rolled her eyes, not that Juliet could *see her.*

"Just go to sleep, that's what you do best when we're looking for UFOs," Dax told her. Her voice sounded like she was grinning, but Juliet couldn't see her face enough through the ski mask to know for sure, so she held back from smacking her without proper evidence. Juliet pulled out her phone and started reading an ebook about extraterrestrial trouble spots in America.

"At least one of us is doing work," Juliet replied, when Dax leaned over and started making fun of her for studying. "I'm trying to actually figure out where we'll find an alien. I don't know if we'll find one in Pierre."

"But isn't it nice?" Dax asked, wiggling back to her own side and continuing to watch the sky, arms folded behind her head. "To just live free."

"I'd like to have some semblance of a plan, thanks," Juliet remarked, going back to her book. Dax ended up reaching over and plucking it out of her hands roughly half an hour, declaring that she was lonely and Juliet needed to pay more attention to her. Juliet rolled her eyes, but Dax either couldn't see it or ignored her - likely the latter, because it was pretty obvious she rolled her eyes - and instead pillowed her head on Juliet's chest and kept her eyes on the sky.

"You can't even see anything," Juliet pointed out. "It's cloudy. More than that, man, it's *snowing*. What do you think you're going to see?"

"I don't think I'll know until I see it," Dax answered, continuing to stare up. Juliet fell asleep first after that, like she usually did, Dax still reclining against her and keeping watch for something that would either try to abduct them or just straight-up kill them. Based on the fact that Juliet woke up a couple hours later when Dax shook her and dragged her back to the ground, none of that happened, but Juliet still had a strange dream about getting kidnapped by aliens and being taken to a big trash compactor.

Working at the deli during the days was okay. Juliet could take it or leave it; she appreciated that it gave her and Dax cash to fill the van with gas and to fill themselves with water and hot food. She and Dax used a little bit of money to get flu shots at a local drugstore drive one day, and Dax needed to take the van to a repair shop and replace the spark plugs one day, but that was about the extent of their expenses at the moment.

It was the nights that Juliet really enjoyed, when she got out of work and Dax picked her up and they found something to do in Pierre. They alternated nights to choose something, Juliet choosing to tour the State House one day, Dax breaking them into an off-season vineyard the next, Juliet bringing them to an aquarium the day after that, on and on through one week and into the next. Dax wound her arm through Juliet's, pointing out a shark above their heads in the aquarium, throwing her arm across Juliet's shoulders as they watched a community production at the neighborhood playhouse. Juliet started to settle into the rhythm of their lives in Pierre, God help her. She knew Dax was getting antsy, starting to look up the next place to go on her phone while Juliet was reading. Juliet tried to enjoy their last days as best as she could, even if no aliens revealed themselves at night, no blinking lights showed up in the night sky to end their journey or give them any hope going forwards. Instead, it was just clouds, the occasional snowfall; helicopters and planes now and then made Dax twitch and point upwards only to be ultimately disappointed.

"Where the hell did you bring us?" Juliet asked, leaning out the window as Dax parked out back of an unassuming building with letters on the side that could only have been painted in the 1970s or earlier. It was Dax's turn to choose their activity, and she had been secretive about it the whole way there.

"Nightclub," Dax answered, turning the van off and clambering into the back. She started changing her clothes from her warm day clothes into something showing a hell of a lot more skin, and Juliet turned back around to watch out the windshield instead.

"Why are we at a nightclub?" Juliet asked, picking at the fraying end of her coat sleeve.

"Because you made me go to the Cultural Heritage Center yesterday," Dax answered, a grin in her voice. "I'm sorry, am I scandalizing you?"

Juliet turned back around, and her heart threw itself against her ribcage at how beautiful Dax looked. "No," Juliet said, dumbly, trying to actually come up with something to say. "I just… Aren't you going to be cold?"

Dax picked up her same worn leather jacket and threw it on over her shimmering black dress. "There. Fixed." She ran her hand over the open patches of skin on her side through the dress. "We never dress up for anything."

"I don't think aliens care what we're wearing," Juliet commented, watching as Dax started to root through her bags. "I'm sorry, have we totally given up on personal space?"

"I'm surprised you still have any concept of personal space when we spent most of our days in a van together," Dax replied, digging out a dress from Juliet's bag and holding it up. "How about this?"

"Won't *I* be cold?" Juliet asked, and Dax rolled her eyes before balling the dress up and throwing it into Juliet's face. She started pulling through her own bags again for a little sack of makeup that looked like a magician's bag.

"It's not cold *inside* the club, dumbass," Dax informed her. "You're a foot from the front door. Nut up or shut up."

Juliet climbed into the back and changed with minimal grumbling, letting Dax shove heels on her feet and slap makeup on her face before she all but dragged her out through the back door of the van. Dax checked her jacket pockets for cash before transferring some of the money to her bra, some to her shoes, some to Juliet's bra, and the last of it to Juliet's shoes while Juliet stared at her. Dax chucked her jacket back into the van before slamming the doors shut, locking the behemoth, and tucking the keys into her bra.

"Don't get lost," Dax whispered in her ear, winding her arm through Juliet's as they entered the nightclub. It was not very much like the movies; there were no bouncers, or red velvet ropes, or anything like that. There was loud music, pulsing lights, people *everywhere*, and - Dax was right - it was hot as hell in there. Dax tugged her over to the bar. "Who's designated tonight?"

"I am," Juliet decided without needing to even think about it, watching two people grind on each other next to her. "Drink as much as you want."

"Don't have to tell me twice." Dax turned back to the bar and stretched up onto her toes to shout her drink of choice to the bartender over the din of voices and music in the nightclub. She got Juliet a virgin margarita, which Juliet sipped at while leaning against the bar, watching Dax slam back two Moscow Mules before getting herself a Baltimore Zoo that she decided to take her time with. She listed against the bar next to Juliet, watching the club throb like it was one organism with too many limbs.

"Have you ever been to a club before?" Dax called over the music, dark red mouth close to Juliet's ear. Juliet shook her head, and Dax nudged at her drink with her free hand. "Finish that up, let's get out there."

Juliet tipped her head back and drank the last dregs of her virgin margarita while Dax turned away from her with an empty glass - when the *hell* - before grabbing her wrist and tugging her towards the dance floor. Juliet abandoned her empty glass and followed her out, not that she had much choice, and let Dax envelop them in the middle of the crowd. She reminded herself there was nobody paying any attention to them, that nobody cared about her and she could do whatever she wanted, that Dax was never going to let anything happen to her.

True to her word, Dax had no sense of personal space. She edged close to Juliet, pushed nearer by the crowd, and let the thumping bass and shoving bodies keep them together. Juliet had only ever seen people dance like Dax was in movies and on pay channels, but here she was, the exact subject of a few confusing dreams Juliet had had in the past few weeks.

"Dance," Dax shouted in her ear, and Juliet tried her best to mimic her movements, tracing the actions of her hips, of her wrists, letting music move her instead of her brain. Dax left only a few times to get drinks, one time to smoke outside while Juliet leaned against the wall beside her, catching her breath. The whole night was something else; it was exhausting, sweltering, and exhilarating, moving like that, having Dax moving like that with *her*. Someone got too close, and Dax edged them away, grinning like a wolf at Juliet, letting her hands fall to her hips, her back. Juliet ached like an open wound, watching Dax move like that. She really was beautiful.

"You look tired," Dax called to her, and Juliet picked up her wrist to check the time, shocked that it had been over three hours. "Are you ready to head back?"

"Whatever you want," Juliet replied, and Dax shook her head, tipping it closer so Juliet's lips were closer to her ear. Juliet repeated herself, louder, and Dax laughed.

"It's not whatever I want," Dax shouted back, turning and striding away before Juliet could ask what the hell she meant by that. Dax got another Baltimore Zoo for herself, glancing to Juliet, who got herself a Shirley Temple. She bit the cherry off and gave Dax the stem to let her continue her attempts at tying into a knot with her tongue. She was more clumsy than usual, trying her best, but the alcohol in her was making her sloppy and happy. She laughed as she pulled a bent stem out of her mouth.

"What's important is that you tried," Juliet told her, and Dax laughed for two minutes while Juliet sipped at her Shirley Temple, pushing the ice around with her straw. When Dax gathered herself, having lost the cherry stem, she threw back the rest of her drink, barely gathered the patience to let Juliet finish hers, and paid their tab. She pulled Juliet outside; once she was out there, she tipped her head back, eyes shut, and took a deep breath. Juliet glanced up, as well.

"Hey, look at that," Juliet pointed out, voice a little rough from shouting so much over the music inside. Her ears were still ringing. "The sky's pretty clear tonight." As she pointed upwards, Dax opened her eyes to look at the moon, and a star streaked through the sky. Dax rubbed at her eyes and looked away.

"It's beautiful," Dax commented before pulling away and heading over to the back of the building to throw up in a bush. Juliet followed and lifted her hair up and back, holding it out of the way while she was sick. She let her finish, then sat with her, the two of them leaning against the building for a little bit while she caught her breath.

"You okay to go home?" Juliet asked, and Dax nodded, leaning her head against Juliet when they stood up, Juliet let her rest there for a while, arm wrapped around her shoulders. Dax just breathed, slowly, one hand fisted in Juliet's dress, white fabric tangled up in tawny skin, knuckles white with the tightness of her grip. Dax eventually pulled away, and Juliet pushed her hair off her forehead while Dax stared into her face.

"Thanks," Dax murmured, reaching out to trace Juliet's hairline from one temple to the other. She touched at the edge of the bandages still covering half of Juliet's face, then pulled away. Juliet helped her get back to the van, though Dax seemed to not need as much help with it as Juliet had originally assumed. She did need a boost up into the passenger seat, and Juliet buckled her in before climbing in herself and taking them back to the campground. Dax spent most of the ride with her head tilted out the open window, chilly wind whipping her hair back away from her face. Juliet handed her two pieces of hard mint gum from one of the cupholders, and Dax chewed absently at them as they drove.

"Do you want to just go to sleep tonight?" Juliet asked, once she pulled into their spot at the campground. Dax shook her head, dragging herself up and out of her seatbelt and her seat, shoving open the door and sliding out. Juliet hurried after her, grabbing the back of her dress to stop her from falling face-first onto the ground. Dax steadied herself, landing her feet on the frozen ground and letting Juliet drape her in a blanket.

"I want to see the aliens," Dax murmured, staring up at the sky. Juliet took her by the hand and led her around to the back of the van, pulling the key from her heel and unlocking the back door before hauling Dax up into it. Dax let her yank her dress off, put her pajamas on, then bundle her up in bathrobes, jackets, a ski mask, and sunglasses before propping her up against the seat and doing the same for herself. Dax watched her sleepily, drowsing now and then before snapping back awake each time. Juliet tugged her ski mask on and nudged Dax up onto the roof with their pillows and blankets. Dax sprawled out, spread-eagle on her stomach, until Juliet pushed at her to move to the side and make space for her.

"Thank you," Dax said, the two of them trapped under blankets and bathrobes and the sky up above. She curled up around Juliet, head tucked into her neck, and fell asleep almost at once. Juliet pressed her hand up underneath her ski mask to feel her skin, make sure she was warm enough. She was sweating a little bit, so Juliet tracked her hand down to Dax's throat, feeling for her pulse point. Her heart pounded steadily against Juliet's fingers. She snuck her arm under Dax and held her close for a while before falling asleep herself.

"Jules," Dax murmured near Juliet's ear, and Juliet swatted at her, pulling away and rolling to her side. Dax's hands yanked her back, and, when Juliet opened her eyes, she saw how close she was to falling off the roof. Dax rolled her onto her back again, staring down at her as the images of Juliet's dreams flickered away from her, flighty memories of flashing lights and loud music escaping her.

"What?" Juliet asked, heart edging back from pounding now that she was no longer in danger of falling off the roof. Dax had pulled off her ski mask and her sunglasses, and Juliet did the same, running her hand through and over her hair to give it lift.

"Do you see that?" Dax asked, pointing up at the sky. Juliet pulled her sunglasses off and squinted up at the dark sky, her eyes still adjusting. "Shit."

"What?" Juliet glanced at her, but Dax didn't look back, too busy scowling at the sky.

"You missed them again," Dax told her. She sat up fully and ran a hand through her snarled hair. Juliet scooted over and started gingerly untangling the knots out of her hair. "The aliens. The UFOs. I saw them."

"Yeah?" Juliet asked, working at her hair. "What did you see?"

"Just like you said," Dax responded, eyes still fixed on the sky, barely flinching when Juliet pulled on her hair. "There were three of them, though. They had red and blue lights flashing on it. They blinked a lot. They did kind of a zig-zag." Dax craned her head to look around at the entirety of the night sky laid out before them. "And now they're gone."

"I'm sure they'll come back," Juliet assured her. She tilted

Dax's head back to look into her face. "Do you want to go to bed?"

"I wish I had a picture," Dax mourned, frowning up at the sky. Her eyes darted over to Juliet's face, and Juliet reached into her pockets and dug out Dax's phone.

"Why don't you write it down?" Juliet suggested, and Dax spent the next fifteen minutes clumsily writing down her experiences in the memo pad on her phone while Juliet combed out her hair. "How's that?"

"That's good," Dax told her, handing the phone back to her. Juliet pocketed it and helped Dax down off the roof. "We should leave in the morning."

"Are you sure?" Juliet asked, sliding Dax down the windshield to the ground before following. Dax nodded before moving drowsily around to the back of the van, letting Juliet do most of the work in guiding her under her covers. Dax turned over onto her side and was asleep in seconds. Juliet slammed the doors shut tightly, locked them from the inside, and curled up next to her to fall back asleep.

The next day found Juliet waking up first, as per usual. The light was coming in at a slant, already leading into afternoon, which Juliet cut herself some slack over since they had gone to sleep so late after working off so much energy. She pulled out her phone from where it was plugged in and started flicking through her bookmarks, looking for something that was nearby. She ended up settling on Yellowstone National Park, since there were so many articles about it, some claiming there were entire fleets of UFOs, some claiming there was an alien base underneath the park.

Plus, she thought, *these pictures look beautiful.* She kept flicking through the pictures the Internet offered for the park until Dax blinked awake and squinted at Juliet, eyes bloodshot.

"I should've drank more water," Dax croaked, ducking her head down to clear her throat. Juliet brushed her hair back from her face and handed her one of their water bottles from under the front seats. Dax sat up cautiously, sipping at the water while Juliet pulled her hair back and started braiding it loosely in a fishtail. Juliet edged towards the van door when she finished, opening it up and waiting for the six seconds it took for Dax to lurch forwards and vomit out the back door and onto the ground outside. Juliet tucked her braid under her shirt for her, to keep it from dangling into her face. She rubbed her back in circles until Dax leaned back against her, catching her breath.

"I fucking hate past-me," Dax groaned, laying back down in the van with her head in Juliet's lap. Juliet stroked through the loose hair at her forehead, letting her nails scratch her scalp.

"I had a good night," Juliet commented, smiling down at Dax. Dax scowled at her and shoved at her weakly before rolling back into the van, hiding under the covers. Juliet stretched into the front seat for more mint gum.

"How about I bring you to the front, we get you showered, brush your teeth, put you in your pajamas, and I'll drive to our next place?" Juliet suggested, giving Dax the mint gum. She started to stroke through her hair again. "You can get some more sleep. Do you want anything to eat?"

"No," Dax mumbled into her pillow, her voice muffled. Juliet dug some of their bread out from their grocery bags and gave Dax two pieces to chew on while she found her more water and some aspirin. Dax took the water and aspirin gratefully, continuing to gnaw at the bread, eating the crusts off first in strips while Juliet drove them to the front house of the campground. She helped a visibly exhausted Dax into the showers, stepped out to let her clean herself, assisted her in brushing her teeth and getting dressed. She was bundled back into the van in record time. Juliet only stopped in town briefly to stop at the pharmacy and to pick up her check from the deli and cash it before they left.

Chapter Eight

Juliet drove carefully, the stereo on the lowest volume she could manage while still hearing it, the directions coming from her phone muted so she could follow it without waking up Dax. She let Dax sleep though, selfishly, she did want to wake her up so she had company. Dax slept on in the back of the van, happy to miss the entire trip. She slept all the way until around 10:00, only halfway through the drive; even then, she only sat up and made bleary, tired conversation while sipping at her water and continuing to bite hunks out of the white bread they had left.

"How are you feeling?" Juliet asked, once or twice, and Dax flipped her off each time. They passed through Mount Rushmore; Juliet stopped, got out, took a picture. She uploaded it to Instagram. She didn't agree with the whole arrangement, but the both of them loved seeing it in person, Juliet thought. It was wonderfully large and elegant. It felt like something bigger than them, and smaller, all at once. Dax fell asleep in the van before Juliet was done looking at it, but they were on the road again before they knew it.

Getting to Yellowstone was a long, arduous road, but a beautiful one, truly magnificent as they drove through the separate winters of South Dakota, Montana, and Wyoming. Juliet was a much less aggressive driver than Dax, but she did end up yelling at a few people in traffic, as well as pointing out the state capitals when they drove by them, Cheyenne being the last of them. Dax, eventually, asked where they were going, and Juliet passed her the phone and asked her to give her directions. Dax hauled herself up into the passenger seat with two pillows and three bathrobes, navigating through the streets of Wyoming for her.

"I think we're here," Juliet pointed out, and Dax snapped out of her half-doze to watch the trees and cabins flick by the window. Juliet stopped outside the wooden registration building to buy them a spot, even though it was nearly three in the morning by the time they actually got there. The night ranger took their cash and showed them to their parking spot with a flashlight, Dax hanging out the window the entire time. Juliet parked, though not as smoothly as Dax typically did, and thanked the night ranger for her trouble. She left Juliet and Dax there as Dax seemed to catch her second - or, possibly, first - wind, hopping out the back of the van and going to investigate the trees. Juliet locked the van behind them and followed after her.

"This place has definitely seen some alien action," Dax commented, feeling along the bark of a tree Juliet couldn't even see the top of, it was so tall and the night was so dark. "I wouldn't be surprised if this was another Area 51, to be honest with you." She leaned in and rapped on the tree trunk with her knuckles, pressing her ear to it like she was expecting it to be hollow. She held out her other hand to Juliet, one finger extended to point at her. "Stop thinking so loud, I can hear you. You're distracting me."

"You can not," Juliet disagreed, but she did step back a little bit. Dax smiled at her, bringing her hands back to the trunk and feeling along it. "Are you still drunk?"

"On life," Dax answered. She stepped back, hands on her hips, and stared down at the tree's roots before picking one to follow. Juliet let Dax lead her all over creation, exploring the campground in its entirety.

"Indian's Landing, eh?" Dax asked when they found the sign. She scoffed. "*I'm* Indian. This place isn't Indian."

"You're Pakistani. Barely; you're American," Juliet corrected, and Dax waved her off.

"Details. Point is, when are they gonna start cleaning this shit up?" Dax gestured to the sign, then to the park as a whole. "Give the nation back, am I right? It's not ours."

"Maybe it's time to go back to sleep, since you're babbling," Juliet suggested, and Dax followed her back to the van, where she refused to do anything even resembling sleep. When Juliet finally dozed off on the roof of the van, Dax was making up stories about the stars in the sky. One of the constellations looked suspiciously like it was flipping Juliet off. Dax kept muttering long into the night, if the way Juliet half-heard her words in her dreams was any indication.

"Isn't this place beautiful?" Juliet woke up to the next morning, as Dax hovered over her on the roof. Juliet blinked up at her, her face chilly, her body warm under the multitude of covers Dax must have stacked up on her. "You picked a good one, Jules, I'll give you that. It's called Indian's Landing, though. *I'm* Indian. This place isn't-"

"You said that," Juliet interrupted her, rubbing at her eye with the back of her hand. "You said that last night. Quit recycling old jokes."

"Maybe you didn't laugh enough last time." Dax leaned back on her hands, watching as Juliet woke up, shaking the sleep off of herself. Juliet's dreams had been filled with Dax's voice and face and the trees high above their heads. Dax was playing with one of Juliet's boots absently, tossing it back and forth between her hands. "What are we gonna do today?"

"Assuming you're feeling better," Juliet said, pushing at her hair with her hands until it was standing up the way she wanted, "then maybe we can go look for jobs in town today."

"What town is Yellowstone even attached to?" Dax asked, throwing the boot up above her head and catching it again, fiddling with the frayed end of one of the laces. Juliet pulled her phone from her pocket and did a quick Internet search.

"West Yellowstone," Juliet told her, and tapped the directions in before sliding down the windshield to the ground. "Let's go."

"I need another shower, man," Dax told her, sniffing at her arms. "Where's the bathroom in this place?"

Juliet helped Dax gather up their toiletries and find the bathrooms and showers. The two of them took their time, enjoying the warmth; Dax languidly brushed out her hair while Juliet self-administered her hormones. The tips of Dax's wet hair started to freeze on the way back, and Dax spent most of the walk lamenting their lack of a hair dryer and proclaiming that she was going to get one before they did anything else in town.

"My hair is way too thick for this," Dax complained, pulling at her slowly-freezing hair, trying to pick the little particles of ice out of the strands before she lost them again. Juliet noted she still had not started wearing her nicotine patches. "I'm sick of it. Why do I bother?"

"Because you're beautiful," Juliet answered without thinking about it. She kept walking without glancing back, and they were in town before she knew it, driving the van through the wide, snowy streets of West Yellowstone. Juliet switched her prescription to the pharmacy in West Yellowstone before she asked Dax to pull over at a huge wooden lodge-looking building with an enormous signboard dangling in the front. Dax left her there to seek a job in what turned out to be a woodsy restaurant while Dax herself sought a hair dryer.

"You're new," the manager said, when Juliet asked her if there was a position available for her for the next couple of weeks. He looked Juliet up and down, uncomfortably sizing her up. Juliet wondered distantly what Dax would think if she was here to watch him. His name tag was handwritten and said *Walter*. His penmanship was terrible. "What do you do?"

"Uhm." Juliet wrapped her hands together behind her back, nails digging into the skin and muscle at the backs of her hands. "I have experience hosting and serving. I can also clean, if that's what you'd like. I'm an okay chef but that's not really where my strengths lie, I'd say I'm-"

"Yeah, whatever," Walter interrupted, cutting her off with a wave of his hand. Her jaw snapped shut and she stopped herself from rocking back on her heels. His gray temples were wet with sweat. "Come back tomorrow at six sharp. In the *morning*. You can fill in for Teddy until he comes back."

"When is Teddy coming back, if you don't mind my asking?" Juliet asked, nails still sharp on her hand. Walter gave her a look that suggested she should have already made herself scarce.

"When he comes back," Walter answered her, as though she were simple. He raised an eyebrow and shooed her away with a heavy flick of the wrist. "Be here at six."

"Yes, sir," Juliet responded, leaving at once. The bartender raised an eyebrow at her as she left, his skin seeming chalky under the lights of the restaurant. Juliet slipped outside and tugged up the collar of her coat against the late February chill. She shoved her hands far enough into her pockets that she almost tore the soft lining of them before setting out down the street towards the pharmacy, picking up her hormones. She headed off in the direction Dax had left in, trying to find any convenience store Dax might have stopped at in her hunt for a hair dryer. The wind whipped at her face as she walked, ice flakes slapping at her cheeks. She kept an eye out for any possible pathways to an underground alien base, but her hopes were not all that high.

"Yo!" Dax shouted, snapping Juliet out of her own head. When Juliet skid to a stop on the snowy sidewalk, Dax stopped, too, the van screeching to a halt right next to her. "You lost?"

"A little bit," Juliet answered, coming up to lean against the open passenger window. Dax raised an eyebrow at her.

"Come here often?" she asked salaciously, grinning with all her teeth. Juliet hauled herself up through the window instead of opening the door, a decision she would have regret more had Dax not laughed so hard at it.

"Did you get your hair dryer?" Juliet inquired politely, dusting the snow and van grime off of herself. "We really have to wash this van."

"The snow will wash it," Dax said, reaching back into the van and fishing around before unearthing a paper bag. She thrust it towards Juliet's lap. "There we go, right there."

"We've got a hair dryer, a six-pack of beer, two lipsticks, a discount ornament shaped like a pickle, a pack of cigarettes, and four chocolate bars," Juliet listed off as she pulled each item out of the bag. She tucked the cigarettes under her leg, between her thigh and the seat, and held up the chocolate bars. "Does that mean we have four new friends?"

"Now you get no new friends," Dax answered, knocking the candy out of her hands while Juliet laughed. "You ruined it. You see what you did? It's soiled now. I hope you're happy. Now none of us get any friends and it's all your fault."

"Jesus Christ, *stop*," Juliet gasped, laughing. Dax smiled, still watching the road. Juliet packed the paper bag back up and set it between her feet. Dax reached down and fished for the pickle ornament, drawing it out and hanging it from the rearview mirror. It dangled high, reflecting sunlight off its plastic green skin. "What do you want for breakfast?"

"Roots and berries," Dax replied, pulling into the parking lot of a diner. She ushered Juliet out without a second thought to exploring local cuisine, which, Juliet could admit, would probably be pretty plain and mostly in need of seasoning.

Yellowstone is beautiful at night in the winter, Juliet thought to herself as they drove back to their campground that night after exploring the few streets in town. It was true, too, not like the other lies she told herself; the park had ravishing views. The two of them parked the van and weaved through the trees on foot. The inch of snow on the cold ground crunched under their boots. When Juliet tipped her head back, the Milky Way stretched through the night sky, filling it with oranges and purples and colors that, as a hospitality major, she struggled to define. As an astronomy minor, she could describe where the Milky Way was in the universe, that 'Milky Way' was a translation from the Latin *via lactea,* which was a translation from the Greek γαλαξίας κύκλος. She had no words for witnessing it above her, feeling like there was nothing stopping her from reaching out and trailing her fingers through its smoky colors, and how all that made her feel.

"Let's break in," Dax whispered, pointing to a wooden sign with *Silex Spring* carved into it in blue letters, faded in the moonlight. Juliet was distracted from the Milky Way back down to Earth. She raised an eyebrow at her.

"I don't know about that," Juliet murmured, peering at the spring. "It's acidic and dangerous. There's a reason there's fences."

"There's a reason we've got arms and legs," Dax argued quietly, but she did not vault the fence like Juliet suspected she might. Instead, she squirmed between the slats of the fence, and motioned for Juliet to do the same. When they were both pressed against the inside of the fence, Dax took Juliet's hand and pulled her to the ground. The grass and dirt were frozen, cold seeping through Juliet's pants, the hard wood of the fence biting into her back. Dax tipped her head back, watching the Milky Way twist past them, slowly, radioactive moss on a river, fish skulking along the bottom of the ocean, food coloring slinking through a glass of milk. She glanced back to the geyser basin, now and then, at its oranges, its blues. The colors that filled that night all had names Juliet had to look up afterwards to get just right: vermillion, gamboge, majorelle, brandeis, medallion, mulberry, juniper, garnet. Porcelain stars on a tablecloth stained with spilled ink, black and rich and still wet, shards of china shattered against the sky.

"Thank you," Dax breathed, a plume of hot air visibly trailing from her mouth to the sky. She reached down and weaved her fingers through Juliet's before tucking their joined hands into Juliet's pocket. Juliet didn't ask what Dax was thanking her for.

It was Dax who fell asleep first. Raven-black hair spilled like oil, soft over their shoulders when Dax's head dropped down in sleep. Terracotta skin shown in the moonlight, under the glow of the Milky Way, her face backlit with an inner luminescence as she slept. Juliet reached up with her free hand and pulled her fingers through her hair, finding a rhythm, keeping herself awake to keep watch over the basin, the skies, and themselves.

Their time in Yellowstone was hard during the day, and incomparably exquisite at night. Juliet absolutely hated her job at the restaurant; her coworkers and managers were miserable people who liked to torture her with menial work and meaningless insults and taunts. Dax took entirely too long after her shift was over to show up and take her away. Juliet waited for her inside the shop next door, a little store styled like a lodge. It housed jewelry and jars and wooden carvings that Juliet recognized as old Shoshone designs. She wandered through the aisles, day after day, rolling the weight of her workday off her shoulders in waves, until Dax came to get her and take her back to the park.

Same as every other place they had been to so far, they stayed up every night, waiting and watching for aliens. They prowled the campgrounds and the park beyond after dark, trying to find trapdoors that might lead from the dirt and the trees into a secret underground military base, perhaps, or an alien site long since covered up and hidden. They prodded at tree trunks and stomped on suspicious swathes of loose earth, but to no avail. Dax had a look of unparalleled glee on her face when they hunted like that. Juliet kept most of her attention on the sky, captivated by the night sky and the waxing moon, nearly full now.

"Why don't you lie down?" Dax suggested, tapping a broken stick against the gnarled roots of a tree that still had a long life to live, Juliet thought. Juliet leaned against the trunk and watched Dax tap a pattern into the ground with her stick. "You look tired."

"My job sucks," Juliet murmured, scuffing her heel through the dew shifting into frost on the dead grass. Dax clicked her tongue.

"Tsk," she murmured. "And here I thought you wanted to stay longer."

She was referencing a conversation the two of them had had in the van on the way to the restaurant that morning; Juliet had suggested they settle in Yellowstone a little longer, since the park was so exquisite, the grounds so expansive, the possibilities so endless. Dax had only nodded to show she had heard her before turning up the music and trying her best to sing along to the notes of the show tunes coming through the speakers.

"I think this place is gorgeous, I really do," Juliet reiterated. "I don't see any reason we shouldn't stay longer."

"How about: your job sucks, it's cold as nuts here, and we haven't found any aliens even though we've been here for almost three weeks?" Dax suggested, snapping her stick in half over her knee and weighing the two pieces in her hands. She tossed the larger half to Juliet and set to breaking the smaller half into tiny pieces.

"Some people search their whole lives for something like this and never find anything," Juliet reminded her. "We've only been here for just under three weeks. That's barely a dent in a place this big. Plus, I mean, look around." Here, Juliet gestured at their surroundings, at the trees that wanted to bloom again so badly, at the moon that so desperately wanted to be full, at the Milky Way that was bursting with life just waiting to prove itself. "We couldn't find somewhere more beautiful."

Dax stared at her, the broken pieces of twig filling her palms. Juliet stared right back, unblinking, unwavering, just patient, letting Dax sift through her thoughts on her own without prodding. Dax finally tipped her hands and let the shards fall to the ground.

"I'll give it until Wednesday," Dax said, eventually. Juliet pulled out her phone to check the date; it was Friday, the 3rd of March. "You can get your last pay from that restaurant, we'll do our last search that night, and we'll head out on Thursday morning if we haven't found anything. How's that sound?"

A deadline sounded weird but fine, Juliet thought. She delicately placed her half of the snapped stick on a higher branch, still attached to the tree, and brushed the dirt off her hands onto her jeans.

"Sounds fine," Juliet said, "if you don't want to stay."

"I don't," Dax agreed. "Not really." She hesitated for a long beat. "I'm sorry."

Juliet looked at her, then away. "Don't be. You've never

wanted to stay anywhere. I'm not expecting that to change." She tucked her hands into her jacket and motioned with a jerk of her chin back in the direction from whence they came. "Maybe it's time to go start our lookout for the night. You in?"

"I'm in," Dax accepted at once, trailing after Juliet until she caught up and matched her footsteps, though her stride was always just an inch or two long, due to her height. Juliet usually made light fun of Dax for not keeping up, but felt as though she was not in the mood that night. They walked in silence, for once. Well, mostly; Dax hummed tunelessly to herself, short snippets of notes with no meanings or real sound to them, tapping her heels against the ground in a broken rhythm as they returned to the van.

Of course, a deadline for them meant a deadline for the aliens, whether they were coming or not. Juliet laid out on top of the van with Dax, the two of them bundled in their blankets and covers and bathrobes and jackets, staring up at the sky. Dax was waiting for something that Juliet suspected was never going to come, no matter how badly they wanted it to. Juliet was more invested in studying the Milky Way, the arc it made over the Park, the millions of stars like pinpricks in the velvet of the sky, revealing the light beyond the veil of their universe.

"You sound like you're thinking something stupid," Dax commented, reaching for her pocket to pull out a cigarette. Juliet stretched her hand out and took the pack from her without so much as looking down. "Come on, man, don't be a-"

"You're not supposed to be smoking," Juliet reminded her without inflection. She pocketed the pack and Dax groaned, throwing herself back against the roof.

"Why can't I smoke? I'm a grown fucking adult, aren't I?" Dax asked, staring up at the sky, eyes glazed with annoyance. Juliet sat up and frowned at her.

"If you're such a grown fucking adult, maybe read a fucking book or something," Juliet spat. She took the pack of cigarettes from her pocket. "You know these are killing you, right? Or do you want to die? Is that it?"

"No, I just-"

"You just *nothing*, Daksha." Juliet turned the pack over in her hand, looking down at the label. "Look at that. Surgeon General's got a warning on here and everything." Juliet kept staring at the label, turning the pack over and over between her fingers, watching the words flip upside down, rightside up, upside down, rightside up, over and over; the frustrations of the past couple weeks came bubbling up to the surface as she did so. She kept her eyes firmly down; the sky would only tie itself to bad memories if she looked at it now. She didn't want to look up in a week, see the stars, and think of the time Dax annoyed the shit out of her.

"I just picked up a bad habit," Dax reminded her. She reached out for the pack, and Juliet's fingers snapped shut around it like a crocodile's jaws, impossible to pry back open.

"A habit you're not trying to break." Juliet glanced up at Dax's face. Her eyes were bright.

"I'm-"

"You're not wearing the nicotine patches," Juliet bit off, before Dax could even lie. "Come on, Daksha. I know you're not." She looked down at the pack again before turning and cocking her arm back, letting it loose in the next moment, pitching the pack far enough into the woods that it was impossible for either of them to see where it went on the dark.

"Oh, come *on*, you son of a-"

"Go get it, if you're such a grown fucking adult," Juliet said simply. She gathered her covers and slid down the windshield without a backwards glance. She could feel all her annoyances and frustrations and angers bubbling just under her surface, popping free through her fingertips and her mouth when she wasn't quick enough to snatch them back. She threw the back doors of the van open, tossed herself and her belongings in, and slammed them shut behind her. She heard Dax shifting around on the roof, grumbling to herself. Juliet shoved Dax's pillow under her head, her own pillow over it, covering her ears and muffling the sounds outside. She let her frustration out in tears, dulling the sounds with the pillows.

Juliet could not quite pinpoint why she was so upset, but she did feel validated in her own emotions. She believed it was more than reasonable for her to feel this way. What right did Dax have to be killing herself like this? When they were working so hard, when all the information she needed to know she was killing herself was at her fingertips, when there were so many reasons not to? Juliet yanked her phone out of her pocket and tapped out a text about it to Angelo, who replied with his apologies, a bunch of emojis, a picture of a

Persian cat he had found in their yard, and reassurances that everything would be better in the morning. She exhaled shakily, her face aching, her head throbbing, and she fell asleep there, alone, in the back of the van, a picture of a white kitten in her hand. She felt irritated, indignant, and sad, burying her face in Dax's pillowcase. It still smelled like her shampoo.

Chapter Nine

A soft rap at the back doors of the van the next morning snapped Juliet into wakefulness; she had always been a light sleeper, and the night in the alley had exacerbated that tendency a little bit more than usual. She pulled the pillow off her head and dragged herself to the back to open one of the doors a crack, peering out into the murky dawn sunlight straggling over the horizon. Dax stood there, staring at a dirty smudge on the closed half of the van doors rather than at Juliet, one hand tugging at the piercings in her left ear.

"What?" Juliet asked, and Dax met her eyes, briefly.

"Are you still mad at me?" Dax looked a little sad, her eyes tired and red. Juliet didn't get upset very often, nor did she tend to show much outward emotion towards any one person. Juliet could understand how it might be jarring when all that came out as suddenly as it had the night before.

"Yeah," Juliet answered honestly, rubbing at one of her eyes with the back of her hand. "Stop smoking, man."

"I'll work on it." Dax motioned to the inside of the van. Her cheeks were flushed; her blankets were wrapped around her tightly. "Can I come in?"

"Sure," Juliet said, scooting away to make room for Dax to fit through the opening without letting in too much cold air. Dax hopped in, hauling herself with her covers and tugging the door shut behind her.

"If it really bothers you, I'll try harder to quit," Dax spoke up, eventually, inevitably. Juliet had just drawn her knees up to her chest, wrapped her arms around them, and put her chin on her knees. "I didn't know it *really* bothered you. I thought it was more of a 'you shouldn't be doing that!' kind of thing."

"You *shouldn't* be doing that," Juliet murmured into her knees. Dax pulled at the end of a lock of her hair, looking a little frustrated, a little sad. *Good,* Juliet thought, vindictively, though the anger was draining out of her.

"I know that," Dax said. She ran her hand through her hair, scratching at the back of her skull, nails skittering on her scalp. "My mom used to do it." Juliet looked up; this felt more like a confession. It was more truthful than any other explanation Dax had given on the topic thus far. "We both worked in the same grocery store when I was in junior high. She used to take smoke breaks, so I picked it up so she would have to talk to me when we took the breaks together." Dax picked at one of her nails, tearing at the edge of one fingernail that had gotten too long. "Joke was on me. She didn't talk to me then, either." Dax scrubbed the back of her hand along her eyelids, the jagged edge of her nail catching a little on her cheek and leaving a light white scratch behind.

Juliet turned without speaking, starting to dig through her bags. She could see Dax watching her in her peripheral, but she kept looking, rooting through her groceries and her toiletries and her clothes until the box of nicotine patches emerged. She tossed it at Dax's chest; Dax caught it, turned the box over in her hands, and read the label on the front. She smiled, just a little bit, the corners of her mouth twitching up against her will.

"I'll talk to you," Juliet reminded her. She tapped the box. "Please."

"Okay." Dax read the instructions on the back of the box before pulling one patch out, tugging the backing off, and pressing it to her arm. She removed her hand and the patch was on, which she had done before, but never with much conviction and never with the need that was in her eyes when she looked at Juliet now.

"Is there a reason you were so upset last night?" Dax asked, voice careful but not soft. "I mean, besides the smokes. Is something bothering you?"

Something in Juliet's chest itched. She half-shrugged. "I don't really know. It all just came out." She scratched at the back of her hand, then met Dax's eyes in a hard look, trying her best to maintain eye contact. "I'm sorry about that. That wasn't fair to you."

"Sometimes it's gotta happen, kid," Dax replied. She tossed the discarded patch backing into the trash bag that hung off the back of the driver's seat. "We've all blown our tops now and then. But, you know what?"

"What?" Juliet asked, rubbing at her face. Her cheeks felt stiff from the tears drying on her face overnight without being washed off.

"I saw aliens last night," Dax told her, leaning in like she was sharing a secret. The two of them, co-conspirators in this whole... whatever it was. This whole *thing*. Maybe even with a capital-T: a Thing.

"Really?" Juliet leaned back against the pillows, a yawn cracking her jaw. Dax laid down next to her, hesitant, not too close. She accepted Juliet's pillow when it was offered to her, since Dax's pillow was already under Juliet's head. "Tell me about them."

Dax grinned, her eyes crinkling a little bit. The mole under her right eye was distracting this close. Her brown eyes, so close to black, had a white spot on the left edge of the left iris. Juliet stared at it, fixated, as Dax spun a yarn about spinning UFOs and flashing lights and beeps coming from the ground, far away. She threw theories this way and that, speculating on the possible continued existence of the base under their very feet, at *that very moment*, she told her, dramatically. Juliet let her rant, her hands tucked against her chest, letting her words become a bedtime story. Dax lightly touched the shell of her ear, then her cheek.

"Why don't you sleep a little more?" Dax suggested, after proposing, wildly, that the aliens had heard them arguing and decided to make themselves known before Juliet and Dax left and the aliens were alone once more. Juliet nodded her agreement, her brain already blurring. Dax withdrew her hand and turned to lay on her stomach, her face still turned towards Juliet. Juliet stared into her eyes, at the mole, at the white fleck, at the long line of her aristocratic nose, at the faint freckles dusted across her cheeks like pinpricks in the velvet of her face, revealing the light beyond the veil of her skin. She reached out and tangled their fingers together before she succumbed to a more restful sleep than she had had the night previous.

When she awoke, Dax was still passed out next to her, snoring lightly into her pillow, hair tangled around her head, eyes flickering under her eyelids, brows drawn together slightly. Juliet pulled out her phone and closed the picture of the pristine, beautiful cat in her brother's lap and, instead, started searching for a new place for them to go. After all, Dax had seen the aliens. There was no reason to stick around Yellowstone any longer after that.

"I think it's time to stop being Boy Scouts," Dax said, out of nowhere, and Juliet yelped before glaring down at her.

"How long have you been awake?" Juliet demanded, and Dax grinned up at her, all teeth.

"Long enough." Dax tugged the covers up a little further. "I stand by it. I think it's time to stop being Boy Scouts, camping out in Yellowstone Park like we're on a goddamn field trip. I'm not here to sell cookies. I'm here to *win*."

"Aren't Girl Scouts the ones that sell cookies?" Juliet corrected, still flicking through her bookmarks. "We can pick up my money from the restaurant today. I was thinking we should go to Idaho. I crave structure."

"Self-aware today, I see," Dax murmured into her pillow, her voice muffled. "Idaho's fine. What's in Idaho? Iaho? Iowa? The fuck'd you say?"

"Idaho, Daksha. Focus." Juliet pulled up her tab with the UFO sightings from Mountain Home, Idaho. "Idaho. Capital city, Boise. They've got reports of flying saucers out that way. Real ones. With blinking lights on them."

"Flying fuckin' saucers, Alva?" Dax sat up, blankets sliding off of her, hair knotted on one side of her head. "Sold. Let's *go*."

"Yellowstone was nice," Juliet commented, as Dax dug up a hairbrush and started ripping it through her soft, snarled hair. Juliet tugged a curtain aside on one of the back windows of the van, peering out at the mid-afternoon sky. She wondered what had happened to her sense of time since Dax had whisked her away to be her sidekick. "I'm glad we came."

Dax's fingers curled briefly on Juliet's shoulder, squeezing the bone, fingertips brushing her clavicle, before she pulled back to keep working at her hair.

"Me, too, kid," Dax answered, and Juliet dug out her toiletry bag for the showers before they hit the road. Dax's hotwired hair dryer left a lot to be desired, but it would have to do.

This drive was shorter than their last one by half, only five hours southwest, which felt like peas compared to their last ride. They stopped, briefly, at a craterous and pockmarked swath of land branded as a national monument, which Juliet was unduly fascinated by.

"It's like Earth created its own little Moon, right here, where we could always keep an eye on it," Juliet commented, rocking back on her heels as she took in the volcanic expanse ahead of them. If she stepped forward, keeping humans and cars and the modern peripherals out of her way, she almost felt as though she really were on the moon. "Isn't that nice?"

"Romantic," Dax agreed, hands shoved in the pockets of her jacket. She had been surly the whole trip, probably wanting to smoke and trying to stop herself. Juliet was more patient with her than she had been in days, and they bundled back into the car after an hour or so of Juliet staring at what Dax eventually told her she could take pictures of and probably experience in virtual reality in the future.

"You won't learn anything new," Dax reminded her. "It's not going to change."

"Yeah, I know," Juliet replied. "I'm sorry."

Dax had only just made a little sound, then stepped closer, letting Juliet look for a while longer, her hand tucked into Juliet's pocket as they stared. Dax's nails were bitten down, even though Juliet had missed that actually happening. Her fingers twitched in their shared pocket now and then, but neither of them commented on it.

They hit the road again eventually, on the way to Mountain Home, Idaho, which held the promise of real-life flying saucers, a job that Juliet would hopefully hate significantly less, views not as spectacular as those at Yellowstone, and a Dax with slightly clearer lungs.

"I was wrong," Juliet said, instantly, once they crested the hill leading into Mountain Home and were greeted with a town set in a valley before a wide expanse of stunning, glorious mountain ranges, frost-tipped blue stretching into the sky like it, too, wanted to reach the moon. "It's beautiful here, too."

"It's beautiful everywhere, if you know where to look," Dax responded, a faux-sage with a nicotine patch and tattoos curling up and down her arms and no reason to be awake except that she was driving. She rolled her head to the side and grinned at Juliet. "You know?"

Juliet smiled at her and turned back to the mountains. "I guess so, yeah."

"She *guesses* so, this girl never believes me," Dax muttered, still grinning away. The mountains extended forever in all directions except towards them, and the van brought them down into the town that lay at the mountains' feet, chugging its way down the hill and into the village's only campground. Dax and Juliet sorted through Juliet's restaurant money and Dax's Mystery Money before paying the ranger up front and finding themselves a place to park. They found a spot where the mountains were still in full view over the tops of cabins and campers and trees, which had the best role models in the world for growth.

"I'll try to find a job in town tomorrow," Juliet promised, checking her old watch. She tapped at the face, and the second hand sluggishly kept ticking. "Is it really 11:31?"

"Sure is," Dax confirmed, whipping out her phone like a pistol from a holster, and pocketing it again with the same twirl of the wrist and prideful enthusiasm that a successful cowboy might have. All she needed was a hat and some spurs and she was due to hit the range. "What the hell are you thinking, Alva? You got a dumb look on your face."

"Learned from the best." Juliet tucked her hands into her jacket as she stood outside the van, leaning against the side and taking in the night sky creeping up over the mountains, stars jumping over the peaks to reveal themselves. "It's pretty warm here, isn't it? We're not that far from Yellowstone. That's weird."

"Yeah, nature's a freak like that," Dax murmured, pulling off her leather jacket and tossing it back through the window of the van. She ducked down and scooped up a rock. "See, look, exhibit B, this rock looks *exactly* like... like if you combined a dolphin and a magic wand. Do you see it?"

"I guess so," Juliet agreed, tilting her head and squinting. It looked more like a pair of sunglasses than anything, she privately believed, but she understood Dax's train of thought better than anything else at the moment. Dax held the rock up to the moonlight.

"Yeah, nature's a freak," Dax repeated. She dropped the rock in one of the deep, nearly cavernous hip pockets of her overalls. "Freak in the streets, freak in the sheets."

"Was 'freak' on your word-a-day calendar, or are you just now learning about the dictionary?" Juliet tipped her head to the side to meet Dax's eyes. "Or a thesaurus? Or have you finally learned to read?"

"I think we both need some fucking sleep, to be honest with you, because you're just spitting random shit now," Dax answered, taking Juliet by the elbow and ushering her up into the back of the van, into her pajamas, and under the covers. Dax fiddled with her rock, twisting it between her fingers before she considered falling asleep.

"What about the aliens?" Juliet asked, her face half-smashed into her pillow. She had no idea if the pillow she was currently buried in was hers or Dax's; they had been so mixed up by this point, it hardly mattered. Dax tossed the rock in the air and caught it deftly.

"We'll find 'em tomorrow," Dax promised. "For now, grasshopper, sleep. Gather your strength. The world will beat on you tomorrow, and you must prepare your aura."

"Shut up," Juliet mumbled into her pillow, and Dax's fingertips brushed the edge of the scar on her cheek before vanishing.

"As you wish, your majesty," Dax whispered back, a grin in her voice, and Juliet's eyes fluttered fully shut to the sound of Dax tossing and catching her rock over and over again beside her. It seemed to bleed into her dreams, where Dax stood in a flowing river, her jeans rolled up to her thighs, skipping a never-ending supply of rocks from her pockets while Juliet struggled not to go over a waterfall. She ended up falling over the edge, in the end, and Dax looked over just in time to meet her eyes in the moment before she plummeted, Niagara Falls without a barrel.

Her eyes snapped open to darkness, to Dax sleeping beside her, her fingers curled around her safe, unskipped rock, and she fell back asleep in moments, her dream long forgotten.

"We're gonna find some real-ass flying saucers tonight," Dax exclaimed in the morning, jolting Juliet out of sleep again. Juliet jerked up, sitting with her back ramrod-straight, breathing heavily. Dax shook her shoulder, dragging her attention over. "Hey. Yeah. Flying saucers. That's what you said, right?"

"What time is it?" Juliet demanded, and Dax picked up her wrist to check her watch for her.

"Mm, it's about 10." Dax dropped her wrist and rocked forward, grinning in Juliet's face. "Now, I know you're gonna go get a boring-ass job, but, tonight, man, *flying saucers*. Can you imagine? With fucking *lights* on them? Damn-"

"Where are the showers in this place?" Juliet asked, rubbing at her eye with the heel of her hand. Dax started weaving her tangled hair into a shitty braid that Juliet reached up and had to disassemble before it got any more knotted than it was. Dax led her to the showers, on a loop through the woods, then a different loop back to the van before they started off into town. Juliet used her phone to find a good intersection to get dropped off at. Dax leaned across the console once Juliet was on the sidewalk, looking down at her through the open window. The temperatures in Mountain Home were in the high fifties, starting to creep towards the sixties; Juliet had her jacket open.

"Don't get lost, now," Dax warned, flipping someone off without looking when they honked and swerved around her. "Remember what I taught you."

'What Dax had taught her' was mostly related to the knife currently strapped to Juliet's calf under her pants and the gun in her bag. Juliet patted the bag before heaving it up higher on her shoulder.

"Good girl," Dax called out the window. She replaced herself in her seat and offered a wave. "Call if you need anything, see you later, bye!" Her 'bye' trailed off as she sped away, her last syllable catching in the breeze left behind by the van. Juliet started heading towards a diner she saw that was open and looked busy, hoping someone might just give her a job in haste. That turned out to be a pretty good idea, since the manager did exactly that. She started her work there immediately, because they were short-staffed for the week and needed an extra hand while one was being offered to them.

Juliet shot off a text to Dax to let her know what she was up to, then one to Angelo with a picture of a service dog someone had brought in (*awh, shit, i fuckin love that french bulldog*, he replied, with eighteen emojis of various dogs, hearts, and smiley faces). Dax sent back a picture of herself in front of a gas station, screaming and pointing up at the cheap gas prices up on the sign above her head. She saved the picture and pocketed her phone for the rest of the shift she had been given. Dax came in before she had finished and ordered herself a coffee. She held the mug up to Juliet.

"Do you mind drinking some so I can put more milk it?" Dax asked, smiling warmly, *clearly* trying to play her. "Please?"

Juliet rolled her eyes, but she drained half the cup, much to Dax's delight, as she could now add as much milk and sugar as her heart desired. The energy rush from chugging that half-cup of coffee sustained Juliet into the night, as her shift wrapped up. Dax tipped her with a twenty shoved in her apron pocket, and Juliet helped clean up a few tables before heading out with her.

"What'd you do today?" Juliet asked, counting through the tips she had made throughout the day. Dax shrugged, sliding across the front of the van to get to the driver's side.

"This and that," she answered, scrounging through her pockets to get her keys. She had wrapped her jacket around her waist at some point, leaving her midriff bare under her crop top. The amount of skin she revealed was... distracting, Juliet privately thought. She wished she could get a closer look at her tattoos. She could see the ones twisting up and down her arms, and she observed them as Dax drove, taking them to a 1950s-themed diner that she had found in town that day for a late dinner. Her tattoos were a mix-match of different styles, ideas, images and words, all sorts of varying things from completely different eras of her life. Juliet was tracing an octopus that trailed up the outside of her right biceps when Dax parked the van with a sudden jerk.

"Get out, madam," Dax instructed, grinning. She hurried around to open Juliet's door for her and offer her a hand to escort her out. At Juliet's confused look, she explained, "Jules, it's the 1950s. You gotta be treated like a *lady*."

"Somehow, 'get out, madam' doesn't strike me as a particularly polite thing to say to a lady," Juliet replied, even as she took Dax's hand and let her help her to the gravel. She thrilled a little bit at Dax's hand wrapped around hers before squashing that feeling. It was nice for someone to treat her like the woman she was, though; back home, everyone remembered her from childhood, and it made a lot of people act weird around her, stilted, even though *she* had never really changed. "So, does that make you the perfect gentleman, then?"

"Hell, no, I'm just far more gentlemanly than you so I'm picking up the slack." Dax crooked her arm and pulled Juliet's hand through the triangle to rest on her wrist. "Someone's gotta watch out for you, kid, and it certainly ain't you."

"It certainly *is* me," Juliet protested, but Dax was already slamming the front doors of the place open and announcing their presence, as well as their intentions to share one milkshake with two straws.

"We never could have done this shit in the real 1950s," Dax commented later, as they split their milkshake and fries. Juliet dipped one of her fries into the milkshake. "Two queer brown ladies sharing a milkshake? No fucking way. They would've hosed us at the door."

"I certainly am glad they didn't," Juliet replied, trying to locate the salt amongst the napkin castle Dax had constructed while they had waited for their order. Dax reached into the castle boldly and withdrew the salt shaker from the bedroom in the west wing. Juliet took it in stride and coated her fries in salt.

"Hey, how come I can't smoke but you can turn your fries into the Dead fuckin' Sea and get high blood pressure and die?" Dax asked, confiscating the salt. Juliet scowled but kept eating them.

"Because smoking is actively killing you and you know it." Juliet swirled her fry in the milkshake a little extra, for spite's sake. Dax smiled a little. "Salt doesn't do too bad by me because I don't eat it all that much."

"I still think you're a hypocrite," Dax replied. She set back to fixing up the tower in the east of the castle while Juliet dug a mini peanut butter cup out of the milkshake. That night found them back at their campground, staring up at the sky, half a grilled cheese sandwich each between them in the takeout box from the diner.

"We should get you a poodle skirt," Dax suggested, out of the blue. Juliet paused in her reading of a secondhand shop find book about American UFO hunters to glance at her.

"Why?" Juliet asked, and Dax shrugged, not meeting her eyes.

"Just think it would work on you." Dax picked up her grilled cheese and narrowly avoided getting crumbs in her eye when she ripped a hunk off and shoved it in her mouth. Juliet returned her attention to the book after a while. The UFO hunters were in Washington, and Juliet thought that might be a beautiful place to visit on her American road trip tour. "Happy birthday, by the way."

"What?" Juliet asked, sitting up in surprise. Dax smirked at her.

"Angelo texted me." Dax smacked her in the chest, and Juliet laughed, brushing her off. "Why the *fuck* didn't you tell me it was your birthday?"

"Because I didn't think it was important! Plus, how do you bring that up? 'By the way, it's my birthday, don't forget to celebrate me'?" Juliet said. Dax grinned and reached behind herself, handing over a flat box.

"Ideally, yeah," Dax said. She motioned for Juliet to come closer, and come closer she did, leaning against Dax's side. She surrendered the box to Juliet. "Open it up."

"You didn't have to get me anything," Juliet said, picking up the box. She tugged at the ribbon when Dax pushed at her hand, smiling.

"Too late." Dax motioned towards the box. "Let's go, open it up."

Juliet pulled the ribbon apart and let it slide down into their laps, opening the lid to find a new pair of glasses. She lifted them up and was delighted to find a sturdy frame, the correct prescription, and no cracks like her current pair had.

"How did you find out my prescription?" Juliet asked, switching out her broken pair for her new one.

"I stole Angelo's number from your phone and texted him." Dax looked Juliet's face over before grinning. "They look good on you."

"Thanks," Juliet said, setting the wrappings aside and relaxing against Dax again.

"I hope it was a good birthday."

"It was a *great* birthday," Juliet assured her. "When's yours?" she asked, because she had long since forgotten what Dax's license told her.

"Before I tell you," Dax said, "you're going to have to believe me when I say it. Because I'm not lying."

"Lay it on me," Juliet said.

"New Year's Day."

"It is *not*," Juliet laughed. Dax smacked her again, this time on the arm.

"I *promise* that it is, I'll even have my dad text me my birth certificate if I have to," Dax told her. Juliet grinned, settling in against Dax's side and opening her book up again.

"I look forward to celebrating," Juliet said. Dax shoved at

her, but left her alone after that, letting her read about the UFO hunters. She fell asleep with her book still open over her chest, her head tucked up under Dax's arm while Dax, presumably, continued to keep watch. Dax had nothing to report in the morning, but then, she rarely did.

"When are you working today?" Dax asked the next morning after she showered, as Juliet listened to the late-night voicemail she had been left by the manager of the place she was working now. Dax was trying her best to blow-dry her hair in the front seat, sifting through sections of her long, thick hair in an effort to get them into a state resembling dry.

"Sounds like from ten until eight," Juliet answered, blowing out a breath that displaced her glasses. She tipped them back into place as she deleted her voicemail. "It's 8:48 now. Do you wanna get breakfast?"

"Shit, yeah, do I ever," Dax replied, and 9:00 found them, Dax with her hair only partially dry, Juliet with her watch out to keep an eye on the time, a plate of pancakes between the two of them on a table at the local diner. Mountain Home was a gorgeous place to settle, the mountains rising high over them wherever they went. Juliet stood outside the diner for a while just looking up at the mountains, the clouds drifting over their heads feeling as though they were extensions of the peaks, dragging them across the skies. Dax stood next to her, picking at her nicotine patch.

"View sure is pretty," Juliet commented, glancing at Dax, who stared back at her for a moment before gesturing back towards the van. Work in Mountain Home was the same as work anywhere else, regardless of the mountains or the view or Dax's smile when she dropped her off that morning. The days passed like they usually did anywhere else. Dax held her hand when they went to the foot of the mountains and stared straight up, necks craned at ninety degree angles to try to see the highest peak. Juliet's squeezed her fingers and reached out to touch the start of the slope, in a slight state of disbelief that she was seeing this, after all her years stuck up in Michigan.

Chapter Ten

Things in Mountain Home were going smoothly. Juliet started to settle in; she was looking at hotels they could stay in, maybe, or an apartment to rent. Once her stint at the restaurant ran out, they decided to keep her on for a little while longer, indefinitely, because she was such good help. She was growing attached. It was *stable*.

Of course, that meant Dax was starting to itch to get out of there. She hated staying in any one place for too long, Juliet noticed, with increasing frequency, since each place they went Dax started to get antsy just as Juliet was settling in. The more antsy Dax got, the more reckless she got, the more argumentative, the more flighty. She argued a little bit more, but Juliet fought back, and they ended up apologizing by the next morning, Juliet combing through Dax's hair, Dax drawing little designs onto Juliet's arms with her Sharpies.

Dax took Juliet to the bar when it started feeling like it was getting close to the end of their time in Idaho. She tossed back a shot or two while Juliet was watching her, but she had no idea what Dax did when they were separated there. She suspected it was a fair amount of drinking, because Dax was leaning against the bar, her head down, laughing to herself, when Juliet came back from the bathroom.

"You ready to go home, Daksha?" Juliet murmured, down by her ear, and Dax agreed, letting Juliet drag her to her feet and lead her outside. She breathed in the fresh mountain air, her eyes squeezed tight. Juliet busied herself tying Dax's hair up into a bun at the back of her head before bundling her into the van. Dax seemed like she hadn't drank as much as she could have - Juliet hadn't seen her putting a glass to her lips all that often, and she was certainly more coherent than she should have been on a night like that. She certainly was acting like she had no filter, though, so maybe she had more than Juliet thought. She rolled her head against the back of the seat to squint at Juliet as they drove.

"Do you even know how beautiful you are?" Dax asked, voice edging in too loud for the confined space of the van. Juliet glanced at her briefly, one eyebrow raised, before redirecting her attention back to the road. "Because you are." Dax reached out, aiming for Juliet's ear, but Juliet flinched without meaning to, an odd habit as of late. She tried to tamp it down, but Dax just murmured an apology for startling her before slowly reaching out towards her forearm. Juliet kept still that time, letting Dax lightly stroke up and down her arm, blunt nails just barely scratching, not even leaving a mark behind.

Dax trailed up to Juliet's cheek, fingertips gentle as they edged along the line of her scar - then further, up towards her hairline. She traced the lines of the pattern she had shaved into Juliet's head, humming to herself as she did so. Juliet parked them back at the campground all too soon, startling Dax out of her trance, regrettably. Dax let go of Juliet to climb into the back, amongst all the covers and pillows and their belongings. She reached up into the front after a moment of hesitation on Juliet's part, grabbing her wrist and tugging her back to join her. Dax lay on her side, staring, transfixed, at Juliet's face.

"Look at your face," Dax whispered. Juliet let her gaze, comfortable enough with her after months in exclusively the company of one another. Dax gave up on staring after a while, choosing instead to burrow close to Juliet, digging her head into Juliet's chest and sighing softly. Her hands grabbed at Juliet's, holding her firm, keeping her close.

"I'm glad you're here," Dax told her, before falling asleep. Juliet kept her eyes open, unblinking, watching the moon falling from the sky through the opened curtains on the back windows. She tried to forget what had happened, even as her mind raced with it. Dax was tactile; Dax was a motormouth; Dax was a loose cannon. She didn't *mean* anything by it. How could she? It made no sense. They were close, yeah, but that was natural when people did what they were doing together.

Remember, Dax told you a while ago that she was queer, Juliet reminded herself, eyes still unseeing, gazing through the window at the trees outside. *Maybe that extends to you. Maybe she's trying to tell you something.*

"We're just friends," Juliet said softly, out loud, to herself. An affirmation. A reminder. She couldn't risk fucking this up, not when Dax was her only friend, her traveling companion. *Do not fuck this up.* "Do *not* fuck this up."

"Mm," Dax murmured in her sleep, shifting restlessly, head ducking in closer to Juliet. She squeezed Juliet's hands, even as Juliet tensed up and froze. Dax seemed to drift right back into deep sleep, leaving Juliet alone with her thoughts all night.

Juliet woke up the next morning to Dax shaking her awake, before the sky had even started to lighten with the sunrise. Juliet cracked open one eye to look up at her, groaning when she saw it was still dark.

"What the- Man, it is still dark out there, go back to sleep," Juliet groaned, turning her face back into her pillow. Dax tugged at her ear until Juliet turned to look grumpily up at her.

"I saw a flying saucer!" Dax exclaimed, which made sense, because it was just starting to edge into April, and it had been a while since they packed up and moved. Even as Dax dragged her outside to locate a flying saucer that seemed to have long since flown far away from the campground, Juliet was already starting to plan where they would head off to now that Dax's cold feet had finally sent her skittering across the ice to the other end of the pond.

"We can pick up your last paycheck from the restaurant and head out today, what do you say?" Dax suggested, throwing her hair up into a messy bun before climbing into the driver's seat, bottle of water in one hand as she started steering them towards the road. Not an easy task, Juliet imagined, but one Dax seemed more than willing to take on as they headed into town. Juliet watched the mountains trail alongside them as they drove, tracing with her eyes the lines where the peaks met the sky. She was going to miss it when they left, just like she missed the Milky Way, the geyser, the river, the orange bridge, the island. Places that, for her, now only existed in memory.

"How about Washington?" Juliet suggested, remembering the

book she had read on one of their first nights there. She reached into the back of the van to dig it out, leafing through it to find the exact chapter that had the information she was looking for. "Lake Stevens. Not Olympia. Says here that they had a few well-documented instances of unidentified flying objects flying over the town when it was foggy one night. This says it moved super fast, had weird sounds coming off of it."

"Hmm." Dax turned smoothly into the parking lot of Juliet's restaurant. "Sounds are new. I say check it out. How far out is Lake Stevens?"

"About nine hours northwest," Juliet answered, heaving herself out of the car to go in and apologize for leaving without any warning at all. The manager gave her a few passive-aggressive comments and sighs, but ultimately gave her her money and sent her on her way. Dax hit the highway as fast as her lead foot and flighty nature would go, Juliet leaning out the open passenger window, letting the wind whip her face as she watched the mountains vanish behind them. She forgave Dax, again, for her nature. It was just how they were. A van was enough for Dax, so it had to be enough for Juliet.

There was less of a sense of urgency to reach their next destination this time, it seemed, as Dax dawdled the whole way to Lake Stevens. She passed through a couple national parks and forests, telling Juliet they were a gift to her because she could sense that she was upset about leaving Mountain Home so abruptly. Juliet looked out over lakes so blue the colors had no names, mountains so tall the numbers couldn't keep up, trees so old they grew and climbed until time told them to wait a little longer. It was hard to love them as much as she loved the places that she kept trying to make into her home, only to have them taken when Dax was done there. She understood, she did. She just wanted to *stay*, just for a little bit. Maybe Big Bay wasn't so bad; maybe that stability was what Juliet needed, and what she craved - roots, her feet tied to the ground, to four walls and a steady job - was okay to want. Adventure was fine, and all, but she wanted more than that, too.

"Here we are," Dax announced, an entire day and a half later, as the sun was setting on March and starting to lead into April. She found them a campground right on the lake, fog settling thick over the van as they parked and paid the ranger for their spot. She paid him up through the next two weeks, Juliet noticed, and she marked in her phone calendar the day they would probably leave. She found a job in town that night, just to get the most money she could out of their pay period without wasting time, speaking with several managers at a few different places before getting a job at the register in a secondhand shop. Dax complained loudly at her the whole time, while simultaneously guiding her to places that looked like they could use an extra hand. Juliet took it in stride, even though her brain and entire body thrummed every time Dax touched her, each point of contact feeling like it lit her on fire at the spot.

"So," Dax said, bare leg dangling over the edge of the van roof like a modern Tom Sawyer, picking at the edge of her nicotine patch. "What now?"

"We wait for the aliens," Juliet answered, stretched out along the roof, hands behind her head as she tried to orient herself under the stars of Washington. The entire state was bewitching, a masterpiece of woods and rain, a state made of almost-rainforest, a wet American jungle of woodlands. "Same as we always do. It's kind of our thing now."

"Think we'll ever find what we're looking for?" Dax asked, head tipped so far upwards and backwards that the smooth line of her throat was growing distracting. *Friends. You're friends.* Juliet cleared her throat and refocused her attention on the sky, watching each shooting star as it shot by their heads, the fog dissipating more and more as the cool night wore on, the chill growing with each tick of the watch tucked up by Juliet's ear.

"I think so," Juliet replied, as honest as she could be, given the phrasing of Dax's question. "I hope so, anyways. That would be nice."

"Yeah, it would be," Dax answered, before tucking herself up into a ball on her side, eyes focused on the skyline, keeping watch as the night wore on. Juliet rubbed at Dax's back and shoulders absently, finding a rhythm that kept them both distracted and quiet on a night that felt tense for reasons unknown, a necessary silence falling between the two of them. Even though Juliet was more active that night, she was still the one who fell asleep first, her alarm set for the next morning so she could get to work at the secondhand shop. She woke up on the roof when the alarm went off, Dax having fallen asleep before she could urge either of them to wake up and get into the back of the van. Dax was curled up next to Juliet, as close as she could get without touching her, a ball on her side with the ends of her hair barely touching Juliet's side.

"Did you see anything last night?" Juliet asked, reaching down to comb her fingers through Dax's hair. Dax hummed and rolled onto her back, staring up at the morning sky with squinting eyes.

"No, nothing yet," Dax murmured sleepily, covering her eyes with her hand and stretching to pop her shoulders. "I'm sure we will soon, though. This place feels like a hot spot, you know what I mean? Do you feel that in the air?" She pressed a yawn into her palm, eyes fluttering shut again. "When do you gotta be at that store?"

"Not until eleven, but I'm there until close," Juliet told her, watching as Dax turned onto her stomach, burying her face in her arms and snuggling back up into sleep.

"And what time is it now?" Dax asked, voice mostly muffled by her forearms. Juliet checked her watch, tapping at it when the second hand stuck but the minute hand kept going. She compared it with the time on her phone before answering.

"Nine forty-five," she told her, rubbing her hands over her face under her glasses. Dax blew a raspberry up at her and buried her face again. "I can just walk down there."

"Like hell you're gonna walk down there," Dax grumbled against the roof before hauling herself up and sliding down the van to the ground. "Let's shower and go, you menace."

"You can sleep when I'm dead," Juliet joked, and Dax threw her a look over her shoulder as she gathered her toiletries in the back of the van.

"You're a fuckin' riot, Alva," Dax deadpanned back. "No, keep going. We're all in fits of laughter hearing your stellar wit. Shine on us all, you son of a- *Goddamn it!*" Dax shook her head, displacing water from her eyes from the open bottle of water Juliet just threw in her face. Juliet lifted one shoulder, trying valiantly not to laugh.

"Shouldn't have mocked me for so long," Juliet said, lifting her chin dramatically, and Dax tackled her right out of the van and onto the ground. She shoved Juliet over until her face was pressed into the dirt and she was calling uncle. Dax leaned back, still sitting on her, and let Juliet twist around onto her back. Juliet stared up at her, catching her breath, while Dax pinned her wrists above her head.

Dax's hair hung into Juliet's face, tickling her mouth and nose. Juliet blew it away from her, but it only caught on her lips. Water dripped from Dax's nose onto the dip above Juliet's lips.

"I'll make sure not to mock you so much next time," Dax murmured. Juliet exhaled in one long, low breath. "Sorry about that."

"No apologies necessary," Juliet replied softly. Dax kept her eyes on her until Juliet's breathing leveled out. She let her go, but Juliet's wrists tingled where she had touched her, like marks were permanently burnt into the skin there, two vices permanently attached to her skin. She rubbed them before Dax stood and offered her a hand up.

The secondhand shop manager turned out to also be the owner and the stock boy. It was the two of them for most of the day, apart from the customers, but he didn't talk to Juliet much. Instead, he instructed her not to leave the register, and he puttered around through the aisles, into the back, organizing and reorganizing, muttering to himself and singing himself songs that Juliet strongly suspected were made up on the spot. He was bad company, so she texted under the counter. Angelo mostly sent back memes and pictures of the cat he had since adopted and placed bows on, and Dax actively texted her back, maintaining a conversation regarding the merits of various heist films and whether or not they could pull off a similar crime. Juliet was halfway through assembling her own casino heist team when her shift ended, and she helped the owner - who finally introduced himself as Josh - close the place up before hopping in Dax's van.

"I think I'd put Pretty Boy Floyd on my team," Dax said by way of a greeting, peeling out of the parking lot and searching for a grocery store to get them food for the next few days. Juliet put in her prescription address change on her phone. "He was a bank robber, wasn't he?"

"Yeah, but I think he was shot by cops. Park there," Juliet instructed, pointing, and Dax followed her orders. Dax shrugged.

"I don't know, man, his name was Pretty Boy Floyd." She parked the van with a jolt and turned to Juliet. "I don't think it gets any better than a guy named Pretty Boy Floyd, do you?"

"What about the Blonde Tigress?" Juliet asked, as they pushed their way through the grocery store, Dax perched inside the cart, Juliet driving her down aisle after aisle. "Eleanor Jarman. *That* was a cool name."

"The Blonde Tigress isn't bad, but neither of us is blonde," Dax pointed out, reaching out to grab a box of Bisquick off the shelf.

"I thought we were picking people for our casino heist," Juliet asked, switching Bisquick out for the cheaper store brand pancake mix.

"No, we've moved on, now we're picking criminal names for ourselves, pay attention." Dax leaned back in the cart, reading the ingredients on the back of the box. "The Blonde Tigress is cool but we both have black hair, so it's not gonna work. Think along the lines of Pretty Boy Floyd, Jules, focus."

"There was one guy named Old Creepy," Juliet informed her as she carefully selected a pack of butter sticks. "I think that might suit you."

Dax reached back to flick Juliet in the forehead before turning her attention back to the store brand pancake mix instructions. Juliet sorted through their cash and their groceries, then stowed the groceries in the van before heading out for the pharmacy to pick up her hormones. When they got back to the campground, she put the groceries away in their places in the van; since she had already started sorting, she spent the next couple hours completely cleaning the van out and organizing all their belongings. Dax sat on top of the van and played music while reading through one of Juliet's alien books.

"What if we get abducted by aliens?" Dax asked through the van's open doors and windows, brushing her thumb along the edges of the pages. Juliet packed the refrigerated groceries like Tetris blocks in Dax's hotwired ice box console and hesitated, thinking through an actual answer to her question.

"I think," Juliet called back, closing the console and sealing it up tight, "it would probably be for experimentation. We're good examples of the human race, don't you think? They'd probably want to probe us, you know. Check out our insides. Or to use us in a zoo. We could be a Vonnegut story."

Dax's head appeared upside-down in the opening at the back of the van. "I don't think I wanna be in a Vonnegut story." Her hair was long enough that it was close to reaching the bottom of the doorway. "I'd rather not be abducted at all, I think."

"What do you want to do with the aliens, then?" Juliet asked, leaning back on her haunches and turning around to face her. "Do you want to travel with them? Talk to them? Just look at their faces?"

"We don't know if they'll have faces, don't be presumptuous." Dax disappeared, then reappeared, lowering herself into the van and reaching for her box of nicotine patches. She peeled hers off her arm and threw it in the trash before digging for a new one. "You know what they say."

"The aliens?"

"No, *they*. Never assume. Makes an ass out of you and me." Dax leaned in, smiling. "Ass, u, me? Get it? Assume?"

"Yeah, I heard you, Daksha," Juliet turned, and Dax's face was only a breath away from hers. She held up her nicotine patch. "What do you want?"

"What?" Dax asked, softly. Juliet raised an eyebrow and ignored how clammy her hands were getting.

"From the aliens," Juliet clarified, and Dax leaned away from her.

"You were right, I want to talk to them." Dax carefully applied her new nicotine patch, all of her attention fixated on making sure the edges were smooth, anal in a way Juliet had never seen her act before. "I want to ask them what's up, you know, on their home planet. On other planets, too, because I'm assuming we aren't the first planet they'll visit, especially 'cause I'm assuming they aren't from our solar system. Otherwise, we probably would've found them by now, right? We've seen Pluto, haven't we? Not saying Pluto's a planet-"

"Because it's *not* a planet-"

"And *God forbid* someone try to tell you that it is," Dax agreed, jokingly pacifying, holding her hands up in surrender. "But what I'm saying is: we know most of what's in our own solar system, right? So, logic dictates that these guys are coming from someplace *else*. Someplace we've never even *dreamt* of before. They're coming from who the heck knows where, right, so they must have a lot to say. I'd have to learn their language, though. But, I guess, I'd hope they'd learn mine, since they are coming to *my* planet and taking *me*, not vice versa- What are you doing?"

Juliet took Dax's wrist in her hand and found a blank patch of skin. "You're always drawing on me. I figured I'd draw on you for a change." She took the Sharpie and started lining her skin with black permanent marker. "Keep talking."

"Right, so, what was I saying? Yeah, they have to learn *my* language if they're gonna go all Christopher Columbus on my ass, *especially* if they go Columbus, because he was the *worst*-" Dax kept yammering, just letting herself riff and spin off; she kept going, and going, as the sun set in the sky and night came on them. Juliet had never been much of an artist, but lineart she could manage. She doodled a miniature version of the van on Dax's arm, delicate with the details. She drew tiny likenesses of the two of them, slowly rising into the air, attached at the hands; a UFO was above them, dragging them up towards the ship. She drew the beam, the night sky, the stars, the trees, all in a carefully straight-edged diamond shape on Dax's arm. When she finished, she sat back and let Dax finish her diatribe against colonialism and the culture of invasion.

"Do you like it?" Juliet asked, once Dax was close enough to being done that it was fair to interrupt her. Dax held her arm up to her face, examining the intricacies of Juliet's drawing. It took a long moment, but she smiled.

"I *love* it," Dax answered, pulling her forearm closer and stretching the skin tight to make out the details. "Is that us? Right here?"

"Yeah, that's us," Juliet confirmed. "Getting abducted by aliens. So we can talk to them. In English."

"I also speak Urdu and Punjabi, never assume, we just talked about this." Dax lowered her arm and motioned for Juliet to join her on the roof.

"And I speak Creole and Spanish, but you don't see me bragging about it," Juliet replied, letting Dax haul her up by the shoulders, her feet scrambling for purchase on the edge of the open door. She leaned over and swung the doors shut to keep the warmth trapped inside as the night grew cool.

"Gracias, mi amiga," Dax murmured, laying down on her back on the roof. "Think we'll get abducted tonight?"

Remembering the date in her phone calendar that signaled the end of their prepaid time at the campground, Juliet said, "I don't think it'll be tonight, no."

"Then we can still try to pull off our heist tonight," Dax said, extending her arm to Juliet, who accepted and curled up next to her, eyes on the sky. "Tell me, are we letting Pretty Boy Floyd onto the team or no? Because, man, I gotta tell you, I think he'd only drag our team down. First of all, he was killed by cops, so, dude clearly isn't very good at being a thief - at least, not for the long con. Second of all, man, he's dead, and I bet he's been dead for, what, eighty years? Ninety years? He's probably dust by now, he'd be useless to us."

"I'm sorry, *that's* the second of all? Also, I didn't know that this hypothetical didn't extend to helping him be alive again," Juliet murmured, yawning. She drowsed off, ten hours of working on her feet catching up to her, while Dax traced patterns into the side of her head and told her all about their heist, who would be on their team, what they would steal, where they would live afterwards, and what the aliens would think of them pulling it off. Juliet had strange dreams about stealing amulets from alien spaceships that night before Dax lured her to their bed.

Chapter Eleven

The next day, Juliet made her manager aware of the fact that she was probably going to have to leave in two weeks' time. She tried not to get used to Lake Stevens, but it was hard for her; she was a settler. She was one of those women in a covered wagon who hopped out in the Wild West and started building a home, *that* was her. Dax was the cowboy, the rogue, who wandered out into the desert for years at a time to prove herself to God, or whatever it was cowboys did. Cowgirls. Cowwomen.

Get your shit together, Juliet thought to herself, even as she imagined herself in petticoats and skirts on some ranch in the middle of the desert back in the heyday. Dax would sit on a horse with a ten-gallon hat and spurs, a grin on her tan face as she left their land for an adventure. *Jesus Christ, Jules, pull it together, what the hell was that?*

Lake Stevens was *nice,* goddamn it. There were parks and beaches and trails. Hell, Juliet had even found a dog park on one of her lunch breaks once, and all the dogs were off their leashes, and she got to pet a bunch of them. If nothing else had made her want to settle down, that sure as heck drove the last nail in the coffin. She itched to stay as much as it seemed Dax was itching to leave, which was no small itch. *More like chicken pox.*

Fuck off, she thought at herself. *Do your job.*

Traveling was fine. It was, really. It *really was.* It was just that it had been months since she had left Big Bay, and she was no closer to being what she wanted to be. All she knew now was what she really wanted from *life,* and that-

Oh. *Well, that's not so bad. To know what you want.*

But still. Couldn't they stay in a motel? Get a damn apartment? Just stop for once?

When Dax pulled up at the secondhand shop on the presumed second to last day, grinning so wide her teeth shone in the street lamp's light, Juliet thought, *Nope*. No, they could not just stop for once. They would keep going until Dax figured out what she was looking for, too. And that was no small feat, either.

"I got a good feeling about tonight," Dax informed her while Juliet made sandwiches in her lap in the passenger seat. Dax drove slower than usual, taking care to avoid potholes and sudden turns, lest ingredients go flying out the open window. "You, me, some aliens. What do you think?"

"I think we should go for it," Juliet agreed, checking her phone briefly. She had an alert for her calendar event for the next day, *time to pack up and go*. She yawned and reached for Dax's iced coffee, taking a long sip. "Jesus Christ, Daksha, this is mostly sugar and milk."

"Nobody asked you to drink my coffee, man." Dax pulled back into their spot at the campground and took the sandwich Juliet offered to her. When they shimmied up onto the roof, Dax wriggled out of her jacket; the mid-April weather had been faithfully staying in the mid-sixties for the past few days, and Dax seemed to heat up fairly easily. Juliet caught sight of a scab on her arm, and she caught Dax's wrist before she could escape her.

"Hey, what the hell?" Dax asked, jerking, but Juliet tightened her grip and pulled her arm up to examine the scab. The scab, as it turned out, was attached to a new and still-healing tattoo. An exact replica, it seemed, of the drawing Juliet had made on her arm, in the same exact spot.

"You got it tattooed?" Juliet hated how emotional she sounded, and tried to swallow around the lump in her throat. "Dax."

"It was a good drawing," Dax explained, tugging her hand back. Juliet let her slip through her fingers. "I liked it. You did a good job. And I like to get tattoos for things that happen in my life. Important things." She gestured between the two of them with a jerky hand. "This is an important thing happening in my life. I wanted to remember it. Feel free to stop me at any time, man, come on."

"I like when you ramble," Juliet answered. She swallowed again, averting her eyes, swiping the heel of her hand under one wet eyelid. Dax reached out hesitantly, touching her shoulder.

"Oh, come on, man, don't cry, it's not that big of a deal." Dax gripped her shoulder, and Juliet turned into her, burying her face in Dax's neck. Juliet let Dax rub circles into her back, even though she kept the tears back, stifling them as best as she could. Dax was already alarmed enough; no need for them to leave tonight, before Juliet could get her paycheck from the secondhand shop.

"Thank you," Juliet offered, when she pulled back. She meant thank you for all of it - for holding her, understanding her, getting the tattoo in the first place. Trusting her, most of all. Dax shrugged, looking down to pick at her nicotine patch.

"Thanks for drawing it, kid," Dax replied, smiling when she glanced back up. Her eyelashes were long and dark. Juliet wished she *were* a better artist, because Dax deserved to be drawn. *Knock it off.*

"So, aliens." Juliet leaned back again, laying neatly on the roof, and Dax sprawled out next to her, limbs everywhere, grinning away. "You have a good feeling?"

"My guy, I got a *great* feeling. An *unparalleled* feeling." She turned her head to Juliet, smiling like she really was going to meet an alien that night. Juliet's attention was drawn down to her tattoo, over and over again. "We're gonna meet an alien tonight. We'll see one, at *least*. I can feel it."

Dax was like a moon, Juliet thought to herself, watching her friend speak, listening to her ramblings and doing her best to catalogue the thoughts that spilled out of her mouth. If moons made their own light, that was Dax, Juliet imagined. It fit her rather well. But, then again, Juliet herself did not feel much like a sun. *You don't need to match each other,* Juliet thought, savagely, but she wanted them to match regardless. Maybe Dax was the sun, after all. She created her own light.

Maybe, Juliet thought, she was a star. The sun was a star, wasn't it? She had the aesthetic of a star. The whole look. Dax would appreciate that, she thought. Dax was a star. Juliet was a moon, then. Reflecting light. Steady. Reliable. Responsible for the tides. The metaphor needed work. Unless it was a simile? Whatever; metaphors suck, and she majored in hospitality, not English. She knew management, service, sustainability. She had no clue whether or not she was a tide or a beach or whatever the hell she had been thinking about.

She was drifting; she had no idea what she had thought, actually, once she considered it more fully. She forced herself back awake, but Dax had already fallen silent; a glance at her confirmed she thought Juliet had fallen asleep. Juliet got a spike in her heart rate when she thought, *This is it. Aliens.* Tonight was the night; Dax wanted to leave the next day, Juliet strongly suspected. She assumed Dax had been lying when she claimed to have seen aliens. Not that it was a big deal, because she understood why Dax was doing it, and lying about seeing aliens, of all things, was not the worst thing Dax could be lying to her about.

The adrenaline kept Juliet awake, watching Dax as she scanned the sky, over and over. It was uncharacteristically clear that night, since Lake Stevens was a foggy town, and Juliet could see each shooting star well enough when she squinted. Dax looked back at her a fair few times, eyes skimming her face as she fake-slept, her eyes snapping shut every time Dax so much as twitched in her direction.

Dax folded her hands over her waist and sighed softly. If Juliet was guessing right, it was near one in the morning, and neither of them had slept; Juliet figured Dax would sleep in the next morning regardless, and Juliet was already prepared not to work the next day, so it didn't really matter. Dax leaned over to check Juliet's watch before twisting and shaking Juliet awake. Nothing moved in the sky - no shooting stars, no helicopters, no airplanes, no birds, and certainly no unidentified flying objects. And yet, here Dax was, urgently squeezing Juliet's shoulder and jostling her into fake-wakefulness.

"What?" Juliet asked, making her voice low and rough, rubbing at her face. Dax was too caught up in her own act to notice any fallacies in Juliet's.

"I saw them, man. The UFOs, right there," and Dax pointed up at the sky, where Juliet had just seen a whole lot of nothing.

So, she *had* been lying. This entire time. It made sense; it only confused Juliet, more than anything else, and reassured her a little bit, because Dax claiming to have seen aliens in every city and town they visited was more than a little concerning. There was nothing there; unless Dax was actually seeing something that did not exist, this was more of a baffling lie than anything that actually aroused concern.

"Was it a flying saucer?" Juliet asked, still rubbing at her eyes.

Dax nodded eagerly.

"Yeah, just like you said."

"Did they go really fast?"

"Yeah!"

"And they had weird lights on the rims?"

"Yes-"

"And the top?"

"Yeah! It's just like the report!"

"Did it make any sounds?" Juliet prodded, and Dax hesitated, just for a breath, before she nodded, barrelling on.

"It did, it made sounds like, you know," and Dax imitated a UFO one might see in a movie. "You know? Like that. I can't believe it."

"Your intuition was right." Juliet scrubbed at her face and yawned, the one part of her performance that was the truth. So, she wasn't really seeing anything; she was just making it up. Probably so they could move on to the next town, Juliet speculated. It made sense.

"Guess so." Dax lowered herself to the ground and helped Juliet and their blankets follow. "Should we head out tomorrow?"

"I'll talk to my manager in the morning, but I'm sure he won't have a problem with me shipping out," Juliet agreed sleepily, letting Dax tuck her in. "Where to next?"

"We'll decide tomorrow," Dax answered. "Get some more sleep. I'll write down everything I noticed about the ships."

"Yeah, you do that." Juliet buried her face in whoever's pillow was closest. Was it really a lie when Juliet knew the truth like she did? It felt like a lie more for Dax's sake than for her own. She let it slide for the night, giving herself over to sleep while Dax tapped her story into her phone beside her in the back of their van.

The next day saw them both waking up soon after noon, just barely drifting into true non-morning territory. Dax blearily drove Juliet into town to pick up her money first. They headed back to the campground afterwards, to wake up more and shower before picking out their next destination. Juliet sorted through their options while Dax blow-dried her hair with her dangerous hot-wired weapon of a blow dryer.

"We've got Nevada-"

"Not yet, nah. I'm not ready to head back to Nevada."

"Yeah, alright. So, Oregon, you know-"

"No, the Oregon Trail is scary. I don't want to die of dysentery. Next."

"Nobody has dysentery in Oregon anymore, Daksha. Not in modern-day Salem. Plus, look at this," Juliet said, offering Dax her phone. Dax flicked through the pictures of a UFO in McMinnville, Oregon in the 1950s. Dax whistled low.

"Yeah, that's an unidentified fuckin' object if I've ever seen one," Dax replied, and Juliet laughed, startled by the joke. Dax tapped in the directions for McMinnville, and set off on their four-hours-plus drive. She seemed more determined this time, driving with purpose, not stopping on her way out to Oregon. The drive was direct, only pausing once at a rest stop so Juliet could self-administer her hormones and use the bathroom and Dax could get them burgers.

It seemed like there were more trees in McMinnville than there were people, based on the sheer amount of sprouting greenery Juliet could see as they drove through the town. It was quaint; that was really the best word Juliet had for the place. Quaint, small, and just so *green*. April was starting to fade into May, and the spring was coming in full force. Trees were filled with new buds and leaves, creating covered bridges out of the roads of the town. There were banners everywhere, signs proclaiming downtown to be a historic district. Juliet watched a nice little building containing a real estate agency pass them by, feeling wistful about the whole thing. Just for shits, she pulled up the agency on her phone, and passed the time looking at houses for sale in town.

They found a campground that let them park in one of their small spots, mixed in with a bunch of huge RVs that completely dwarfed their ratty van in both quality and size. Dax made sure the sky above the van was clear of trees and obstructions. The whole place was much nicer than any of the other hole-in-the-wall woodsman's yards they had stayed in so far. When they retreated to the glass office building to pay for their stay, Juliet redirected her attention; she liked the surprise of not knowing when the aliens might show up. She had a newfound fun in wondering why Dax might be making up these stories and when the next white lie might come.

The town was gorgeous, small, and welcoming. Dax even

seemed to light up with how comfortable the place was, enjoying their moments walking down the street, the van left in the parking lot at the edge of the so-called historic downtown. Dax tucked her arm through Juliet's and pointed out dresses and toys and displays in storefront windows.

"If cartoon princesses' ideals collided with TV romance movies, this place is it," Dax commented, the two of them watching a cheery Easter puppet show in the window of a vintage toy shop. Just the fact that a vintage toy shop even existed was an agreement in itself. Juliet nodded, dropping her head against Dax's shoulder and exhaling, happy.

She *liked* McMinnville. She got a job in a nice little boutique, like she was right on Main Street, USA, some kind of idyllic image of a perfect American town. She hoped against hope that Dax would never see any aliens, and maybe they should stay there forever. Juliet liked going in to work, walking in from the edge of town and helping little kids find outfits for their kindergarten graduations and makeup for young people trying to paint themselves in a new light. She wanted to stay there for as long as they could.

She thought Dax might have been able to tell that, too. That Juliet was happier there than she had been anyplace else they had gone so far. She took her into town pretty often, coming up with excuses for odds and ends she needed from local stores. She still disappeared during the day, while Juliet was working, but she spent a good amount of time without any 'good feelings' about possible aliens coming to McMinnville. They looked at the pictures of the UFOs from McMinnville, now and then. Dax found a little novelty shop that had copies of the old issue of the magazine that the original UFO photographs were featured in.

"If we stay here until the 12th," Juliet pointed out, motioning up to a banner high above them as they walked down the street downtown after Juliet's shift, "then we can go to their UFO festival." The banner had green aliens and brightly-colored UFOs all over it, hand-painted. Probably by a bunch of morally straight and ethnically diverse kids from the local middle school. It was April 22nd already; they would have to stay in town for another three weeks to make it to the UFO festival. Dax seemed to be doing the same math in her head, but coming to a different conclusion on whether or not it was worth it. "It could be fun. I wouldn't mind staying here that long.

This is a… It's a really nice town." Trying to keep her cards close to her chest, trying not to reveal her hand. Dax was being kind, looking away from her face. "I don't mind waiting."

Dax glanced at her, then away. Her eyes scanned the street: the shops, the trees, the people bustling here and there. Maybe she was inventing another UFO to see. "I guess I don't mind, either," Dax offered. Juliet turned her face to hide her smile. "Why don't we go get ice cream, then? There's a place we haven't tried yet, right around the corner - see, there." Dax pointed, and started for the store, and Juliet followed, trusting her footsteps.

Juliet's manager at the boutique - a little place called Adam's - was a charming older woman named Sandy, whose father was the titular Adam, a man who loved fashion and had always dreamed of owning a place like Sandy owned now. Juliet worked with Sandy and two other employees, Leslie and Dorian, every day except Mondays, when the boutique was closed. Dax tended to take off Mondays, as well, from wherever it was she went and whatever it was she did those days. They started learning the names of people in town, recognizing different places they could go for good meals, cheap prices, good quality items. They started to make acquaintances; God help her, Juliet felt like she even had a couple of friends. She even met up with Dorian a couple times for supper when Dax didn't pick her up in time by dinner. She was making *friends*, putting down *roots*. It was *nice*, goddamn it.

Dax was being good to her, too. Dax was usually good to her, but she was being *nice*, moreso than *good*, doing little things for her just to make her smile. She was good at that, too. May 2nd found them at a Renaissance Faire outside of town, the two of them in gowns that Dorian had dug up from old inventories in the back of their stock room. Dax kept trying to tug at the hoops and petticoats under her skirts, but Juliet took her hand and led her around, letting her examine the different kinds of food options they offered while Juliet poked around the little shops.

"Gotcha some fudge," Dax told her, handing her a little paper bag. She had a leg of some sort of meat in the other hand. She held it up towards Juliet. "They told me it's mutton. I told them that's a fake meat. They told me I had spunk." She motioned with the leg at Juliet, who leaned down and took a bite out of it with her teeth. "It was a whole thing. But, now, mutton, see?"

"I do see, thank you." Juliet closed her fingers over Dax's hand to keep it steady so she could take another chunk of meat out. Dax's thumb hesitated before touching the corner of her mouth, swiping.

"You had, uhm... Meat. Juice. Sorry." Dax turned away, licking her thumb clean and starting to look over the armor in the shop Juliet was in. She made short work of the mutton, offering Juliet bites when she saw her glancing at it. Juliet mostly focused on looking through the shops, lifting her skirts up to stop them from dragging in the dirt as she moved from kiosk to kiosk. She got pine needles caught up in the folds anyways, but it mostly just made the skirts smell nice, so she left them.

Juliet was nibbling at one of her fudge pieces, trying to make it last, when someone tapped on her shoulder from behind. She started to turn, but Dax stopped her, keeping her facing forwards.

"Sorry, I didn't mean to startle you," Dax murmured. "I just wanted you to put your hand down- There, yeah, just like that. Sorry. Hold on." Dax's hands reached around Juliet's neck, settling something in the hollow of her throat. Whatever it was fell down a little bit when Dax returned to the back of Juliet's neck, landing on her chest, and Juliet craned her head down as best as she could to see the charm. It was a gem, bright red, set in a small golden lion's head. There was no way it could be real gold or a real gem, but it was beyond beautiful. She reached up to rub the necklace between her fingers as Dax hooked the back of it against the top knob of Juliet's spine.

"I thought this looked good for you," Dax told her, before clearing her throat. "I thought you'd like it. Do you like it?"

"I do, it's beautiful," Juliet answered. She put the fudge back in the paper bag and stuffed it into her purse. "How much is it?"

"It's a gift," Dax said, reaching out with a grip on Juliet's upper arms to turn her around. "It looks nice. You look pretty."

"Thank you," Juliet replied, a little confused. She forced her eyebrows to smooth back out so she looked less puzzled than she felt. "So do you. What's that about?"

"I just thought you'd like it." Dax reached into Juliet's handbag to grab a piece of fudge, taking a chunk out of it to fill her mouth. "This is good fudge, right?"

"Right," Juliet agreed, incredulous. Dax rubbed at the back of her neck. After a long moment, she stepped away, heading over to look at another display like she actually cared about it. She ended up getting herself two gloves made of thin wire with metal leaves set into it, the foil wrapping around her wrist, the back of her hand, and her knuckles delicately. She wore them as they left the faire, her hands glistening on the steering wheel. Juliet kept fingering her necklace, half of her attention captivated by it, even when they drove into town to get a cheaper dinner than anything the renaissance faire offered. They got burgers and strolled through town in their gowns, drinking ice cream sodas and enjoying each other's company. Dax's lies faded to the back of her mind; she imagined they were only a way to achieve moments like these.

"I'm glad you came to Big Bay," Juliet commented, out of the blue, if only because she had been thinking it and thought Dax deserved to hear it. "Nobody ever comes to Big Bay. But I'm glad you ended up there."

Dax licked whipped cream off her upper lip before smiling. "Me, too, kid." She reached down and squeezed Juliet's hand. The sun setting in the trees was breathtaking; Dax seemed to shine in the setting sunlight. Her own personal star.

Everything felt right in McMinnville. Dax kept pulling little things, things that she seemed to think Juliet would never notice. Things like asking Sandy to push Juliet's hours back a little bit when Juliet had had a rough night sleeping the night before, or showing up with dinner for her after a long shift when she knew Juliet would rather climb into the back of the van and relax rather than go out or make anything. She took her on walks, indulged her in her little homegrown fantasies.

It made the whole thing all the harder when, right before the UFO festival came into town, Juliet started noticing Dax getting antsy again. She shared her concerns, brief and lacking detail though they were, with Dorian at their shared lunch break.

"Just tell her you want to stay," Dorian suggested, licking mustard off of his wrist. "It's a nice place to live. I'm sure she'd like it if she gave it more of a chance."

"She doesn't want to give *any* place a chance," Juliet told him, keeping her eyes on her sandwich. She put it back down in her plastic container with a sigh. "She doesn't like staying in one place too long."

"You guys have been here a while, though," Dorian pointed out. "Maybe she does like it here, but she just feels like she's gotta keep going, you know? If that's what you guys always do, maybe she still thinks she has to. I mean, she might not be actually *thinking* that exactly, but, like. Her subconscious. You know?"

"Yeah, I know what you mean." Juliet put her chin in her hand, picking at the crust on her sandwich with her free fingers. "I'll try to talk to her, but she's not a fan of talking about feelings."

"I hate to break it to you, but neither are you, Juliet," Dorian commented, taking another bite of his reheated burger. "One of you has gotta get one of those books about getting in touch with your inner demons or something before you both die of emotional constipation."

After that enlightening talk left Juliet feeling more antsy than anything, she tried three separate times to try to talk to Dax about staying in McMinnville in a more permanent way, but Dax brushed her off each time. She started showing Juliet places they could go next, even as they walked from booth to booth at the UFO festival. Dax had left her jacket in the van, so her fully-healed tattoo of Juliet's drawing was in full display and was well-liked by other festival attendees.

"What do you think about this place?" Dax asked, looking at a display in a booth about military-related UFO sightings. It was about a sighting in Carson Sink, Nevada. "It says two Air Force dudes recorded an actual unidentified flying object. Government approved, man. Must be something, they don't let just anything slip to us. Plus, it's Carson Sink. That's almost Carson City. You like state capitals."

"Carson Sink isn't even kind of Carson City. And, besides, I thought you weren't ready to go back to Nevada?" Juliet asked, trying to seem only mildly interested when, in reality, her heart was already pounding, and half of her mind was occupied with how she was going to say goodbye to Dorian, Sandy, and Leslie.

"I could get behind it for something this good," Dax replied. "Plus, it says they took off from Hamilton Field. You like history. It's Alexander Hamilton."

"Well, I-"

"How far is Carson Sink from here?" Dax asked the couple running the booth, showing them the display she had been looking at and discussing the sighting with them. Juliet ran her fingers over the papers in the display, trying to read the words but unable to focus on them. The lion's head necklace felt heavy in the hollow of her throat.

That night, after the festival, the two of them lay on the van roof in the RV park, a balloon shaped like an alien floating above their heads, tied to the handle of the back door. Juliet rubbed at her necklace anxiously, glancing at Dax now and then as Dax played a block-stacking game on her phone.

"Do you think you'd ever want to settle down somewhere?" Juliet blurted out, instead of leading up to it more elegantly, with actual conversation. Dax turned to her slightly, one eyebrow raised. She kept playing her game. "Not, like, now, you know. I'm just, you know. Wondering. If you might. In the future. Curious."

"Yeah, I don't know," Dax answered. She let a straight line of four slide into the wrong spot; she frowned slightly. "I don't know if that's really me, you know? You know."

"I know," Juliet said, falling silent again. She let herself fall asleep, amongst Dax's occasional nervous glance in her direction. The next morning, when she woke up inside the van, Dax told her she had seen a spaceship the night before, what a coincidence, with the UFO festival in town and everything. Juliet talked to Sandy and gave her notice; Sandy let her go with a hug and the rest of her money for the pay period, even though she was going to miss the whole next week of it. Sandy just stroked Juliet's cheek and hugged her again.

"I'm gonna miss you, Juliet," Dorian told her, squeezing her tight and seemingly refusing to let her go. Dax was sitting on the hood of the van outside the boutique, picking at her nicotine patch, her sunglasses taking up most of her face. "You always have a place to stay if you decide to come visit, you hear me?"

"Loud and clear," Juliet murmured into his neck. Dorian released her, kissing her on the forehead. Dax glanced up at them, a frown between her eyes. "I'm going to miss you guys, too. I'll text you, I promise."

"You be good, you hear me?" Dorian said as she left. "Use your words." Juliet smiled over her shoulder at him with an exaggerated shrug, and he flipped her off. She waved out the passenger's side window until the boutique vanished from her sight.

"Carson Sink, here we come," Dax announced, shattering

Juliet's quiet, sad thoughts. Juliet rested her forehead against the glass of the rolled-up window. Dax's phone told them it would take eleven hours to get to Carson Sink, so Juliet shut her eyes, letting the music from the soundtrack sing-along CD Dax had put in the player wash over her and trying to forget how she was feeling. She struggled to remember the excitement she had once had, attempting instead to siphon off of Dax's joy for a little while. She fell asleep with the charm of her necklace wrapped up in her hand.

Chapter Twelve

"Hey, kid, wake up," Dax exclaimed, smacking at Juliet's leg. Juliet blinked up at her groggily. "Can you grab my phone, find a different route? This one's got a shitload of traffic."

"Yeah, sure," Juliet told her, sitting up and rubbing at her face. She slapped lightly at her cheeks and reached for the phone. Tapping in a new route, a text came through with an address in Nevada. She frowned and swiped the text away, respecting Dax's privacy, but she wondered if that had anything to do with where Dax went during the day while Juliet worked.

"Hey," Juliet started, setting the phone back on its stand against the dashboard. "Where, uhm… You make money? Where do you…"

"Jules, kid, come on," Dax replied, reading the directions for her exit to take the backroads out of traffic. "I thought we didn't talk about that, you know. I thought we had an understanding on that one."

"No, yeah, you're right, I'm sorry," Juliet murmured. She kept quiet the rest of the way to Carson Sink, letting sing-along songs fill the car when Dax turned the music up. Dax sang along, but Juliet pressed her forehead to the window and just listened.

Carson Sink was everything McMinnville was not - which was to say, it was literally nothing. It had no houses, no people, no trees. It was a pebbled, wet-looking, barren wasteland as far as Juliet could see - which was fairly far, since there was nothing to obstruct her vision on its way to the horizon. The two of them parked alongside Carson Sink and got out of the van, standing up on top of the roof to look over the area.

"Well," Dax said, hands on her hips, surveying the land. "Guess we're gonna have to head back to Lovelock."

"You mean, you don't want to stay in this desolate hunk of wet sand? Why ever not?" Juliet asked, and Dax lightly shoved at her shoulder. "We could always stay in that ghost town. Rochester, wasn't it? Looked like a mining place. Maybe we'll find some gold."

"Fuck off, Alva," Dax laughed. She threw an arm around Juliet's shoulders and motioned to the entire hot wasteland. "Everything the sun hits could be ours."

"Wow, really? This'll all be mine?" Juliet joked, playing along. Dax leaned in and kissed her temple, grinning, before she swung herself back down into the van. Juliet followed, and the two of them drove back to Lovelock, Nevada, finding themselves a little clearing to park in, since the tiny town had no campground. They slept on the roof that night, staring up at the desert sky and watching the stars streak by, free of light pollution out in the middle of nowhere.

Dax drove Juliet into town the next day, leaving her at a movie theater before vanishing. Juliet strolled down the street, hands in her pockets. She found a boutique that reminded her somewhat of Adam's, and she reached for the door, but found that it felt wrong without Sandy or Dorian waiting for her inside. She sent Dorian a text and moved on autopilot to the building next door, which turned out to be a little hotel.

"Are you looking for any one position in particular?" Juliet asked, standing politely opposite the concierge and manager at the reception desk. "Literally, any job. I'm gonna be here for a week or two, I just want to make some cash. Please."

"We need a bellman," the manager told her, after a few moments talking with the concierge and two receptionists. He nodded his head in the direction of a man in a uniform and cap standing by the seating area of the lobby. "Scott's our bellman, right there, but his mother just died and he's been a little distracted, understandably. We could use an assistant for him until he gets back on track. How's that sound?"

"That sounds perfect," Juliet agreed, and started working that day, wearing an old bellman's uniform from the back that fit her rather imperfectly. She had forgotten why, exactly, she had chosen hospitality for a major, but she liked coming back into something that actually utilized four years of her life's work. Dax texted her and picked her up at the time she gave. The two of them explored the tiny town of Lovelock together that night.

The entire place, as it turned out, was a romantic tourist trap, essentially. Balloon rides over the town and out into the desert, wedding chapels and meadows all over the place, and a plaza with lovers' locks. Juliet was reading the sign leading into the little plaza, learning the explanations behind the lovers' locks, when Dax came over and held out a lock for them.

"Doesn't have to be a romantic love thing," Dax murmured, offering her palm, the lock square in the center of it. Juliet took it, flipping it over in her hands. Dax hesitated, then took it back, carving their initials into one side with key to their van. She surrendered it again, and Juliet found a spot on the fence to secure the lock. The two of them stood, watching the sun set beyond the plaza, until day faded into night over Lovelock.

The next couple of days were not easy days for Juliet; she tried to settle back into the rhythm of a new city, to forget McMinnville and move on, like Dax was doing. She liked working at the hotel; Scott was a good guy, easy to work with, and Juliet didn't mind spending her days helping him out when he was too distracted to work.

Partway through the week, though, Dax didn't text her asking what time she needed to be picked up. She didn't call her, or send a Snapchat, or come and pick her up after her shift ended. Juliet waited until the parking lot was completely dark before she called, but Dax's phone went to voicemail. She called twice more before getting a sandwich from the corner store, catching a movie at the theater, and heading back to their clearing in the complete and utter darkness, lit only occasionally by streetlights. Sure enough, when she got to the clearing, there was nothing and no one there. She threw her hands up in the air, the only sound in the clearing her palms smacking her thighs when she let them fall.

"Daksha?" she called into the darkness. No answer. "Daksha?" She picked up her phone again, craning her neck to look around the corner. "Dax? Hello?" Nope. *Fuck. What the hell?*

Juliet ended up sleeping tucked up behind a rock, under a makeshift tent of sticks and fronds, using her jacket as a blanket that she rolled her whole body up into. She fingered her necklace throughout the night, keeping the metal warmer than she was, held tight in her palm. When she woke up the next morning, shivering from the cold of the night and of the ground beneath her, there was still no van. She called Dax's phone again, and still she got no answer. Icy fear started to sink into her chest, moreso than the anger of the night before. Something had happened, probably; something had happened to Dax and she was unable to come back.

Maybe she left, Juliet's mind traitorously whispered to her. *You scared her off, after everything you said in McMinnville. Nice work. Now she's gone and you're stranded. You'll never see her again. You'll-*

"Shut up," Juliet said out loud, rubbing at her eye and sitting up. She fixed her jacket in place again and head off on the long walk back into town for the hotel. She tried to stay focused at work, but, between her and Scott, they had about the mental capacity and attention of one entire employee, rather than two. Juliet texted Dax every half hour or so, but none of them were answered. She called on her lunch break, but got her voicemail again. She got choked up leaving the voicemail this time, but tried her best not to actually cry on the recording. She held it in until she hung up, and then she cried in the employees' back room, fear clawing at her chest. She waited in the parking lot until dark, again, and then even further, waiting for Dax to come for her. She stood there until she saw one of the hotel visitors watching her through their room window, and she left after the third time the curtain flickered. She grabbed another sandwich and head for the clearing again, in case Dax had come back and fallen asleep or something, maybe, *anything.*

No, nothing, nothing at the clearing, nothing down the road. Nothing at all. *Fucking goddamnit, fuck, fuck, what do I do?* Cops? No, not the cops. But... but, maybe the cops? *Shit.* If Dax wasn't back by the next day, Juliet was already making plans to find the police station in town and file a missing person report. She knew that movies and television shows usually had a waiting period to file missing person reports, but she didn't think that was an actual real thing.

Juliet used her phone - slowly dying, without the charger in their van to fill the battery back up every night - to map out the path to the police station in Lovelock before she started to search again. Her chest ached; her hands shook with adrenaline, muscles pulled with fearful tension. She stared, wide-eyed, across the sand and dirt, and still no van came. She tossed her phone between her hands before calling Dax's number again. Still no answer, still the voicemail, still a choked-up and fearful message for Juliet to leave. She felt herself growing exhausted, hungry, but could do nothing to fix it; she could feel herself starting to lose her grip on what was happening, but still hoped against hope that Dax might actually come back, and in one piece. God, Juliet hoped she was all in one piece, still okay. She dialed 9-1-1 a few times as she searched before giving up, knowing Dax would be embarrassed if she called and everything turned out okay.

Logically, Juliet assumed this had something to do with where Dax went every day while Juliet worked, in any given city or town. It *had* to. It just… It had to. What the hell else could it be? The thought of what Dax could be doing… Worse and worse scenarios flitted through Juliet's mind's eye, plaguing her every moment. She itched to do something, and so she kept looking into the night, searching through back alleys and behind buildings. She started to wander through clearings, through sandy desert meadows, through tourist trap sightseeing spots, getting shakier and losing more hope with each empty spot she searched. Her phone died somewhere along the way, and she curled up on a bench near town, near the plaza with their lovers' lock on it, and cleaned off her tear-wet face with her sleeve. Her necklace dangled into her face when she ducked her head, bumping against her nose; it felt like a taunt.

"Yo," a voice said over her, and Juliet's head snapped up, tears steadily streaming down her face. Dax stood over her, a scratch over one eye, looking a little tired but otherwise unharmed. Juliet rocketed to her feet, but reached out only tentatively, half-worried she was seeing an illusion. When her fingers met Dax's solid arm, she threw herself at her, throwing her up in her arms and burying her face in Dax's neck.

"Whoa, kid, are you alright?" Dax asked, wrapping her arms around Juliet and rubbing up and down her back. "I'm so sorry I disappeared like that on you last night, something came up and my phone died out in the desert and I-"

"You can *never* do that to me again," Juliet ordered, voice trembling uncontrollably, her hands shaking like things possessed. She stepped back, framing Dax's face in her hands. "*Never*. Do you understand me, Dax? I can't go through that again. I *can't*. Where the *fuck* have you been?"

"Oh, man, you're filthy, Jules, I should've-"

"There's a lot of things you *should've*," Juliet interrupted, tired and scared, exhaustion leaking into her relief, tension seeping out of her, fear and anger warring in her still. "What the fuck *was* that? Where did you go?"

"Whenever I leave," Dax explained, wrapping Juliet's hands up in hers, holding her still, "I just... I take ads on Craigslist. And this one, the guy was looking for someone to get messed up with, and we ended up in the desert and I just... Lost track of time? I guess?"

"You *guess*?" Juliet asked incredulously, pulling her hands out of Dax's and stepping away, yanking her hands through her hair, scratching rough nails against her scalp. "You guess. Fantastic. You take Craigslist ads to go out in the desert and get messed up, and I slept under some sticks and thought you were dead. Amazing."

"Usually it doesn't-"

"Usually it doesn't go like that?" Juliet finished for her. "Really? Well, this time it did, Daksha. My *God*." She pressed the heels of her hands to her eyes and exhaled shakily. "No more Craigslist ads without telling me."

"But I-"

"No more," Juliet repeated firmly, hands still pressed into her eyes, "Craigslists ads. Without telling me. Or I'm walking. Daksha, I swear, I will go home. I can't keep doing this. I can't, I can't, I just-" Her voice broke on a sob, and she dropped her hands to clasp against her mouth, starting to cry all over again, uncontrollable, a release of tension and rage and the clawing, aching fear. Dax pulled her into her arms again and stroked her head, her back, her arms, anywhere she could reach, shushing her, soothing her.

"I promise," Dax whispered into her ear, and Juliet shook, hands trapped between their chests, face pressed into Dax's skin, hot and slick with tears. "I promise, Juliet. It's going to be okay."

"I'm *so* mad at you," Juliet spat angrily into Dax's neck. Dax kept rubbing her back without a hitch. The rest of Juliet's words caught in her throat, too afraid that one barb might catch Dax wrong and she would be alone again. She swallowed them back. The embrace had lasted too long; Juliet forced Dax away from her in an effort to hold onto her anger.

"That's okay," Dax assured her softly. "I am, too. It's never going to happen again. We're both okay."

Dax and Juliet sat on the bench for a long time after that. The sun fully set, leaving behind a blue-purple dusk and a dark, cloudy night - no stars, no moon, no aliens or UFOs. Dax reached out, hesitantly, after a while, and Juliet let her take her hand, and only that, unwilling to let her go, angry though she was.

"I'm still mad," Juliet informed Dax as they piled into the van to go to the clearing and sleep for the night. "I can't *believe* you. You should've at least told me where you were going. Do you know how irresponsible that was?"

"Yeah, I do, *Mom*," Dax answered, but her expression was soft and concerned. "I got a lot of cash from it-"

"I would rather have you," Juliet interrupted, and Dax glanced back at her. Juliet was busy was rubbing at a weird stain on the window with her sleeve, using that as an excuse not to look back and make eye contact. Dax reached over and pat Juliet's knee before continuing to drive. The clearing wasn't hard to find, and Dax inspected Juliet's little shelter.

"I'm so sorry," Dax whispered. Juliet put her hands on her hips, looking at the stick tent for a moment before kicking it all over.

"Make it up to me," Juliet said, heading back for the van. She climbed up onto the roof with most of the blankets, making up for the cold night hours after the fact, and Dax joined her after a bit of pensive staring near the rock.

"I won't go anymore," Dax promised, and Juliet let her under the blankets. Dax curled up against her, and Juliet let her arm wind around her shoulders, holding her close, still grateful she was real and whole and safe. "I won't answer the ads anymore unless we both decide it's okay. I'll try to get jobs in town instead, like you do. Okay?"

"Okay," Juliet replied softly. She buried her head in Dax's hair, nose brushing along her scalp. "Okay. Thank you."

"Thank *you*," Dax murmured against Juliet's shoulder. Juliet squeezed her.

"I just want you to be safe."

"I know."

A beat.

"I want to leave," Juliet told her, and Dax nodded automatically.

"Yeah, sure." She adjusted her position, situating herself so the two of them could see each other's faces. "We'll go get your money from the hotel tomorrow and head out. Anywhere you want."

Somehow, Juliet didn't think that McMinnville counted as 'anywhere'. She resolved to find somewhere in California, maybe. A populated area, no deserts, no places to get lost. Sacramento, maybe. Can't go wrong with a state capital. Maybe somewhere near an ocean; she still hadn't seen an ocean. She pulled Dax close again and fell silent. Dax fell asleep before Juliet that night, but she relished the warmth and the comforting knowledge of Dax's safety and closeness. Her fading anger left space for open, rushing relief, and she pressed her face to Dax's hair and let herself cry again while Dax slept, letting herself feel for a moment without any restriction

Chapter Thirteen

The next morning, Juliet woke up before Dax, as per usual, and started searching for a new place to go. She had had very minimal opportunity to search for a place during her time in Lovelock, so she flicked through her bookmarks while Dax slept. Dax's head was pillowed on Juliet's chest as she snored lightly, one arm flung up around Juliet's head, fingers tangled in her hair. Juliet sorted through her websites, eventually finding an incident in Huron, California where UFOs had been spotted fairly recently.

Dax woke up a little while before Juliet's usual shift would have begun at the hotel, groggily lifting her head to look directly into Juliet's eyes. "Mornin'."

"Good morning," Juliet murmured back, and Dax burrowed her head into Juliet's neck, sighing softly, warm breath against her throat. Juliet stroked her hair back from her face, dropping her phone next to them in the back of their van. "I'm still pretty mad at you, you know."

"Yeah, I know," Dax answered. She propped her chin up on Juliet's chest and smiled at her. "I'll make it up to you."

Juliet's heart thudded in her chest, picking up speed as she looked down at Dax's sleepy face. Dax scratched at Juliet's head before heaving herself up into sitting, rubbing her hands over her face. She grimaced, but Juliet just kept staring up at her, relief and anger and something she had been half-suppressing warring intensely in her chest.

"I gotta take a shower," Dax stated matter-of-factly, stretching her arms up above her head to pop her shoulders and elbows. She groaned, then dropped her arms, yawning. "I'm sure you do, too, kid. You slept on the ground."

"Asshole."

"I'll keep apologizing." Dax started gathering up her toiletries and Juliet's, tossing them all into a canvas bag. "I saw a gas station a little down the way. Baths in the sink?"

"Sounds good," Juliet agreed, locating her shoes in the tangle of blankets and pillows and clothes that their bed had become. Dax pulled her in for an unexpected hug, squeezing her tight and burying her face in Juliet's neck. Juliet hesitated out of surprise before slowly embracing her. "What's this for?"

"I love you," Dax told her, and Juliet was abruptly nauseous from the sudden onslaught of emotion filling her stomach and chest. "I don't want you to think that I don't, just because I fucked up. Because I do. You're the best thing that's happened to me in a long time, all right?"

"Yeah, all right," Juliet murmured back. She exhaled shakily. "I love you, too. I was just worried about you, that's all."

"That's not all," Dax replied, "but thank you." She squeezed Juliet and released her. "Where are we heading to next, kid? You're the navigator, I'm just the pilot."

"We're like our own starship crew," Juliet commented, and Dax smacked the back of her head lightly.

"Quit being a fuckin' nerd, where are we going?"

"I found a nice place." Juliet pulled out her phone and brought up the reports she had been reading. "It's called Huron, California. The map says we go through Sacramento on the way there. It's just a nice little California town." She turned to Dax, a little jolt of fear going through her unexpectedly, and seemingly without cause. *Chill out.* "What do you think?"

"I think it looks perfect," Dax replied. "I trust you. Good choice." She kicked open the back doors of the van and slid out, pulling the bag of toiletries and Juliet's wrist with her. "Too bad this place was a wash. We're not even in the actual place the UFO was spotted, you know, that's probably why. There's no fuckin' UFOs in Lovelock. No wonder we didn't see anything." She motioned for Juliet to crouch down before she jumped up onto her back. "Hiya!"

Juliet straightened up and released Dax, letting her fall on her ass in the sand. Dax sputtered up at her before wrapping her arms around Juliet's knees and tripping her. Juliet smacked right into the sand, laughing all the while, and it took them a healthy amount of wrestling in the dirt before they called a truce, gathered their belongings, and hiked their way to the gas station. It took a while in the bathroom to scrub each other down with paper towels to get them to a respectable state of cleanliness and acceptable hygiene again; they each brushed their teeth more than once, and Juliet gave Dax's hair the hardest wash she had in weeks. Helping Dax wash was doing weird things to her chest, which she tried her best to ignore until she could suitably sort her emotions out into boxes and shove them away for the season. Dax helped her administer her hormones with gentle hands on her thigh, and Juliet tried far too hard not to make eye contact while they did it.

Once they were back in the van, Dax drove straight into town to the hotel. Juliet gave her two minutes' notice and picked up her due payments before hopping right back into the passenger's seat. The two of them head off for Huron, leaving Nevada behind, hopefully never to return to the horrible desert and every terrible thought and memory it now held for Juliet. She cranked down her window, Dax doing the same, and they let old disco soundtracks blast through the van as they abandoned Nevada for good.

"Did you know I can dance?" Dax offered, after nearly an hour of silence on Juliet's end. Dax caught her off guard with the question; Juliet frowned up at her, their eyes unable to meet due to the sunglasses on both their faces. In fairness to Juliet and her silence, she had been trying to work through the strange thumping in her chest that came every time Dax so much as glanced at her, or she at Dax.

"You can not dance," Juliet argued, folding her arms across her chest. Dax laughed, returning her attention to the road.

"I can so dance," Dax disagreed. "My father used to be a dance instructor when he was young. When he moved to America, he taught traditional Pakistani dances. So, he taught me. I eventually wanted to learn other types, too." Dax turned to grin at Juliet. Her teeth were getting whiter every day. "It was kind of my thing."

"You can *not* dance," Juliet challenged. "No, I won't believe that one, nice try. I'm not *that* gullible."

"You're *so* fuckin' on, Alva," Dax exclaimed, yanking the van over to the side of the empty highway without a second thought. She dragged Juliet out of the car and over to the front of the van, Juliet perched on the hood, Dax standing right in the dusty breakdown lane in a chopped-up dress, her leather jacket, and sneakers laced up to her ankles. She untied them and placed them neatly next to Juliet on the hood, her jacket folded up beside them.

"Watch this, you bastard," Dax prefaced herself, before raising her hands and moving into an unbelievably intricate dance. Juliet was hypnotized by her movements, by the way she hummed music she must have remembered from her childhood under her breath as she moved, by the flicks of her wrists and ankles, by the smooth motions of her hips as she danced. When she did stop, breathless, five minutes later, Juliet was caught off-guard by how far she was leaning off the hood, her chin in her hands as she watched.

"Holy shit," Juliet commented, as Dax bent in half to catch her breath. "You really can dance, can't you?"

"Sure fuckin' can." Dax stretched up again and held out her hand for her shoes. "I specialize in Khattak dance and Bhangra dance, which are two popular traditional forms. I can also do some tap and ballet, and a little hip-hop, but I never finished that course." She did a little flair-flick move with her wrists before continuing to tie her shoes. "I also do magic tricks."

"Really?" Juliet asked, willing to believe anything Dax told her by then. Dax grinned, reaching into through the window of the van and retrieving out a deck of worn cards. Returning to Juliet, she made a show of shuffling the cards back and forth between her hands, stepping into the brackets of Juliet's legs to get closer. She held out the cards.

"Pick one," Dax offered, spreading them out for her. Juliet raised an eyebrow, but pulled one out and looked at it. The queen of hearts. *Typical.* "Great, got it memorized? Good. Put it back." Juliet did so. Dax stared hard at her face, shuffling the cards up again before catching them by the edges and flicking them all into Juliet's face. Juliet sputtered and lashed out, smacking them away from her, but one caught on her glasses. Dax reached out and plucked it off, turning the face of the card towards Juliet.

"No fuckin' way," Juliet laughed, picking the queen of hearts from Dax's fingers. "How the hell did you do that?"

"A good magician never reveals her secrets," Dax told her. "But a good dancer can - it's all in the hips, just like everything else in life. Now, help me pick up the cards, they're getting all dirty."

The two of them were back on the road in record time, but Juliet could only stare out the windshield, unseeing; the memory of Dax - Dax dancing, Dax pressing in close, her hips moving, her eyes smiling, her whole face lighting up - was far too much, and Juliet felt a little fried from the events of the past day and a half. She exhaled shakily, rubbing at her face with her hands, and Dax was grinning at her when she looked up.

"We're almost in Huron," Dax told her. "You can start your new life. Again."

"I don't think I need to this time," Juliet replied honestly, and Dax's smile softened a little before she turned her attention back to the road. *That*, that *fucking* face, was just another memory to add to the pictures flipping through Juliet's mind. She let her head fall back against the headrest of her seat, the wind whipping her face. She was grateful for her sunglasses to protect her. Dax turned up the soft glam rock song currently slamming into their eardrums, letting it flow over them and fill the silence that Dax accepted from Juliet as her default setting.

Sacramento was a gorgeous city to visit, the two of them stopping on the Tower Bridge to look over the edge into sky-blue water, their own hazy selves reflected back up at them, shimmering from hundreds of feet below. Dax leaned her head against Juliet's shoulder, smiling happily as they watched the afternoon sun start to fade into evening, and Juliet let herself put an arm around Dax and enjoy the moment.

The magic hour made an orange-purple blur out of the city, the two of them driving to a hill and looking out over what felt like the entirety of California, sitting on a bench under a lamplight that flickered to life when darkness came. Dax stood up on the bench, stretching her arms high above her. Juliet wrapped her fingers around Dax's ankle to keep her from floating away. By the time the sky was black and the city was white, lit up with headlights, streetlights, and house lights, Dax was plainly itching to get back on the road. Juliet let her bring them all the way to Huron that night.

"Are we still staying in the van?" Dax asked, slowing down next to a campground that boasted its vacancy in neon letters. Juliet considered saying no; in the end, she said yes. Dax took them into the campground and found them a spot to sleep. She found them beef jerky and a jar of peanut butter and brought both up to the roof with their pillows and blankets. Juliet followed at her heels, fixated on the back of Dax's head.

"I missed you," Dax told her, quietly, ripping a strip of cheap jerky to shreds with her hands. She tucked her head up against Juliet's neck, cheek pressed to her lion's head necklace; she squeezed her eyes shut, and Juliet ran her fingers through Dax's hair gently, grounding herself in her presence.

"I like working at hotels," Juliet commented. She had been silent for a while, just scratching at Dax's scalp slowly as the two of them sat on the roof of the van. "I think I should keep doing that."

"Yeah?" Dax sat up a little bit, better able to meet Juliet's eyes from her new angle. "Well, you majored in hospitality, didn't you? I always thought you were wasted as a waitress. A wastress, if you-"

"Knock it off."

"Well, we'll find you a job in a hotel." Dax settled back in, jerking them both backwards so they could lay down on the roof, shrouded in blankets, the sky a roof over their heads. Juliet yearned for something more solid, for once. The stars seemed so far away. "Get some rest, kid. We'll find somewhere to be in the morning."

"I love you," Juliet offered through hard teeth, her mouth cold. Dax buried her face in Juliet's chest and exhaled slowly. Juliet kept her eyes on the sky.

"I love you, too," Dax promised. Juliet wrapped an arm around her and tried to remember if she had seen a hotel in town on their way to the campground. Dax slept deeply.

The next morning saw them waking up on the roof, neither of them having gained the strength to haul the other down into the van during the night. The campground had a shower that Dax sprinted to in an effort to get there before anyone else could beat her, while Juliet hauled their toiletries and followed at a normal pace. She helped Dax wash her hair out, combing out sand and grit, cleaning each strand to the best of their ability. Dax all but wrestled Juliet into the shower and scrubbed her down, cleansing her of the night spent outside, of the fear and anxiety, of the anger. Juliet leaned against the wall, watched Dax comb out her hair while she held the blowdryer, and took a few deep breaths.

The sign near the center of town declared Huron to be The Heart of the Valley, but the town had essentially nothing in it but people and half-closed businesses. Juliet changed her prescription address on her phone, then dragged Dax to a rundown hotel that could have passed as a drugstore in an old western movie, pleading on both of their behalves for jobs. Dax got minimum wage on the housekeeping staff, Juliet getting a little more for a guest service job, with the condition that they were temporary staff. It was edging into late May, and their new boss told them that the summertime was busy enough to warrant hiring them. She was bold, tall, and heavy, with a loud voice and a caring edge to her decisions and to her eyes as she looked them over.

"You don't need to beg me for a job," she told them. She had introduced herself as Señorita Flores, and shook their hands vigorously before they left, ready to return the next day to work. Dax looked at her uniform with barely-disguised trepidation, but she kept her head turned down, face aimed in the opposite direction from Juliet, so Juliet pretended not to notice.

"I like this town," Juliet commented as they walked down the main street of the small city. Their uniforms, a lunch for the day, Juliet's hormone prescription, and their wallets were all crammed in the backpack Dax carried, and Dax hesitantly slipped her hand into Juliet's partway through their stroll. Juliet squeezed, nails sharp against the fine bones in the back of Dax's hand, but Dax smiled at her anyways.

"It's not bad," Dax agreed. Juliet wondered how much of it was for her benefit, and how much of it was true. She looked down, watching her feet on the sidewalk as they walked, careful not to step on any cracks. Juliet lightly pinched the back of her hand.

"I want you to know, you can do whatever you'd like," Juliet told her. "Really. You can do what you'd like. I'd just… I'd like to know before you do it. So I can make plans, and know that you're safe, and everything. Is that okay?"

Dax glanced up at her, holding her hand tightly enough that when she stopped, Juliet stopped, as well. "I don't want you to feel like you-"

"I don't feel anything bad," Juliet assured her. "I promise. I just want to know you're safe. If we're going to be doing this together, I don't want to hold you back. I just want to do this… *together*. Is that okay?"

Dax studied her face for a moment, brown eyes darting back

and forth between hers, before she yanked Juliet in to hug her.

"We're doing this together," Dax agreed. "I'll run things by you, and you'll run things by me. We'll talk about things we want. Deal?"

Juliet hesitated, considering how she thought about settling down in every city they had been going to lately. The look on Dax's face, though, and the smile she had on her lips, and the light she had in her eyes, made her forget about all that. Juliet nodded.

"Better communication. Deal." Juliet let Dax kiss her on the cheek and start walking once more, grabbing her hand again as they went. *And besides,* Juliet thought to herself, *it's not so bad traveling. There's so much to do still.*

"I'd like to see how you work anyways, Alva," Dax commented as they went, finally finding a place to set up their lunch. "You're always going off, being a professional, all hot in your uniforms. Maybe it'll do me some good."

"Maybe," Juliet murmured, laying out the towel she had brought to serve as their picnic blanket. She kept her eyes firmly on the ground, trying her best not to read too much into anything Dax said to her. It was a wildly difficult task.

"Did you make this or did we buy it?" Dax asked, unearthing the container filled with salad Juliet had packed. Juliet dug in the bag for their bowls and disposable utensil packages.

"I made it," Juliet told her, "but it tastes good, I promise. It's got avocado, steamed broccoli, soy sauce, some garlic, curry…"

"Jesus *Christ*, I love you," Dax commented. She popped the top on the container and started poking around for the broccoli while Juliet forced her grip on her spoon to loosen.

Life with Dax got a lot more intimate, for lack of a better word, after everything that happened in Nevada. She vanished significantly less, choosing instead to spend those gaps of time with Juliet, exploring the town and its outskirts, reading at her side, working with her at the hotel with Señorita Flores. All of the intervals in the day that used to be filled with Juliet working by herself, thinking to herself, imagining various scenarios and wondering what she might do next, were now filled with Dax. Dax working at her side, showing off the rooms that she had cleaned and how well she had done. Dax eating dinner with her, the two of them sitting cross-legged on the roof of the van, watching the sky with only a small part of their attention. Dax exploring with her, keeping her company, investigating their new town at her side. Dax *talking* with her, asking her questions, maintaining conversations, spending *time* with her.

Juliet tried not to get used to it. She tried, and she tried *hard*, not to read anything into it. She had had close friends in high school, in college; she had even had best friends, the kinds of friends she had shared everything with, went everywhere with. She knew the signs of a friendship developing beyond the platonic, and she tried to stick on her path. She tried *so hard*. Unfortunately, she was typically a good employee, but not always a great person.

"Hey," Dax whispered, sidling up to her at work, a mop in her hands. Juliet manned the guest services counter in the lobby, and Dax tended to stop and talk to her every time she passed through. "Hey, guess what the guy in 203 left in his bed?"

Juliet blew out a harsh breath. "Daksha, *please* don't-"

"*Shit*," Dax told her anyways, halfway to laughing, face red. "I was so pissed! What kind of a mammering, beef-witted *dewberry-*"

"What the fuck are you saying, Daksha?" Juliet interrupted her, and Dax leaned in to kiss her cheek, starting to laugh.

"I heard a kid saying it in the hall earlier." Dax pulled back to lean back against the desk. She picked absently at the nicotine patch on her arm. Her hair swung over her shoulder down her back, a long plait that Juliet had braided for her that morning. Loose pieces fell over her forehead in inky curls that Juliet's fingers itched to brush back behind her ears. "Kids are weird."

"Sure are." Juliet shoved her away, the both of them grinning as Dax swatted her with the end of the mop. "Oh, *you-*"

"Oh, me," Dax laughed, nicking her in the ankle with the mop before hopping out of reach. "Back to work, Alva."

"You're telling me," Juliet replied, stuffing everything she was feeling back down.

The thing was, she was no longer limited to just wanting to settle down, or just wanting to kiss Dax, or just wanting to go home. She wanted to put roots down and *make* a home, with Dax, specifically. It was too much to want, and yet.

And yet.

"Why do you have to yell?" Juliet asked, playfully rubbing at her own ear as they sat atop the van. According to her watch, it was nearing midnight, but Dax showed no signs of slowing down and going to sleep.

"Because I don't think you can hear me very well," Dax teased. She helped Juliet administer her hormones before she stretched out to reach for her jacket where it lay by their empty takeout boxes. She reached into the pocket and pulled out a little paper bag. "I did get us these, though."

"What are 'these'?" Juliet asked, leaning over, and Dax pushed her back. "*Daksha.*"

"*Jules,*" Dax imitated. She reached into the paper bag and pulled out two eye masks. "They were cheap at the store when I was grabbing lunch today. You know that your phone always wakes me up in the mornings, you fucker. I figured you'd like one, too, since you always end up near the window and the light gets on your face." She dangled one of the eye masks from her finger by its string, and Juliet snatched it from her. "In fact, I have an idea."

"Your ideas always get me into trouble," Juliet commented. She fingered the material of the eye mask, soft, thick cotton between the pads of her fingers. "What is it?"

"Let's test your hearing," Dax suggested. She tapped at the eye mask with her nail. Her face seemed to shine as if lit from within, even though the glow must have come from the light of their phones. Her hair fell over her shoulders in waves. The mole under her eye was drastic in the shine; the piercings in her left ear shimmered.

"Okay," Juliet agreed stupidly. Dax leaned forwards to pull the mask up and over Juliet's face, sufficiently blinding her. She adjusted it until Juliet's vision went entirely black, until it no longer mattered if her eyes were opened or closed. She focused more on her hearing, on the shuffle of Dax in front of her.

"Can you hear me now?" Dax laughed, edging away. Juliet nodded. "Good. You know, I really didn't have a plan going forward this far. We're not very good at games."

"We're okay at them," Juliet disagreed. Dax's voice dropped a little further off, and Juliet strained to hear. The crickets in the woods beside them chirped, like they knew they now had an audience. The leaves rustled in the trees, bursting with summer weight and anxious to move in the hot winds of early June. She could hear Dax breathing, most of all. The blanket underneath her seemed scratchy in comparison to her even breaths.

"Can you hear me now?" Dax repeated, voice softer and

further away. Juliet nodded again. Dax shifted. "Now?" Her voice was quieter again, but closer this time. Juliet nodded once more. "How about now?" She edged towards a whisper as she got closer. Juliet hesitated, then reached out. Dax clicked her tongue. "Don't cheat."

"I can hear you." Juliet readjusted herself where she sat, getting her legs folded up under her so she could lean up on her haunches. "I can still hear you."

"Can you hear me?" Dax asked, impossibly soft, a rustle exactly like the wind through the leaves. She was close.

"I can," Juliet told her. She tried not to swallow too loudly as her heart pounded in her chest, through her neck, her hands tingling, feet feeling numb as adrenaline coursed through her.

"Now?" Dax asked again. Her murmur was more a breath than anything, the air from her lungs breezing over Juliet's face. Juliet blinked, eyelashes dragging against cotton. Her nose prickled, her eyes growing hot.

"Yeah," Juliet answered. She wondered how far forward she would need to lean, or if Dax would do it for her. She was trying to listen for movement when Dax tapped her on the nose and laughed.

"Guess your hearing isn't so bad after all," Dax commented, pulling away, and Juliet wanted to reach for her, to grab her wrist and see if her pulse pounded just the same, to ask why she was playing games, to find out if this is real, if she even knew what she was doing.

"Guess not," Juliet said shakily. She rubbed at her mouth, eye mask still in place. She listened to the silence the crickets left behind. It felt mocking.

"You gonna leave that on all night, kid?" Dax asked, and Juliet made herself smile.

"Isn't that kind of the point?" Juliet shot back, and Dax laughed again. Juliet listened to the van groan under her weight as Dax sprawled out, her head falling into Juliet's lap. Juliet readjusted for comfort before tipping her head back and pulling off the eye mask. Her eyes got used to the darkness of the sky quickly after the darkness of the mask, the only differences being the slight wave of the black leaves and the shimmering of faraway stars. "I wish there were aliens here."

"Me, too, buddy." Dax grabbed her own eye mask and pulled it over her forehead like a headband. "Me, too."

The very next night, Dax shook her awake, tugging off her eye mask to point at the sky and recount a sighting that she almost certainly made up, the only other option being she hallucinated it. Juliet listened and nodded and thought a change of pace might be nice, even as her knees knocked all the way to the passenger side seat of the van. A different scene might do her some good. Huron was too raw after everything that happened in Nevada, anyways. An Internet search told them Arizona would do the trick, even if it wasn't Phoenix.

"You're telling Señorita Flores we're leaving," Juliet called as they washed their hair the next day. Dax scoffed back over the wall separating them.

"No problem, she'll be glad to be rid of me," Dax answered. Juliet wondered how that could be possible.

Huron had made Juliet want to put down roots, but so had every place before it. Juliet wondered if any place would be any different; she wondered if, maybe, it wasn't the places doing it to her, but rather her doing it to the places. Projecting. Letting her imagination go wild, putting things where they most certainly did not belong. She scrubbed hard at her face and let the water cleanse her.

Snowflake was ten hours out from Huron. Dax carefully chose the path on her phone's map that took them through three separate national parks, detouring up towards the Grand Canyon when they started to see signs for it. They got there as the sun started to sink, an Arizona sky painted heavily with purples and blues and reds that Juliet could only stare at, hands in the pockets of her shorts. Dax threw her arm around Juliet's shoulders and stood with her while the sun sank low enough to let the stars fill the sky.

"That's not just a big hole," Dax commented, looking down over the edge. She whistled, smiling. "That's a *huge* hole." Her grin let Juliet laugh for a few moments, over the weak joke and around the two of them, echoing off the canyon walls. Juliet let herself settle behind Dax, her chin at the crown of Dax's head, and they watched the canyon until it was too dark and the ranger started making eyes at them as he cycled through.

"How far until Snowflake, kid?" Dax asked, kicking the van into a trembling sort of action. According to Juliet's map, it was three hours; before she knew it, they were on the road, following the half-moon through the hot Arizona June. Juliet pushed the refrigerator console shut and sat on top of it, resting along Dax's side, listening to her softly sing along to hits from their childhood as the road kicked up gravel under their tires. Snowflake seemed like it was only twenty minutes away during a ride like that.

Finding an RV park in Snowflake was not at all difficult, and between the two of them they had enough change in their pockets to pay the rate at the front cabin without needing to find an ATM. When Dax dragged her up onto the roof, Juliet made good use of the free WiFi by scrolling through Angelo's Instagram. Dax waxed poetic about the potential she saw in each individual star as she commented on an Instagram video of Angelo's gorgeous and spoiled cat, which he had since named Lady Eloise Delphine Alva. He insisted on typing out her full name whenever he mentioned her.

"What do you think," Dax began, while Juliet watched the video; in it, Lady Eloise simply napped, fur braided and dotted with pink bows. Dax frowned, stopping herself. Juliet glanced at her.

"I think a lot of things," Juliet answered, watching her face. The corner of Dax's mouth twitched, but that was it. "More than I think you'd be able to understand, to be honest."

"No, no, I mean…" Dax sighed, then reclined, letting her head fall into Juliet's lap. Juliet just rested her wrists on Dax's forehead and kept commenting on the cat videos. "What do you think about…" Dax frowned, then sighed, then stopped. "Never mind."

"Suit yourself," Juliet murmured, watching Lady Eloise chase a laser pointer. "Let me know when you have a thought again."

"Can do," Dax replied, turning over so she could side-eye the night sky. She fell asleep pretty soon after that, which was rare. Juliet hesitated before setting her phone aside. She let her fingers trail through Dax's hair, lank with the need to be washed. The color was still rich, dark hair against dark skin against dark sky.

They found the showers easily the next day, Dax spending an inordinate amount of time solely focused on brushing her teeth while Juliet combed out her hair for her. Dax watched her evenly through the cloudy mirror.

"Are you going to get a job here?" Juliet asked, separating Dax's hair into sections. Dax hummed a little bit, ignoring her for a moment as she finished brushing her teeth and spit into the sink.

"Yeah, I will," Dax told her, mouth still foamy as she stuck her head under the faucet and rinsed. "I don't know if I'm gonna work with you again, though. I'm not really a housekeeper type."

"Are you any type?" Juliet asked. She kept Dax's hair held high above their heads. Dax laughed at her.

"I'm your type," Dax answered. Juliet shifted so Dax's hair hid her expression from the mirror as she tried to get her pulse down to a less thundering level. "I'll look around. Who knows what'll catch my attention, you know? Maybe I'll become a brain surgeon or something."

"Oh, so you did see the 'Help Wanted' sign in the hospital window when we drove by, good," Juliet replied, and Dax flicked water at her. Juliet gently tugged her back so she could finish combing her hair. "There's a lot out there for you."

"In Snowflake?" Dax seemed disbelieving. Juliet rolled her eyes; she suspected Dax may have seen it in the mirror.

"Everywhere. Yes, including Snowflake," Juliet added, when Dax's mouth was already opening to argue with her. "You have a lot of opportunities. You should do what *you* want to do. Isn't that the point of all this?"

"I guess." Dax's eyes tracked the movements of Juliet's hands as Juliet began French-braiding her hair for her, humming under her breath as she worked. Dax reached back to pinch her in the side. "What do you think I should do?"

"I think it matters more what you think you should do, don't you?" Juliet offered. Dax shrugged lightly.

"I care what you think," Dax told her. "I do. I trust you. What do you think?"

Juliet paused. Dax granted her the time to sift through her thoughts. There were a great deal of jobs Dax would likely be good at, and even more jobs she would be absolutely abysmal at. However, they were in Arizona, and Lord help Juliet if she ever permanently lived in Arizona, so whatever she did here would only be temporary. A few weeks, maybe. A couple of months at most. Something she could flit in and out of, something she could use as a short trial.

"Maybe you could be a dance instructor," Juliet offered. Dax made eye contact with her in the mirror. "How often do people in Arizona get to learn Pakistani dances?"

"Probably not very often," Dax answered. She leaned back against Juliet, considering. "Maybe. Maybe I will." She rubbed at her cheek, eyes distracted now. "Any other ideas?"

"Stunt person? Musician? Cab driver? You truly have limited talents," Juliet suggested, and Dax reached back to smack her. Juliet tied off her French braid and let her hair fall against her back. "Look around in town. Who knows what you'll find, you know?"

"I guess," Dax agreed, and the two of them walked their way to the center of town from the campground. Dax insisted on Juliet carrying her for the final leg, and carry her she did, so long as Dax kept pouring water in her mouth from the bottle in her hand.

"See? Right there," Juliet insisted, pointing out a combination dojo/dance studio. She stopped outside of it and let Dax slide down to her feet. "See if they want someone to teach a Pakistani dance class for a little while. Teach some kids the basics for a couple weeks. Let them know it only goes until we have to leave." And at that, Juliet's throat caught the slightest bit, the lump in the back of it that meant that she wished their journey seemed less endless and more... *more*.

"I guess," Dax said again. She passed the water bottle off to Juliet and knocked off a quick salute to her. "Meet me in that little blue diner we saw near the gas station once you're done, yeah?"

"Yeah," Juliet agreed, and Dax vanished inside the establishment. Hands in the pockets of her shorts, Juliet left her there, strolling down the road to try and find a hotel or a bed-and-breakfast of any sort. The first motel she came upon she was turned out from, insisting they did not need or want her kind of help, which she pretended not to understand. This happened, too, in her second and third stops. The fourth place she found, though, a bed-and-breakfast with a little boy playing with dolls on the floor of the lobby, welcomed her more warmly than the others did.

"Well, we've been looking for a clerk, haven't we?" the old man asked of his wife, who nodded eagerly and took her hand.

"I can only work until my roommate decides she wants to leave again," Juliet told them. The old man turned to his wife, and the two of them ushered Juliet into their dining room and sat her down with store biscuits and a cup of coffee while she told them a bare-bones version of her life story up until that point. The expressions on their faces just seemed to pull the words right out of her.

"You can work here until you leave, of course you can," the old woman asserted. Her name, as it turned out, was Emily. Her husband's name was Earl. This, inexplicably, made Juliet smile at them.

"Are you sure?" Juliet asked, and Emily nodded eagerly, clasping Juliet's hand between her own.

"We've been looking for a clerk," Emily assured her again. Earl nodded beside her. Juliet left them that day with a front desk job and a renewed vigor for Snowflake.

She met up with Dax at the little blue diner, finding her already halfway through a slice of pie with an unidentifiable filling.

"They said it's the town specialty," Dax informed her, motioning to the seat across from her. Juliet scooted across the booth and helped herself to a sip from Dax's Shirley Temple. "I don't even know if it's a fruit or not."

"You're a fruit," Juliet commented, and Dax laughed, pointing her fork at her.

"You're quick," Dax said. "How'd it go?"

"I got a job as a front desk clerk at a b-and-b down the road. They asked me about my entire life and assured me that it would be the content of my character and not the color of my skin that secured my position there." Juliet accepted the mug of coffee that the waitress set down in front of her. "How 'bout you?"

"You're now looking at the semiweekly and on-a-strict-temporary-basis-Ms.-Paracha traditional dance instructor for ages six to fourteen," Dax informed her, spreading her arms wide. "I also have picked up a little bit of side work-"

"*Daksha-*"

"Don't *Daksha* me, Juliet, I'm very well-behaved and I haven't done a damn thing wrong. Open up," Dax instructed, holding out a forkful of Unidentifiable Pie, and Juliet accepted the bite. "I'm just helping a guy down at the record store-"

"*Okay*, who's gonna play you in the indie movie they make about you-"

"*You* are the one who is ill-behaved, if anyone," Dax cut her off. "Stop interrupting me. I'm gonna help him out on the days I'm not dancing. We'll see what I like."

"Sure we will," Juliet said, taking the fork and another bite of the pie. "What in the hell *is* this?"

"Fuck if I know." Dax raised her hand and asked the waitress for two more slices of the pie, please and thank you, and another

Shirley Temple, if she didn't mind. With her own slice of pie and her own Shirley Temple finally in hand, Juliet happily listened to Dax's ramblings about how Snowflake was a hotbed of extraterrestrial activity and the extreme likelihood that their waitress was one of the aliens in a disguise, or maybe that *they* were the ones in a disguise. Juliet just nodded, ate her weird pie, and listened without thinking.

Chapter Fourteen

Snowflake was good. Too good, probably, because Juliet had a burgeoning bad habit of self-indulgence, inclining more and more towards just letting herself be happy and never anticipating the negative consequences of it all. She went to work for Emily and Earl every single day; she came back to the campground every single night. Dax always got back earlier than her, so she would come and pick her up, usually with some sort of dinner in hand - typically made off the *exceedingly dangerous* hot plate in the back of the van - and a grin on her face.

"Guess what I did today," Dax instructed on the second day in July. Juliet raised an eyebrow at her, even as she accepted the subpar quesadilla that was thrust into her lap on a paper plate.

"What did you do today?" Juliet asked, and Dax wagged her finger at her, steering away from the bed-and-breakfast with one hand.

"Uh-uh, I said *guess*, and guess you shall," Dax replied. She curved her wrist elegantly, twisting towards the highway, which was unusual. She usually tended to keep to the town when they got out of work. Juliet swallowed the chicken and cheese in her mouth.

"Uhm…" She leaned against the window, reading the signs flickering by her. "You were stalked by a private investigator?"

"Nope."

"The FBI told you that we were too close on their tails and needed to back off?"

"Someday, but no, not today."

146

Juliet hummed to herself. "Did you decide it was time to leave? Because if you did, I didn't get to tell Emily and Earl and I-"

"No, no, I didn't," Dax interrupted. She rolled her window down and pointed to the left as she pulled up to a dinky little square block of a building with a guy leaning against the broken door. "I found us a fun activity."

"Daksha, *what-*"

"Hi," Dax said to the man, so smoothly, letting her sunglasses slide down her nose. "What've you got for me?"

"Fifteen dollars a car," the man responded, barely looking up, and Dax dug into the pocket of her shorts and came up with a ten and a five. The man handed her back a ticket off a red carnival roll and rambled off a short string of numbers. Dax tipped an imaginary hat to him and sped off through a clearing in the trees in front of them.

"Do you mind switching the radio to that?" Dax asked, and Juliet realized, belatedly, that the numbers were the call for a local station. She cleaned her hands on a shred of paper towel and twisted the radio knob until she found the numbers. Dax parked as Juliet finally got the radio to work, and Juliet peered through the windshield to find an enormous white screen set before the falling sun and the grove of trees behind it.

"Are we-"

"Drive-in theater," Dax exclaimed. She took Juliet's paper towel and plate and crammed them in the trash bag behind them so she could clap Juliet on the shoulder. "I found us a *drive-in theater*, Jules. You can save your accolades, I'll take them later tonight."

"What's playing?" Juliet asked, watching as Dax started gathering up their blankets and pillows and a cloth grocery bag of snacks. Juliet took two bottles of water out with her, following Dax up to the roof.

"Creature double-feature," Dax told her, snapping out the covers on the roof. She stood precariously on the ledge of her van's open window, and Juliet braced her with a hand stretched to press against the small of her back. "Thanks, big guy."

"No problem," Juliet said. Dax accepted the push up that Juliet gave her and settled on top of the van with a hand out for Juliet to take. Juliet grasped it, ignoring the thrill of warmth that had started with her hand on Dax's back and had started to throb behind her eyes from holding her hand, and let her haul her up.

"We're going to be seeing *Frankenstein* and *Bride of Frankenstein*," Dax told her, standing up. Her t-shirt settled loose on her, white against dark skin, hair tumbling down her back, sunglasses wide against her handsome face, and Juliet forced herself to look away, heart thrumming in her chest. She tried to remember the low-key anger she had been trying to hold onto from Dax's stunt in Nevada, but it was fading fast. She barely had the time to examine why it was going away. She was starting to grasp at straws, she knew it.

When Dax sat down next to her, though, throwing an arm around her shoulders, laughing near her ear, soft hair tickling Juliet's arm, she could hardly bring herself to care.

"Do you want to be Frankenstein or his bride?" Dax asked, and Juliet shrugged with one shoulder. Dax turned and started to trace the scar zigging on Juliet's cheek, down to the one zagging across her shoulder.

"Technically, Frankenstein is the scientist," Juliet corrected, and Dax shoved her down into the blankets and smacked her with a pillow. "Frankenstein's Monster is the Creature!"

"Shut up!" Dax laughed, throwing the pillow down over her head and ducking when Juliet threw a bag of chips at her. Juliet picked up the pillow, and Dax lunged, hair catching against the last rays of the setting sun as she settled herself over Juliet, catching her breath. Her chest heaved against Juliet's.

"No," Juliet said, belatedly, but Dax had already seemed to stop listening, staring down at Juliet's face. Juliet swallowed, willing her heartbeat to quiet down or at least *slow* down, pounding into her throat as it was, probably incredibly obvious to Dax when she was studying her like that.

"You can be the bride, if you want," Dax told her. Soft, so soft. Juliet reached up and tentatively touched the shell of Dax's ear, then tucked her hair up behind it so it would stop dangling in her face and tickling her nose. Dax's thumb was pressed hard into the end of her scar, thumbnail pushing into the fleshy space between her neck and her shoulder. Juliet exhaled shakily.

"Okay," Juliet said. Dax's thumb made one small circle against her skin, her eyes flickering up to Juliet's, darting from one eye to the other; they were so close it was impossible to look into both at the same time. Dax exhaled this time, and then sat up and away, and Juliet felt abruptly cold in the space left behind.

"That means I'm Frankenstein's Monster," Dax said, reaching back to start braiding her hair. Juliet kept staring up, the back of her head still pressed against the blankets. The sky was purple. She sighed.

"You get way more screen time than I do," Juliet replied faux-casually. She tried to shove the entire experience into the box she had labeled 'Weird Friendship Moments with Dax,' which had only grown since the two of them had gotten closer after Nevada. The moment refused to stay in there, though, and she forced back her hope like dry-swallowing a pill; it settled in her throat in just the same way. Dax glanced at her from the corner of her eye, and Juliet pretended not to see.

"Do you want popcorn from the concession stand?" Dax asked, and Juliet shook her head, reaching blindly into the snack bag and coming up with a bag of tortilla chips and a box of chocolate-covered raisins.

"I'm set," Juliet told her. Dax took the tortilla chips and leaned over the edge of the roof to reach inside the van. Juliet held her ankles while she dug the guacamole out of the fridge console. The movie flickered to life the moment the sun hit the edge of the horizon and vanished, and the two of them settled with their heads side-by-side. Juliet had seen this movie plenty of times before, but it took on a unique charm with Dax pressed along her side like a barnacle, making bad jokes and gesturing wildly with her little hands. She kept glancing upwards and commenting about what might happen if an alien showed up right then, right there, of all times and places, and how nobody would believe it.

Juliet, for her part, was far more hypnotized by Dax than she was by the movies. She kept herself distracted by thinking over her own anger and her own forgiveness of Dax, of her nature; she stared at her tattoo, the tattoo Juliet had drawn for her, the one that would stay with Dax for the rest of her life, regardless of whether or not that life was spent with Juliet.

As that thought struck her only partway through the first movie, she realized she did want to spend the rest of her life with Dax. She turned her face away and pressed the heels of her hands to her eyes, focusing on the pulsing red and grey behind her eyelids instead of on the thought that had caused instant and simultaneous nausea and desire. She exhaled, and Dax rubbed her back.

"You alright, kid?" Dax asked, and Juliet released her eyes, her glasses sliding back down into place. When she turned to Dax, she was met with a concerned expression, with worried eyes and a frowning mouth.

"I'm fine," Juliet told her, the undisputed master of half-truths. She reached back and took Dax's hand in her own. "Watch the movie. We paid good money to be here."

"Fine," Dax said, leaving her be. They both knew Juliet was highly unlikely to share anything until she was good and ready to do so; Juliet was just happy that Dax seemed to have gotten to a point of near-complete understanding of her and knew when to leave well enough alone. Dax still shifted closer to her, snuggling up against her side, even if she might deny it if she was called out on it, and probably never would have called it 'snuggling.' Juliet forced herself to take a deep breath and settle a little more; she felt a sort of strange buoyancy all over, like her heart, in its haste, had started pumping helium through her veins instead of blood.

"You can talk to me," Dax whispered softly, a few minutes into *Bride of Frankenstein*. "I'm sorry if I... I don't want to make you..." Dax broke off, and Juliet looked up at her.

"I'm not upset with you," Juliet told her, bewildered. "I wouldn't- That's not why- Daksha, I'm not upset."

"One of us will need to finish a sentence one day," Dax joked quietly, and Juliet knocked their foreheads together. "Someone will probably need to force us to, though."

"Let 'em try," Juliet murmured. Dax studied her face for a moment before she dropped her head into Juliet's pillowed arms, pressing her face against Juliet's shoulder. Her eyelashes tickled Juliet's scar. She seemed to be asleep, but Juliet wondered if she might not be; she watched the screen, but not the movie.

She wanted to let Dax sleep - or at least do whatever she was doing, lay and recharge, pressed along Juliet like that, comfortable and comforting - but the two of them had to leave once the movie ended. Juliet propped her head in one hand, her cheek fitting against the curve of her palm and her long fingers. She regarded Dax for a little while longer, studying her relaxed face, the curl of her against her body. She reached out and gently pushed a loose strand from her braid back from her face.

"Daksha," Juliet said. "Dax. You have to wake up, we have to go back to the campground."

"Mm?" Dax turned onto her back, and Juliet had almost instant regret. She reached out and grasped Dax's shoulder, shaking her into full awareness. "Jesus, Jules, what do you *want?*"

"We have to leave, the movies are over," Juliet told her, and Dax groaned but let Juliet drag her and their pillows, blankets, and snacks down into the back of the van.

"Drive," Dax instructed, tossing the keys blindly out of her nest of covers. Juliet snatched the keys out of the air with only the smallest of fumbles. "You remember the way back?"

"We'll get there," Juliet assured her. She spun the keys on her finger as she shut up the back of the van, brushed the last of the garbage off the roof and into a trash barrel, and hopped up into the driver's seat.

Driving the van, when it was this late and Juliet was dizzyingly high off Dax's night-long closeness, was a bit like sitting on Dax's shoulders and asking her to run, Juliet imagined. The van seemed to be an extension of Dax, in a way. Though Juliet rarely drove it, every time she did felt like an honor, like a bit of trust taken from Dax's hands and placed into Juliet's. Dax's head now sleepily pressed against the console next to Juliet's elbow, blinking up at her tiredly as they drove.

"How're you doing?" Juliet asked, and Dax only made a soft humming sound, shutting her eyes again. The street lights flicked across her dark face. Juliet glanced at the road, then back down, briefly combing her fingers through Dax's loose hair.

"Mm," Dax murmured. "Thanks."

"Anytime," Juliet replied. Dax reached up and held onto her elbow as she drove, fingers draped languidly over the crease of her arm. Juliet kept both of her hands on the wheel after that.

Getting them back to the campground was easy compared to getting herself into the back of the van, when Dax was half-asleep and boneless. She mostly required moving, though she was dead weight and wanted to stay close to Juliet, like her own exquisite form of torture that Juliet could hardly bring herself to mind. Dax drooped over her, yawning and sighing in her face, tucking her head under Juliet's chin, and Juliet let her settle there, sleep evading her for hours afterwards.

The next few weeks of Snowflake passed in (unsurprisingly) a similarly repressed state. Juliet bottled her feelings up, and Dax kept being herself; the two of them worked separately, and came together for dinner and whatever they decided to do afterwards. Usually it was Dax who pulled out a stop or two and found them a fun activity for the night, but Juliet was known to bring Dax somewhere she might enjoy. She found her a vintage car show, one night, and Dax spent so much energy there, so long into the night, that Juliet essentially had to carry her all the way back to the van.

Snowflake was a small and insignificant town, but as July became August and August started to edge into September, Juliet found herself caring about Arizona more than she could have thought possible. Juliet had tried not to get attached to anywhere since McMinnville, or attached to anyone since Lovelock, but both of those principles seemed to fly out the window in the face of their time spent in Snowflake. She knew the people in town; the pharmacists at the pharmacy she got her hormones from, the waitresses at the diner they usually ate breakfast at, the teenage grocery store clerks who worked after school. They both seemed to love it in Snowflake. Juliet had considered the possibility she was projecting her own happiness onto Dax, but it even seemed like Dax was enjoying their time there; she kept working at the dance studio, the other half of her time spent in the record store. Juliet kept up with Emily and Earl at the bed-and-breakfast.

Getting one's hopes up was a tricky business, Juliet thought, as they watched Dax's class of nine-year-olds trip their way through Dax's choreography. Dax offered her a piece of cherry licorice out of her hand, like it meant nothing for her to share her food, for Juliet to bite candy from her fingers. Over time, it had come to be nothing; it was just how they were. Coexisting in such a way that they were prone to intimacy, like they were inseparable and had begun to function as one person with two bodies, rather than as two separate people. It was an exceedingly tricky business, she believed, as Dax's brow creased while she watched her students. Juliet kept her hands in her lap and tried not to get nervous at the idea of this being a culmination of any sort, except of the talents of her students. Dax was flicking through her calendar on her phone at intermission; the months seemed to have flown by since Big Bay, and yet Dax looked frustrated as she tapped at the memos on her phone. Juliet stared straight ahead, trying to distract herself from whatever small hurricane was brewing in the folding chair beside her.

Dax was called to the stage afterwards, and she squeezed Juliet's arm before she stood, offering her a look that Juliet was completely unable to decipher in the split second it was shown to her. Her heart started pounding of its own accord, before her mind even caught up. Dax was thanked for her hard work by the owner of the dance studio, and praised for all she had done in the weeks prior teaching the girls the basics of traditional dance, and how she had only been there on a temporary basis but, oh, what a wonderful job she did in the short time she was there.

The time they spent in Snowflake was starting to feel short, now that the instructor mentioned it; what had, only moments ago, seemed to stretch on infinitely, appeared now to have been the blink of an eye. On stage, Dax received a bouquet of flowers and hugs from her students; in her seat, Juliet tried not to cry for what she knew she was going to lose.

"So," Dax said, one hand in her pocket as they left the town hall. The other hand held her bouquet of grocery store flowers; she had worn a dress for the occasion and kept her brown leather jacket over it. She kept snapping the lid on and off the chapstick in her pocket as they reached the van in the parking lot.

"So?" Juliet prompted, when Dax chose not to continue. Dax exhaled, pulling her hand out of her pocket only to pick at the nicotine patch under her sleeve. "Daksha."

"Juliet." Dax turned to her, stopping in her tracks. She stopped and put the flowers on the hood of the van. "You know-"

"Dax-"

"We can't stay here forever," Dax told her, and Juliet shook her head, glancing down at her feet. "We haven't seen anything-"

"You *know* it's not about that-"

"We go where we go because we want to find something," Dax reminded her. "Aliens. UFOs. That's why we're doing this. We're not... We're not bargain-hunting for somewhere to live. Why would we want somewhere to live?"

"Why wouldn't we?" Juliet shot back. "Why wouldn't that be our goal?"

"You know as well as I do that that's not why we do it," Dax said, and Juliet stuffed her hands in her own pockets, glancing up, to the side, trying not to settle on Dax's face. She could feel her dark eyes staring through her, hot like coals on the side of her face as she let her attention slide to the back door of their van.

"Then why do we do it?" Juliet asked, and Dax shifted, putting herself in Juliet's peripheral. Juliet forced herself to look up and meet her eyes.

"What?" Dax adjusted her stance once, then again, fidgeting in place. She tucked her hair behind one ear, then the other. "What do you mean?"

"You know what I mean," Juliet told her. Her face felt hot, Dax seeming more like Hephaestus than Aphrodite in that moment. "Why are we doing this?"

"Because why not, Jules? Why would we stay at home and let ourselves be nothing? Why settle down?" Dax stepped closer to her, and Juliet tipped her head forward without thinking about it. Her instincts knew her better than she did, but her mind knew to hold back. "Why would I want to end up like my mom? Just fucking around for no reason, letting myself turn into nothing, letting everybody down?" Dax stopped suddenly and looked hard into Juliet's face. "Oh, my God. I let *you* down, didn't I?"

"What? No-"

"But I did," Dax interrupted. "I let you down. I can't believe-God*damn- it*, damn it!" Dax turned away from her, pacing towards the van, and away. Juliet stood, startled, watching her jerk back and forth. "I'm just, I'm just trying to do... Jules, do you know what I'm trying to do?"

"No," Juliet answered honestly. "No, you have to tell me. Talk to me. I don't know what you want if you don't tell me."

Dax stopped, tipping back on her heels before closing the distance between them again. This close together, she smelled like worn leather and the soap they shared and her cherry licorice candies. She lifted her chin to look Juliet in the eye. "I don't want to be my mother."

"You're not," Juliet told her. "You're not, Daksha."

"But I am," Dax said, "and I don't want to be." She fidgeted again, adjusting her stance. She squared her shoulders and stood still. "I didn't want to stay in New York. I wanted to do other things. I wanted to find... aliens, you know? I still do. I want to find something more. Something bigger." Her eyes flicked up; Juliet followed the line of her sight up to the sky. A star shot by. "I know there's something bigger than me. I just have to find it."

"That makes sense," Juliet said, to fill the silence. Dax looked at her; Juliet kept looking up.

"Does it?" Dax asked, and Juliet nodded, turning her head down.

"It does," Juliet told her. "I get it. I didn't want to stay in Big Bay. I didn't want to live with my parents. I knew what I didn't want to do, but I didn't know what I *did* want to do." Juliet shrugged with one shoulder. She wished, vaguely, as her fingers twitched with nothing to touch, that she had long hair again. "I still don't know what I want."

"Don't you want to find that out, then?" Dax asked. Juliet glanced upwards again. Dax reached out and tangled their fingers together, squeezing her hand. Juliet shut her eyes and exhaled slowly, trying not to let her breath shake.

"I do," Juliet replied. "I do. I just… I *like* Snowflake."

"But do you *want* Snowflake?" Dax pushed. "Do you like Snowflake enough to live here forever? Do you want to settle down here? That's what you have to ask yourself." Dax tightened her grip on her hand, and Juliet opened her eyes.

Juliet had a flash of it - of living in Snowflake forever, of working at the bed-and-breakfast until she was old enough to retire, of finding someone roughly Dax's size and shape to fill the gap and spending her life with them. Snowflake flickered in her imagination; it was the only part she didn't mind losing. Snowflake was hot, and dry, and it was good for the moment but not good forever. Juliet realized, with a start, that she wanted winters, and she wanted change, and she wanted her own bed-and-breakfast, and she wanted someone *exactly* Dax's size and shape to spend her life with.

"It's not Snowflake that I want," Juliet said, and hoped it didn't seem as obvious to Dax as it sounded to her. Dax nodded and let her go.

"Then we'll leave," Dax told her. "We'll find somewhere else. There's something bigger and better than us out there."

"Nothing's bigger and better than you," Juliet replied. Dax stared up at her, a little twitch pulling the corner of her lips up.

"You're too good for me," Dax said. She stepped forward and wrapped her arms around Juliet, and Juliet let her settle there, Dax's head pressed over her heart like an immovable weight, the lion's head necklace digging into their skin between them, her arms constricting and pleasantly tight. She sighed and relaxed, bending to embrace Dax in return. "We'll find something else. Who knows? Maybe we'll find a UFO after all."

"Maybe," Juliet replied. Snowflake seemed like dust on her heels after all that; she led Dax back to the van and let her drive them out to the bed-and-breakfast, where she gave Emily and Earl her address in Big Bay and asked them not to forget about her. She thanked them for being so kind to her, and they thanked her just the same. Dax stopped in at the record store on their way out. She ran in while Juliet worked on weaving the bouquet into a wreath to hang from the inside of the back window.

"We're all set," Dax assured her, sliding back into the driver's seat. Juliet gave Snowflake a glance over her shoulder and let fresh nostalgia wash over her for a moment, thinking fondly of the time they had spent there. It was comfortable, but it was too hot. It was familiar, but it was impermanent. "Are you all set, Jules?"

"Yeah," Juliet said. She watched Snowflake for another long moment before she pulled her head back into the van and stuck her arm out the window instead. "Let's go."

"Where to?" Dax asked, throwing the van back into drive and setting off down the highway out of Snowflake. Juliet shrugged, dropping her sunglasses on her nose and shutting her eyes.

"Wherever you think we should go," Juliet answered, and Dax yanked a map out of the glovebox and spread it out on the dashboard. Juliet opened her eyes to watch her as she pulled over to the side of the road and studied the southernmost part of the map. She had red stickers all over the United States, and she lifted the biggest one of them all up to read the text underneath.

"How does Roswell sound?" Dax suggested, grinning, white teeth sharp against dark lips and sky. Juliet nodded and relaxed back against her seat.

"Sounds like the perfect place to find something bigger than us," Juliet told her. "Even if it's not the capital of New Mexico."

Dax laughed and leaned over to kiss her on the cheek. Juliet busied herself with folding up the map and replacing it in the glove box, pulling up the directions on her phone when Dax started complaining. She kept her head to the window so the wind whipping into the van could cool her burning face. It was not until halfway through the drive that Juliet realized they had never even visited Apache-Sitgreaves National Forest, the entire reason they had come to Snowflake, where the supposed alien abduction they had come to check out had actually taken place. She kept the realization to herself.

Chapter Fifteen

Roswell was, on a normal drive, a good six hours and change outside of Snowflake. Dax, though, gave in to Juliet's less-than-subtle hints about stopping in Gila National Forest and passing through Cibola National Forest. Dax leaned against the car while Juliet held up her skirt and stood barefoot in the Gila River, staring up at the peaks that towered over them.

"Come on, sweetheart, up and at 'em," Dax called down to her. Juliet watched the moon shimmer against the cliffs for a little while longer before she climbed the hill back to their parking spot. In Cibola National Forest, they drove to the highest peak they could find and hiked the rest of the way up. The sun was nearly ready to come up over the horizon as they settled down on the ground, Juliet spreading out her cardigan for the two of them to sit on. They had to wait for a little bit for the actual sunrise, since the sky had only started to lighten from black to cornflower blue. Clouds lazily drifted by them while Dax dozed against Juliet's shoulder, and Juliet made up small stories about the animals she saw around them. She was partway through a winding tale about a self-conscious red-tailed hawk when the orange peak of sun started to edge over the horizon.

"Daksha," Juliet whispered, and Dax lifted her head sleepily, squinting at the skyline. The orange spread like spilled juice over the blue linen tablecloth of the sky. Dax drowsed, mostly watching the sunrise; Juliet mostly watched Dax. By the time the pinks and yellows of early morning had started to streak over their heads, Juliet half-carried Dax back down to the van, bundled her up in the back, and started driving the last leg to Roswell. Dax slept for the fours hours it took to get there, curled up on her side, her hand stretched up onto the console, fingertips resting lightly against Juliet's bare thigh, thumb lightly touching the band-aid from her last injection. Juliet, with more than a little effort, kept her eyes on the road. The pickle ornament they had picked up in Wyoming still hung from the rearview mirror, glittering in the sunlight.

Juliet was going to let Dax sleep until she woke up on her own, but driving through Roswell on their way to an RV park was a one-of-a-kind experience. She reached down and squeezed Dax's hand, and Dax glanced up at her blearily.

"What'd you... What is that?" Dax asked, abruptly distracted by a huge, lumpy statue depiction of a green alien. She sat up and wriggled her way into the passenger seat at once, narrowly avoiding kicking Juliet in the head as she did so.

"You missed a sign earlier that said 'Extraterrestrial Highway,'" Juliet informed her, "but I think that alien is enough proof that we have arrived in Roswell."

"Holy shit," Dax breathed, and that about summed it up. Nearly everywhere they looked had at least one alien decoration, be it a lumpy statue, a UFO on the front lawn, or a fast-food chain restaurant with an *Aliens Welcome!* sign hanging from its logo. Dax rolled down her window and stuck her head out. Her hair streamed behind her as she laughed. "It's Roswell!"

"It's Roswell," Juliet agreed, smiling at Dax's joy. They stopped at a similarly-festive restaurant shaped like a UFO, where they made a stranger take a picture of them together in front of the building. Juliet sent the picture to her parents and her brothers. Angelo replied almost instantly with a picture of Lady Eloise napping in a sunbeam; Lorenzo sent back a thumbs-up emoji. Her mom ended up calling her, so Juliet ducked out to the parking lot to take the call while Dax got them breakfast sandwiches.

"How are you doing, sweetheart? You don't really call or email me all that much," Bea was already saying when Juliet picked up the phone. Juliet sat down heavily on the curb. "Are you eating enough? How are you feeling?"

"I'm feeling fine, Mama," Juliet assured her, rubbing at the shaved back of her head.

"Are you still taking your hormones? You didn't say if you were eating enough. You aren't eating enough, are you?" Bea continued, and Juliet sighed.

"Bea, let the kid answer, will you?" Abe interrupted, and Juliet laughed.

"Am I on speaker?" Juliet asked, and Bea assured her that she was. "Hi, Dad."

"Hi. How's tricks?" Abe asked, and Juliet recounted her most interesting stories since the last time she had called a few weeks prior, in Snowflake, until she reached the point in her story where they arrived in Roswell.

"Do you think you'll be home to visit soon, sweetheart?" Bea asked, when Juliet caught herself talking about Dax *again,* without a particular point to the story except to talk about Dax. She made herself stop and shut up.

"I hope so," Juliet told her. "I want to see you guys, I miss you. We should Skype more."

"Your father doesn't like Skype," Bea reminded her daughter, and Abe laughed once.

"Your brothers don't do a good job of explaining it, I'll tell you that much," Abe told her, before the conversation got tangled up in her parents sharing stories about the Big Bay adventures of Lady Eloise. Dax came and sat next to her in the middle of a story about Lady Eloise's newest friend down the street. She offered Juliet a sandwich.

"Is that Daksha?" Bea asked, and when Juliet confirmed that it was, Bea insisted she be put on speaker, as well. "Hello, Daksha!"

"Hi, Mrs. Alva," Dax replied. "How've you been?"

"Honey, I've been just fine. You *have* to call me Bea, or I swear, baby, I will start calling you Ms. Paracha and you will be just as uncomfortable as I am."

"Yes, Bea."

"Mama, why do you have to bother Daksha like that?" Juliet asked, and Dax raised her eyebrows, stifling a laugh.

"Don't you give me attitude, Juliet Alva. I brought you in this world, and I can take you out of it," Bea threatened, and Dax started openly laughing. "You, too, Daksha, don't think I won't take you with her."

"Yes, Mama," Juliet murmured at the same time Dax laughed, "Yes, ma'am, Bea."

"You two take care, okay? Daddy and I have gotta go to work," Bea said, and she and Abe said their goodbyes before hanging up. Dax coaxed Juliet back into the restaurant so they could eat their breakfast sandwiches in the relative peace of the alien-themed fast food joint. After Dax made Juliet jump up to take a picture with the astronaut hanging from the playground, she deemed herself sufficiently ready to go, and the two of them hit the road.

Roswell was about what Juliet had come to expect from a town built on a long-debunked alien conspiracy. It was heavily influenced by Mexico over the border, and the resulting clash of cultures had ended up with a town that fascinated Dax on every corner they turned. She insisted on visiting the UFO museums the second day they were there, since the first day was filled with grocery stops, hormone prescription pickups, naps, and job hunts. Dax was working at the fast food joint they had stopped at, flipping burgers and taking orders happily. Juliet wound up at a little motel where she had to wear a pink polo shirt with an alien emblem on the breast.

That weekend day brought them to the Roswell Museum, which they left after only a short while. They visited an aviation museum instead, and Juliet listened to Dax spin conspiracy theory after conspiracy theory as she viewed each and every aircraft in the building. Dax's self-proclaimed highlight of the trip came on the second weekend after they got there, however, when they visited the actual crash site where an actual UFO did not actually crash. Dax was so excited about visiting the site, though, that Juliet kept her mouth shut about her opinions.

"Can you believe it?" Dax exclaimed, taking dozens of pictures of Juliet with the entry signs, with the site markers, with the grass, with the sky. Juliet eventually stopped paying attention to posing and just started looking around the site. "Can we get any *closer* to the action?"

"I actually think it was just a weather balloon or something," Juliet pointed out, but Dax had already moved on, taking pictures of Juliet in front of one of the informative plaques littered around the place. Juliet paused beside it to actually read it, but it had the same information as all the rest. "Do you think any aliens live under the ground here, Daksha?"

"Well, let's fuckin' find out," Dax insisted, pocketing her phone and dropping to the ground. She felt along the sand and patches of grass and dusty dirt for whatever it was she was searching for - a handle to a door, maybe, or an alien's hand reaching up for her. Juliet stuck her hands in her pockets and started paying attention to the clouds speeding by over their heads.

"Suspicious," Dax commented, and Juliet glanced at her briefly. "What is?"

"The clouds," Dax elaborated. "Pretty suspicious, how fast they're going," she added. "Almost like something is influencing them."

"Almost," Juliet agreed, tipping her head back to continue watching them. Dax appeared at her side and let out a long sigh. Juliet glanced at her out of the corner of her eye and waited for her to continue.

"I just feel like they won't come *back* here, you know?" Dax told her. Juliet nodded, rocking back on her heels. "There's no reason. They already got busted here. And, you know, this isn't really a hub of human activity. Maybe they went somewhere else, you know. Exploring a little more."

"Maybe." Juliet turned her head down to look at Dax fully. "What are you thinking?"

"I'm just thinking maybe our two weeks here is enough, is all," Dax offered. She lifted one shoulder. "We might've done all we can do here, you know. Us. The human race, too. I think-"

"We can go," Juliet interrupted. Dax raised an eyebrow at her.

"Are you sure?" Dax asked, and Juliet gave her a shrug of her own.

"I don't see why not," Juliet said. She pulled out her phone and started flipping through her bookmarks for anything close by. "We haven't been able to do much here, it's mostly tourist stuff. Plus, you're right. I don't think what we're looking for is here."

"No," Dax agreed. "No, I think you're right. I don't think it is."

"Great," Juliet said. She handed her phone over.

"What's this?"

"That is Levelland, Texas," Juliet informed her, leaning over her and the phone to scroll down the page. "It's not Austin, but it does have one of the most widely-witnessed UFO sightings in history."

Dax looked up, excitement lighting her eyes; Juliet wondered if maybe she should have been looking at this from Dax's point of view all along, and come along for the ride, rather than waiting for something that might never come.

"Really?" Dax asked, cutting off Juliet's thoughts before they could fully form, and Juliet nodded.

"Really and truly," Juliet assured her. Dax tightened her grip on Juliet's phone and started scrolling through the website.

"Holy shit," Dax commented, "look. Look how many reports came in on the same *night*, Jules. And they all saw the same thing. There's a really good chance this'll work out."

"And it's been decades, and nobody really visits for UFO purposes," Juliet pointed out. "So, I bet the aliens would want to come back and check it out again, right?"

Dax's whole face lit up; her eyes were brighter than they had been in a while, and the exhilaration of Roswell and Levelland combined seemed to fill her up to bursting with light from the inside-out. She stretched up and kissed Juliet on the cheek, returning her phone to her.

"Let's go be irresponsible," Juliet said, and Dax punched her on the arm, leading the way back to the van. The van had certainly seen better days, Juliet mused as they approached it; the sides were a little beaten, and it showed its age. It had been this way since they first met, though, and the sight of the van brought Juliet a fonder feeling than it had when she first saw it. It brought with it sensations of home and warmth that could only come with time.

Dax slid across the hood on her way to the driver's side, hopping in and jamming in the keys before Juliet's door was even shut. With the utmost irresponsibility and with maximum recklessness and excitement, the two of them left their jobs with their first (and last) paychecks in hand, paid off their time at the RV park, and left Roswell like a comet.

Compared to the other drives they had made, the distance from Roswell to Levelland was almost laughably short. There was no park to stop at on the way through, no interesting sights, no giant balls of twine or huge wooden cows. They stopped off for dinner just inside of the Texas border, at the midway point on the two-and-a-half-hour drive, finding themselves in a microscopically small town that barely showed up on the Internet.

"What do you think will happen in Levelland?" Juliet asked, because getting Dax started on one topic was typically enough for her to monologue for an entire meal. Dax fiddled with the bendy straw she had stuck into her Scotch. Juliet had already confiscated her keys the moment she had ordered it; she stuck to a virgin Texas tea.

"I think we're going to find something," Dax offered, simple as that. "But, I don't know... I don't think it's *here* we're going to find it. It's soon, though. This is a stepping stone. I know it is."

"Tell me what we're finding," Juliet encouraged. She sipped her tea. Dax started talking and did not stop through their meal, through their shared dessert, back onto the road with Juliet at the wheel. Juliet split the driving time fairly evenly with Dax at this point; she knew the ins and outs of the van like she knew the ins and outs of Dax herself. Dax lounged in the passenger seat, the street lights flicking over her face in the encroaching darkness. Juliet glanced at her, then back ahead.

"Oh, I need more nicotine patches," Dax exclaimed, as they zoomed past a sign for an upcoming gas station. Juliet pulled over gracefully, checking the nozzle for the gas tank and finding it wanting.

"We need gas, too," Juliet pointed out, coaxing the van up to one of the pumps and parking easily. Dax motioned for her to join her inside the mini-mart.

While Juliet roamed the aisles, perusing her options for a snack for the night, Dax found the slushie machine. She was leaning against it when Juliet found her, seemingly distracted by the drip of sticky red melting out of one of the nozzles. She was facing the shelf of nicotine patch boxes, but the trickle of slush seemed far more captivating to her just then. Juliet heard a car door slam by the gas pumps outside, and Dax jerked out of her trance, glancing out the dirty front windows. Following her gaze, Juliet saw that everything outside was dark, the parking lot difficult to see set against the oppressive fluorescent brightness of the lights inside the mini-mart, but Juliet could just make out the van's shape outside by the pumps.

"You gonna pick something, lady?" the young girl behind the counter asked, looking barely old enough to need nicotine patches, let alone sell them. Dax seemed to consider her for a moment before she pushed away from the wall and dropped a box of nicotine patches on the counter. Juliet snuck her bag of chocolate-covered raisins next to the box. The little girl rang them up while Juliet waited a pace behind her, rocking back and forth on her heels.

"Twenty on six," Dax told the girl, digging her worn wallet out of her pocket. The leather slid against Dax's palm as she pulled out a twenty and a ten and handed them over. The girl gave her a handful of coins and her box.

"Have a nice day," the girl said absently, returning her attention to her notebook on the counter. Juliet watched as Dax glanced outside at the night sky, then back to the girl, raising an eyebrow, but she was thoroughly ignored. Juliet hid a smile with her downturned head as Dax swiped the patches and the chocolate-covered raisins up off the counter and left the mini-mart.

"Fill 'er up," Dax called, startling Juliet, who had been on her way to sprawling herself across the roof of the van. She clambered up and lay down anyways, punch-drunk off the night and the thrill that the day had left thrumming under her skin. Juliet lifted her head, and Dax was backlit by the dying dirty lights of the gas pump roof above them, dark skin and hair outlined in brutal faded yellow. "Got twenty ready for her."

"Where do you plan on going with that twenty, anyways?" Juliet asked, watching as Dax pocketed her patches, tossed the bag of candy up to Juliet, and yanked the lid off the tank. "We're almost in Levelland already." Dax jammed the gas nozzle into the tank in response. Juliet wondered if she could feel her eyes burning onto the back of her neck. Dax pulled the trigger.

"I just want us to drive," Dax answered. Juliet stuck her legs over the edge of the van, letting her feet dangle near Dax's face. Dax swatted at her ankle.

"That's fair," Juliet said, and Dax seemed to agree. They waited for the last drops of gas to trickle out, sticky like the slushie Dax had been so transfixed by, before Dax shook the nozzle off. Juliet slid off the roof, landing on shaky feet on the pavement next to Dax. Juliet watched her for a moment, attention lingering until Dax glanced her way and made eye contact. Juliet held it, more confident than usual, before she reached up and rubbed a fist against her eye underneath her glasses. She fixed the frames and left, abandoning Dax by the gas pump in favor of climbing back into the driver's side of the van.

In the side view mirror, Juliet watched lazily as Dax shook out the nozzle one last time and replaced it on the pump. It sounded like she had to slam her body weight against the gas tank lid to get it to stick, and Juliet stuck her head out the window, stretching her full height up to see Dax over the roof's edge.

"If you want us to drive, Paracha, get in and we'll drive," Juliet called, and Dax flipped her off. Juliet didn't laugh, but she smiled, ducking back in through the window, and Dax joined her in the front seat of the van. Juliet turned to her, head rolling against the back of her seat, watching Dax with a smile. "Do you want me to take us away from all this, Daksha?"

"I do," Dax agreed, and Juliet's cheeks lit up, feeling hot like burners. Juliet turned the van back on and offered her a grin.

"Your wish is my command," Juliet assured her, grabbing the stick shift and shoving it until she got the van started. She let the engine rumble for a minute before throwing the stick shift and peeling out of the gas station lot. Juliet fell silent, a habit familiar to the both of them and comfortable by this point in their journey together. Dax let her head tip to look out the window as the trees sped by, stars turning into streaks and smudges from their speed. Juliet spent most of her time watching the road, and the rest of her time watching Dax.

Dax only deigned to stir and turn to Juliet when they were pulling off the road at another rest stop. Even then, she didn't speak until the van was taking shaky steps off the road and into a grassy clearing.

"What are you doing?" Dax asked. She stuck her hand out the window; the night air brushed against their faces.

"I think we've been driving long enough," Juliet answered. She jammed the car into park and leaned back against her seat. When she glanced at Dax, she met her eyes; Dax held the gaze for a moment, brave, before looking away. The retreat felt almost like cowardice.

"We've barely driven," Dax pointed out, and Juliet shrugged, pointing up at the sky above them.

"But it's beautiful," Juliet pointed out. "There was a rest stop, and I- I guess, I don't know, I just figured there would be a lot of lights in Levelland and I wanted to be able-"

"Chill out, Jules, you're going to give yourself a stroke," Dax laughed. "Fine. Get out. I want to relax." Dax pushed her own car door with her shoulder until it gave and popped open. She left it ajar and circled around to the front of the van. She waved once at Juliet before climbing up onto the hood and scaling the windshield to reach the roof. Juliet followed her through the window on the driver's side.

She found Dax already stretched out, looking up at the stars.

Juliet tipped her head back, dragging her attention away from staring at Dax as she considered the stars' beauty and lied to herself. Her heart thudded dangerously against her chest until she laid down at Dax's side, only a handful of hesitant minutes later. Dax tugged a nicotine patch out of the box in her pocket and jokingly offered it to Juliet. Juliet shook her head, barely looking at her, face still burning. Dax shrugged, sitting up and unwrapping the patch to press against her skin.

"Why did you keep smoking?" Juliet asked, laying back against the roof of the van, attention fixed on the sky. "Before?" Her eyes flickered to Dax when she didn't answer right away. Instead, Dax pulled her old lighter out of her pocket and flicked at it, throwing their profiles into light, then out of it, firelight switching on and off at her fingertips. Juliet wondered would it be like to smoke like Dax once had, to hold her breath until her lungs burned with smoke and ash and all the other things she kept inside. Juliet exhaled, and Dax's eyes tracked the movement of her chest as she breathed.

"Because I wanted to die, but I didn't want it to happen right away," Dax eventually answered, laying down next to Juliet again, the two of them neatly crammed together between the rails on top of the van. Dax turned her head towards Juliet, smiling when Juliet glanced down at her, pocketing her lighter and casting them both in darkness. Juliet reached up and tucked a lock of Dax's hair behind her ear before withdrawing her hand.

Dax remained silent, and Juliet soon turned her attention back to the sky. She was still quite aware of Dax's attention on the side of her face; eventually, Juliet just turned back to look at her once more. She didn't speak. Juliet didn't need her to. The two of them stared at each other; if Juliet stared hard enough, she could see herself in Dax's pupils, the trees and the stars around them reflected in her dark irises. Dax's brow furrowed slightly, her expression becoming a little frustrated, and Juliet understood.

Juliet was the first one to give up, because of *course* she was. She turned her attention back to the sky, pretending that the shooting stars she saw every now and then were the most interesting things the night could offer. Dax stared at the side of her face for a little while longer - she could feel it, the holes burning in the side of her face, and she wanted everything she could barely think to ask for - before she surrendered, too, and turned back to the sky. Eventually, Dax's hand made its way down to Juliet's. She just touched the back of her hand - light, careful, a hunter stalking a deer - before drawing away. She let their hands rest side-by-side on the chilled metal of the roof, and Juliet exhaled shakily, fighting the urge to follow Dax's bad example and smoke cigarette after cigarette until her chest was packed with ash and her head was stuffed with smoke and she didn't have to pretend anymore.

Chapter Sixteen

Pulling into Levelland was like shaking off shackles, in a way, Juliet thought. She felt a similar lightness to her limbs, and the sensations the rest area had left inside of her had all but left. The feel of Dax's hand against the back of her own burned hot like an iron, but Juliet planned to keep that all to herself. She could not help but wonder what, if anything, Dax had meant by it; if she had wanted to hold her hand, or if she was just being friendly, or if it was a mistake, and she had meant nothing by it at all. She privately believed that Dax must have felt the tension between them, too. She imagined that Dax was on edge, and that Dax always wanted to kiss her, and that Dax felt all of these *things* that Juliet had no name for but that belonged almost exclusively to her relationship with Dax. She worried she was projecting. She kept her thoughts to herself.

"Look at that," Dax pointed out as they drove. Juliet craned her neck to see what Dax was talking about. "I bet we could get up there."

As it turned out, "that" was a tremendously tall water tower, *Levelland* painted across the front, wrapping around the old panels in bold black lettering. It was illuminated from below, and Juliet made a mental note to return there later in their stay.

"What do you want to do in Levelland?" Juliet asked, and Dax collapsed back in her seat, rolling her window down, then up, then down again.

"I don't think I want to stay here too long," Dax admitted. "It feels like a pit stop. This isn't where we're finding it."

"What's 'it'?" Juliet asked, and Dax only shrugged. "Alright. So, what *do* you want to do, if you don't want to stay too long?"

"Well, let's give it a couple days," Dax suggested. "Just to make sure I'm not wrong. I'm sure we can pick up odd jobs. Or even just take a couple days off, you know. It wouldn't kill us to take a break."

"I suppose it wouldn't," Juliet agreed. She kept her eyes on the directions her phone was giving her to the nearest campground. Dax started braiding her own hair over her shoulder. Juliet forced herself to pay attention to anything but that, and settled on the road as a substitute.

"Anything good in Levelland besides the UFOs?" Dax asked, and Juliet shrugged. Dax pulled her own phone and started searching, her face illuminated in the glow of her screen.

Creeping into October as they were had Juliet expecting cold weather, a lifetime of Michigan temperatures preparing her for icy winds when she rolled her window down. Texas, though, was nothing like Michigan, and the wind that whipped her face was warm and weak and brought the smell of meat cooking on the grill wafting through the van. Juliet relaxed, one arm hanging out the open window, the other hand holding tight to the steering wheel.

"Says here that Levelland is called the 'City of Mosaics,'" Dax informed her. "They've got some art collections, a couple of libraries, a shopping district. They've got a vendor show." Dax glanced up at her, white teeth flashing in the light from her phone as she smiled. "Texas stuff."

"We've never been Texas gals, have we?" Juliet asked, and Dax laughed, shutting her phone off and pocketing it. "I can pick up my prescriptions here, at the very least. We can spend a few days looking at all the water towers and mosaics Levelland can offer us."

"Sounds good to me," Dax agreed, leaning out her window, letting the wind whip into her face, blowing her hair out behind her. She rested her elbows against the car door, resting casually as they sped along through the darkness. The campground was not too much further, and fairly cheap to boot; they parked in the space they were assigned, and Dax wasted no time hauling Juliet and their blankets up to the roof.

"Who knows?" Dax commented, snapping out the quilt to lay on top of. Juliet crouched in the corner, out of the way, snacking on a bag of convenience store almonds. "Maybe we'll find a good memory here."

Dax dragged Juliet over to use as a pillow, propping her head up on Juliet's chest. Juliet tried not to let her heart beat too fiercely, her breaths come quickly, should they lead Dax to any conclusions that Juliet would prefer she not draw. Dax stayed awake for a rather long time; Juliet dozed off long before her. The gentle stroke of Dax's fingertips over Juliet's temples, tracing down over the shell of her ear to her shoulder, softly running the length of her scar, to her elbow, to her knuckles. Dax's light attentions and the clouded and warm night sky above them led Juliet off into sleep.

If it was Dax's soft touch and tender mannerisms that brought her to sleep, it was the other side of her coin - her noisiness, her need for attention, and the wanting sun driving her eyes open for the day - that woke Juliet up the next morning. Dax shook her shoulder in a vice-like grip, and Juliet's half-awake mind briefly entertained the dreamlike notion that she was trapped in an iron box before she opened one eye.

"What do you want?" Juliet asked, and Dax grinned, still sleep-mussed. Her tangled hair swung into Juliet's eyes and mouth.

"The City of Mosaics," Dax reminded her. Juliet laughed, tossing Dax off of her. Dax, in turn, dragged Juliet down the windshield, quilts and all, to the hood of the van, then to the dusty ground below. She wrestled her over onto her back, pinning her wrists to the ground. "Show me the art, Jules."

"I'm looking at it," Juliet replied. Dax's expression softened, her mouth turning from a grin into something closer to a sweet smile. Her eyes gentled. Juliet shoved her off. "Let's find a shower. You smell disgusting."

"It's from sleeping on you all night," Dax shot back, throwing a blanket over Juliet's head. Dax straightened out the roof and the quilts while Juliet gathered their toiletries in their bags and sought out the bathhouse on the campground's little paper map. Showering was quick and easy; brushing Dax's hair out was an ordeal that took the both of them to complete with any kind of speed. Juliet braided her hair for her while Dax ordered Juliet's prescription at the local pharmacy and called around for something to do that day.

"Looks like we'll be checking out some art collections and the vendor show today," Dax informed her, as Juliet finished pinning up Dax's crown of tight braids. "How's that sound?"

"Sounds fine." Juliet inched out of the van and hopped out, stretching her legs, sighing when her kneecaps popped into place. She turned to say something to Dax, but immediately found herself distracted, her attention fixed on Dax's full lips as she mouthed the words of whatever she was reading on her phone. Her brow creased slightly, a small dent appearing between her heavy, dark eyebrows, and she glanced up at Juliet. Her eyes lit up, near-blackness seeming to be backlit by her newfound excitement, and her mouth twisted up at the corners, cherry-red and dimpled. The mole under her right eye and the freckles dusted across her nose seemed like a bright moon and stars in the night sky of her face. Juliet almost told her how much she loved her, the words bubbling up in her like water in a boiling pot; her lid almost popped off before Dax spoke up and, unknowingly, saved her.

"What're you staring at?" Dax said, and her mouth moved like waves on a shore, enticing, dizzying. "We have mosaics to see."

I want to kiss you, Juliet thought.

"Sure, yeah," Juliet said.

Dax drove them to all the art collections they could find; though they were small, they were interesting, and Juliet tried her best to distract herself from Dax. She found Dax in every piece of art she looked at; every painting seemed to have the exact shade of her skin in its paints, every sculpture had a shape that seemed to fit on Dax's body. Juliet felt flushed all day, her hands tingling, her heart beating into her throat. She felt overwhelmed whenever she looked at Dax, lately; it was becoming irrepressible, these feelings she kept bottled up inside of her.

"Why don't we go to the water tower?" Dax suggested, when they had picked up Juliet's prescriptions and perused the vendor show. Juliet had found herself a simple dress at the fair for an easy five dollars and was in the process of changing into it in the back of the van when Dax had made her suggestion.

"Yeah, sure," Juliet agreed, keeping her eyes down so as not to make eye contact with Dax through the rearview mirror. "Just don't make any sudden turns."

Dax jerked the van a little bit on purpose, making Juliet tip over and start laughing. Dax turned to look at her briefly, grinning before she turned back to the road. Once their eye contact was broken, Juliet dropped her head into her hands and tried to take deep enough breaths to calm herself down.

The water tower overlooking Levelland was at least one hundred feet up, if not higher. Juliet stared up at it, neck craned backwards; Dax was already heading up the ladder. She stopped, hooking her arm around to dangle herself backwards, smiling at Juliet. Her hair was a little loose, wisps of black falling around her face. She looked like a woodland queen, Juliet thought fleetingly, before stuffing the emotions back down.

"Aren't you coming?" Dax asked, and Juliet nodded, willing to follow Dax anywhere, even the top of a tall and impossibly frightening water tower in Texas. The climb was difficult; any time she glanced back, it seemed almost certain that she was going to slip and fall all the way down. She found, though, that she didn't have too hard of a time looking up and keeping her attention on Dax as they climbed. Dax reached the top and hauled herself up before pivoting to offer Juliet a hand. Once they were both safely on the landing, they scooted until they were secured behind the barrier around the edge, their legs dangling into the open air. Juliet glanced down at her feet, had a brief vision of herself slipping between the bars and falling, and exhaled slowly.

"Hey," Dax said softly. "You're going to be okay." She reached out and took Juliet's hand in hers, squeezing tightly. She let their hands rest in her lap. "I won't let you fall."

Too late, Juliet thought desperately. She let her head rest on Dax's shoulder instead of speaking, her heart pounding in her throat. She was starting to spiral out of control, her thoughts starting to pulse, thinking that maybe she should just confess what she had been feeling, that maybe Dax felt the same way and just hadn't been able to tell her. She could feel her hand getting sweaty, but Dax stayed quiet and didn't make a comment. Juliet took a shaky breath.

"I love you," Juliet said, a little too hard, a little too fast. Dax glanced at her, shifting a little to look her in the face.

"I love you, too, kid," Dax replied. She kissed Juliet's forehead, and Juliet's eyes fluttered shut. "You're safe with me."

"I love you," Juliet repeated, stupidly. Dax twisted, pulling one leg up under her, and Juliet tracked her every movement with the flicks of her eyes. Dax pulled her head in, pushing their foreheads together and keeping eye contact with her.

"I know," Dax assured her. "You're okay with me. I'm gonna

keep you safe up here. Don't freak out."

"I'm not," Juliet replied. Even if she was freaking out, it was for different reasons than Dax seemed to think. "I'm not."

Dax's eyes darted down, then back up. Juliet's breath caught in her throat. They stayed there for a moment, Juliet's forehead feeling hot and clammy pressed up against Dax's, staring at one another. Dax, eventually, squeezed Juliet's hand and pulled back. To Juliet, the new distance seemed like miles.

"Levelland didn't have as much for us as I would've liked," Dax commented, looking back out over the town. "I don't think it has what we're looking for. Do you?"

The sky was cloudless; high over Texas, the sky twinkled with stars that were as far away as Dax seemed in that moment. Juliet shook her head; there was nothing in the sky that night for them, nothing for them to find.

"No UFO disasters tonight," Juliet said, aiming for funny and coming up choked. "Nothing to see here."

"Maybe we'll come back someday," Dax said. "Maybe. But I just feel like... What we're looking for? It's not here."

"Do you wanna head out?" Juliet asked, and Dax paused. She shrugged.

"In the morning." Dax shifted them slightly so she could lean against Juliet, her head on Juliet's shoulder. Juliet shut her eyes to stop the unshed tears from spilling out; her heart throbbed against her ribs. She kept in her deep breaths and let Dax rest. Looking out over Levelland - the low buildings, the dusty earth, the lights filling the town below and the sky above - she felt a little more grounded, but was happiest when Dax eventually roused enough to suggest they return to the van. Juliet slept beside Dax, staring at the side of the van, at her belongings mixed up with Dax's, and found herself struggling to fall asleep. Dax slept turned away from her, her back facing Juliet; this ended up being Juliet's saving grace, because being forced to look away from Dax's face eventually allowed her to let her guard down enough to fall asleep.

Juliet woke up to the van already moving. She sat up, squinting in the sunlight that peeked through the windshield into the back of the van. She shifted around, rubbing at her eye with the heel of her hand. Dax was sitting up in the front seat, leaning half-out the window, humming along to the low jazz music coming out of the radio. The sun glinted off Dax's sunglasses into Juliet's face. Juliet slid her glasses on and leaned over the console, resting her head on her folded arms.

"Where are we going?" Juliet asked, and Dax jumped, the van swerving into the next lane. She straightened them out, swearing the whole way.

"God*damn* you, Alva," Dax laughed, shoving Juliet's face into the other seat with her open palm. "I'm gonna get you a bell, I swear to God."

"You didn't answer me," Juliet murmured, yawning. Dax released her and let her sit up; Juliet dragged herself into the front seat, scrubbing at her face with her hands.

"It's a surprise," Dax replied. Juliet let her head list against the closed window, the breeze from Dax's side of the van brushing against her face as she dozed in and out of awareness. Dax kept singing softly under her breath as the Texas dirt kicked up under their tires, their wheels seemingly the only set on the road. Dax shook Juliet out of her hazy half-sleep when they pulled over for lunch.

"This is Dayton, Texas," Dax informed her, picking out an outfit for Juliet to wear while Juliet brushed her teeth with water from one of their bottles. "This is home to one of the only UFO cases to ever actually go to court. People said it was hazardous to their health."

"And this is your surprise location?" Juliet asked, pausing to spit toothpaste into a trash barrel outside the van. Dax laughed.

"No, I'm not bringing you somewhere where you'd be in danger from alien radiation," Dax told her. "I'm a good friend."

"I'm starting to think *you* might be an alien, to be honest," Juliet laughed. Dax shoved a dress into her arms.

"Don't let the secret spill," she said with a wink. She slammed the back doors of the van shut and went inside to get them a table. Juliet dressed in a rush, squashing her emotions in favor of her hunger. By the time she tugged her shoes on, fixed her hair up, and got herself inside, Dax was already sipping at a Shirley Temple.

"It's a virgin," Dax assured her. She slid the second Shirley Temple across the table, and Juliet took it as she sat down, sipping absently as Dax flipped through the menu with her. "Damn, I'm starving. I feel like I've been up for days."

"How long were you driving?" Juliet asked, flipping the menu page.

"Nine hours."

Juliet choked on her breath. "*Nine* hours? Why the hell-"

"I couldn't sleep," Dax admitted, like having driven nine hours barely mattered. "I waited until you fell asleep and I started driving. I just had one of those nights."

Juliet scanned Dax's face, but it seemed like she was being honest. Dax distracted her with pointing out menu items she thought Juliet might like, and Juliet let herself be sidetracked.

It was a lunch like every other lunch they had shared in their time together; Dax got something disgusting and piled high with toppings, mustard dribbling down her wrist, ducking her head down to lick all the way up her forearm while grinning wide at Juliet. Juliet ate neatly, brandishing her knife and fork like weapons against her diner meal. Dax talked incessantly, like always; Juliet listened and prodded her along, like always; the conversation drifted around aliens, then to their memories, then to wild fantasies, like always. What had changed was Juliet.

She had realized for some time that the feelings she was harboring for Dax were like a crush, a slow tipping point, standing at the tip of an iceberg and hoping she wouldn't slide down the side into the ocean. It was then, though - then, sitting at that diner in the middle of nowhere, watching Dax lick the salt off her fries, listening to her chatter about what might happen if they became shepherds in Switzerland - that she realized she was in love with her. Her heart throbbed inside of her chest like an open wound, a sensation like it was trying to pulse blood out of her mouth. Juliet looked down and swallowed hard, suddenly losing her appetite; she pushed her plate away and put her chin in her hand.

"How you doin', kid?" Dax asked, snapping a fry in half with her front teeth. Juliet's heart surged into her throat.

"Really, really well," Juliet assured her. "I'm good. I'm really good."

She obsessed on this thought until lunch was finished, until they left for Dax's secret destination, and for the entirety of their drive. Dax turned up her music, a CD of electro swing tunes, and seemed content to let Juliet drift in her own thoughts. She was unaware that Juliet's thoughts consisted almost entirely of *holy shit I'm in love with her oh no holy shit* on repeat, but that was Juliet's business for the time being.

Despite having driven nine hours the previous night into the morning, lunch seemed to have revitalized her, and Dax drove the remaining five hours to their mystery destination without a complaint. Juliet offered up half of the conversation when Dax did talk, prodding her along so she would monologue without needing contribution. Mostly, Juliet focused on shaking feeling back into her hands and trying not to dwell on the emotions currently surging through her like bolts in a plasma ball.

"We're here," Dax told her, and Juliet started paying attention to her surroundings just in time to notice a sign declaring them to be crossing into New Orleans. She wondered absently how far away Baton Rouge was.

"You didn't," Juliet laughed, rolling down her window and leaning out, the breeze slapping her face. They hadn't been in a real city for some time, sticking to the smaller towns that UFOs apparently preferred, if their tour was any indication.

"I sure did." Dax tapped Juliet's watch. "Did you see what day it is?"

"No," Juliet replied, smiling. "Will my watch tell me?"

"Shut up," Dax said. "It's Halloween, Juliet. Get into the mood. There's a parade in New Orleans that's calling our name, *and* a number of sonic booms and light formations have been spotted here in the last few years. I bet we'll find something here."

"We don't have any costumes," Juliet pointed out, and Dax leaned over to smile at her.

"You sleep like the dead." Dax jerked her thumb over her shoulder to the back of the van. "I stopped at the store. Go look."

Juliet climbed into the back of the van while Dax drove them to a concrete travel park in the city. Juliet dug through their belongings until she found two new and unfamiliar paper bags. She rooted through, pulling out a dress that must have been Dax's, since it was too short for Juliet - a long costume gown, the black fabric slipping through Juliet's fingers like silk, gold threads and embellishments making the piece beautiful. There was a black-gold masquerade mask underneath, and a cheap twisted-up hoop skirt.

"No, the other bag, that one's not for you," Dax called over her shoulder. Juliet packed the paper bag back up and opened the other one, finding a dress that would actually fit her, all white with silver thread and designs catching the sunlight. A matching masquerade mask and a second cheap hook skirt were packed up underneath. She examined the corset bodice of the dress, fingering the ends of the laces. "Do you like it?"

"What?" Juliet lifted her head, still looking at the dress. "Oh, yes. Very much, thank you, it's beautiful. What do I owe you for it?"

"Wearing it," Dax replied. Juliet turned to look at her, and Dax glanced at her in the rearview mirror. "What's mine is yours. Also, vice versa, I think. Yeah?"

"Yeah," Juliet answered. "Yeah, I think so."

"Well, it's a masquerade Halloween parade," Dax told her, once they had paid and parked in the travel park. "And it starts in an hour and a half, so you better get dressed so we can do our makeup and my hair, because God knows I love going all out for Halloween."

"Do you?" Juliet asked, digging through Dax's makeup bag. Dax turned the van off and climbed into the back with her.

"I was an amazing space princess last year," Dax said. "Remind me to show you the pictures sometime. Maybe we can choose our own theme next year."

"Next year?" Juliet asked, and Dax paused, almost unnoticeably, before continuing to pull her costume pieces out of her paper bag.

"Yeah, next year, we'll figure out a good one." Dax kicked the back door of the van open and scooted out, undressing to her underclothes for all the world to see before demanding Juliet's assistance in pulling the hoop skirt into place and helping her into the dress. She finished in a fair amount of time, and Juliet made Dax stand between her legs so she could braid her hair and style it for her, wrapping it up and pinning it like a crown around her head. Dax started working on her own makeup while Juliet wiggled into her own dress and positioned her hair how she wanted it. She adjusted her lion's head necklace against her chest just so and settled.

Dax doing her makeup and painting her up was hypnotizing that night more than it had ever been before. It set Juliet completely on edge, her hands tingling numbly, her back breaking into a cold sweat. She kept her eyes shut for as long as she could, until Dax asked her softly to open her eyes so she could paint her lower eyelid. Dax stared into her eyes, seeming like a Victorian angel, her hair a halo, her face a Renaissance portrait. She smiled; Juliet's heart thudded painfully.

By the time they were ready to go, it was almost time for the parade. Dax slipped her heels on and handed Juliet hers, and the two of them chose to forego the van and walk the short distance to the parade route. Night fell hard and fast on the march over, and the crowds only got thicker the closer they got. Dax took her by the hand and led her to the front lines of the parade, and her hand felt heavy in hers, a warm iron wrapped around her fingers. Whenever she glanced back to check on Juliet, her eyes dark against her skin, her makeup, and her dark mask. The gold on her face caught the streetlights and reflected against her irises. Juliet could barely pay attention to the crowd around her or to the parade as it started, painted performers filling the streets, floats decked out in decorations and bright golden lights starting their slow path through the streets.

"What do you think?" Dax asked, shouting over the din of music and voices that filled New Orleans. Lights lit up the sky above them; fleetingly, Juliet believed they might have been aliens. A beaded necklace thrown her way bounced off her temple, and Dax's laugh could have powered the entire city for a month.

"I love it," Juliet called back. Dax squeezed her hand and pulled her closer, the crowd shoving them up against one another. The darkness seemed to throb around them, a backdrop for the parade to exist against. Pounding music hammered through her veins, her heart pulsing with each low beat of the bass, pulse fluttering in her wrist, her throat. The world seemed to narrow down like a tunnel, focusing down on one point: Dax, who turned and laughed, smiling widely, white teeth, whites of her eyes, dark red paint on her lips, dusted with gold. Dax was saying something, but it could have been anything; the hypnotic sound of her voice filled Juliet's ears. Dax was everything, in that moment and in every moment before, and in every moment since; it seemed like there could be nothing else.

Being well and truly fucked seemed like it was Juliet's new hobby, she contemplated in the back of her mind, while the rest of her was entirely focused on Dax. Dax's dress clung tightly to her, a sheen of sweat against her dark skin, warm and rich like a deep brown ochre, shining in the lights. A bead of sweat rolled down from her temple, locks of her hair falling into her face, and time seemed to slow down. The crowd fell away; the floats only served to backlight

Dax.

"Hey, are you okay?" Dax asked, and Juliet let go of her hand, reaching up and cupping Dax's face in her hands. She pulled her close, looking down at her, and, in an instant, Dax seemed as fixated on Juliet as Juliet was on her.

"Can I-" Juliet began, and Dax nodded vigorously, the question hanging between them. It vanished in the next hard beat of Juliet's heart, as she dropped her head down and crushed her lips to Dax's, using her hold on her face to keep them together. Dax stretched up onto her toes and wound her arms around Juliet's neck, wrists crossing in the air behind her. She tilted her head, soft, letting Juliet take control. Juliet guided her mouth open gently, then pushed harder, kissing her like she had never kissed another human being. Dax tightened her grip, hands pressing hard against the base of her neck. When Juliet finally lifted her head, Dax's lipstick was smudged, gold edging around the edges of her lips, her mouth a deep red and gilded blur, sparkling on her face.

"I love you," Juliet shouted, more firmly than she had on the water tower, and Dax threw her lovely head back, glowing from within, glittering in the lights from the Day of the Dead float passing behind her. The column of her throat was ravishing.

"I can't believe you," Dax laughed. She reached up to take Juliet's head in her hands, yanking her back down to kiss again, grinning through it. Their masks pressed together; the sharp corner of Dax's cheap gold disguise dug into Juliet's cheek, but it was the most exquisite sensation she had ever had the grace to feel. "I can't *believe* you!"

Juliet took her words into her mouth and swallowed them like moonbeams. She pulled back and gave her a smile, and Dax's hoop skirt bounced off of Juliet's when she surged forwards again. The parade continued behind them, necklaces bouncing off of the two of them like pinballs, the crowd around them pushing and pulling like rip tidal waves, shoving them closer until Juliet felt like Dax was a part of her costume.

"Do you want to go home?" Dax called over the crowd and the pounding music, and Juliet nodded eagerly. She took her by the hand again and jerked her forward, leading her out of the horde. Juliet felt like the sea of people must have parted around them; why would it not? Why would people not clear the way for Dax, why would they not take care with her as if she were the most precious thing in the world?

They went home, to the van, stumbling the whole way there because Dax refused to take off her heels and refused to stop trying to kiss Juliet while still moving. Juliet half-carried her back, Dax hanging happily off of her, hands wrapped like vices around one another. When they got back, Juliet hauled Dax into the back of the van bodily. Dax made short work of their hoop skirts, untying them and bundling them up in the front seats, out of their way. Juliet tore her mask off, and Dax hers; the dresses were harder to get out of, but they were both in slips in a short enough period of time. In just their smudged makeup, sparkling hair, and underskirts, they sat up on their knees and stared at each other.

"Why did you never say anything?" Dax asked, finally. The silence shattered. Juliet lunged forwards, meeting Dax as she moved at the same time, pushing her down into the pillows.

"I didn't want to scare you," Juliet confessed, mouth to Dax's throat. Dax twined her fingers in Juliet's hair. "You're the best friend I've ever had."

"And you're mine." Dax tugged lightly, and Juliet lifted her head to meet Dax's eyes. "I love you, too. You know that."

"Now I do." Juliet leaned in and kissed her again, softer. Dax traced the curve of Juliet's ear, the scar on her cheek, the curve of her throat. She pressed the pad of her thumb to the dip of her chest, the lion's heart necklace bouncing against the knob of her wrist.

"I've always loved you, kid," Dax said quietly. Juliet pressed her forehead to Dax's and smiled, her heart filling her chest and her head, throbbing gently, pounding to remind her she was alive, alive, *alive*, and finally *living*.

"I love you, too, Dax," Juliet murmured. She exhaled shakily, half-laughing, and Dax pulled her into a close embrace, smudging lipstick over Juliet's cheek as they went, glitter catching on her eyelashes and sparkling like shooting stars.

Chapter Seventeen

"Hey," Juliet heard. She blinked once, then slammed her eyes shut against the sunlight pressing hard against her face through the van windows. She squinted and barely made out Dax hovering above her. "You awake?"

"I am now," Juliet murmured. She pushed Dax away so she could sit up. Dax handed her her glasses, and she slid them on, feeling the smudge of lipstick against her cheek, glitter smeared over her nose and forehead. She grimaced at the tacky feeling it left on her skin.

"How'd you sleep?" Dax asked. When Juliet opened her mouth to answer, Dax darted in, pressing a kiss to her mouth, then withdrew. Juliet smiled, drawing Dax back in to kiss again.

"I slept fine," Juliet mumbled against Dax's skin. Dax laughed. "How about you?"

"I couldn't sleep," Dax told her. "I was too excited."

"Oh, what were you excited by?" Juliet asked, and Dax kicked open the back door of the van. Juliet started laughing, wrapping her blanket around herself as a shield against the breeze as she watched Dax scramble up onto the roof. "*Daksha.*"

"Always so formal," Dax said. Her head reappeared, dangling upside down, hair brushing the edge of the van floor. She extended a hand to Juliet. "Come on, kid."

"Fine." Juliet put her hand in Dax's and let herself be hauled up to the roof. It was easily somewhere around noon; the sun blazed down on them, feeling like it might have been seventy degrees.

November in New Orleans felt just like July in Big Bay. The summery breeze brushed her face gently as it passed; everything felt more sharp, her senses more acute, the world around them more beautiful. The travel park around them was more concrete than nature, but the sky above them was vast and the smell of the city was sweet. She wondered if Dax felt the same way; she wanted to think so. The dopey smile on Dax's face led her to believe she might.

"I heard a sonic boom last night," Dax told her, her voice hushed like someone might overhear them.

"Are you sure it was a sonic boom?" Juliet whispered back. "Since there was a parade last night and we're in New Orleans?"

"I know what I heard, man," Dax said. She leaned back against the roof of the van; when Juliet joined her laying down, she let her head rest on Juliet's chest, reaching for her hand to play with her fingers. "New Orleans has a history of extraterrestrial sonic booms. Think we'll see something tonight?"

Juliet knew they wouldn't. "Yeah," she said anyways. "I think we might." She fidgeted a little; Dax raised her head to look at her. "Don't give me that look."

"Don't wiggle so much." Dax propped her chin in her hand. "You okay?"

"Should we talk about it?" Juliet asked, before she could lose her nerve. Dax raised an eyebrow at her; when nothing else was forthcoming, she sat up.

"What's to talk about?" Dax asked. "I love you. You love me. Right?"

"Right," Juliet said.

"And I want to be with you," Dax said. "And you want to be with me?"

"I do," Juliet said.

"Okay, so, we love each other, and we want to be with each other," Dax said. She smiled. "So, we'll love each other, and we'll be together."

Juliet watched Dax's face hesitantly for a moment before she felt the corners of her own mouth turn up, without her even needing to tell them to. "Really?"

"Really. Look, Jules-" and here Dax reached out and picked up Juliet's hand, "-I love you. Really. I'm- I thought you might've- but then I was worried I was misreading it. Because. Because, you know,

I've done that before. But when you… I don't know." She kept her eyes down, focusing on the way Juliet's fingers moved under hers. "I'm glad. I don't want to do anything to fuck this up."

"If you haven't by now, Daksha-"

"Come *on*, with the 'Daksha'-"

"Then I don't think you will," Juliet said. Joy was cloudlike in her head, filling every empty space and every spare thought until it occupied her entire mind. She pulled Dax's hand up to her mouth and kissed the back of it. Dax leaned forward until their foreheads were pressed together.

"You need a shower," Dax said softly. Juliet laughed.

"We both need a shower," Juliet replied. She kissed Dax once before wriggling away and sliding off the roof.

Dax as a girlfriend was about the same as Dax as a best friend, just with drastically more kissing and slightly more hand-holding. The two of them took to New Orleans that day with renewed vigor; the city was full of experiences waiting to be had, and more than a week's worth of adventures to have. With no jobs restricting them while they were in Louisiana, each day had something new to do, something fun to try. One day it was Frenchmen Street, exploring the flea markets, the vintage boutiques, and jazz bistros by day and hopping from one nightclub to another once the sun set. The next day it was Royal Street; the day after that, Jackson Square. The French Quarter got a lot of their attention, and nightclubs became Dax's new favorite activity.

The thing about New Orleans was that every day could bring a new experience, even if they visited the same place they had been at just the day before. Juliet found herself bringing Dax back to venues they had already been to just to see if she could get Dax to smile in a different way, if they could kiss in a different corner, if they could find a new dance to learn together.

As thrilling as New Orleans was, Dax was tenfold. Every beam of sunlight that struck her face, every syllable of sound that came out of her mouth, every brush of fingertips that touched Juliet's body; every inch of her was intoxicating. It enhanced New Orleans to the point where she returned to the van overstimulated every night. Juliet's memories of her days were oversaturated with color and sound and touch, with smells she could barely catalogue and sights she could hardly make sense of. In the center of every memory was

Dax, charming as ever, painted in excruciating detail, and damned if Juliet didn't mind at all. She loved her; nothing else mattered.

"Hey," Dax whispered. Juliet's head was pillowed on Dax's chest, and she was already well on her way to sleep. The sky above New Orleans had less stars than some of their other stops had had, but there were still enough that, when Juliet opened her eyes, it looked like the sky behind Dax's head was freckled.

"What's up?" Juliet asked. She sat up, rubbing at her eyes, yawning and stretching. Dax inched up beside her, arms around her knees, drawing her legs to her chest. Her head was turned up, her hair trailing loosely down her back. Juliet followed her gaze and found herself staring at the moon, and realized, abruptly, that she was about to lose everything New Orleans had been giving her for the past couple of weeks.

"I saw it," Dax told her, and Juliet pressed the heels of her hands against her eyes and exhaled quietly.

"What'd you see?" Juliet asked. Dax reached out, and Juliet scooted closer, letting Dax drape her arm across her shoulders.

"It was, like, seven orange lights, little globes, and they all moved in formation," Dax said, showing Juliet the movement with her free hand, sending it soaring through the air. "Like that, see? They kept changing around, moving around. It was *so* cool."

"It sounds cool," Juliet said around a yawn. "What do you think?"

"What do I think about what?" Dax asked, still looking up at the sky. She turned her attention to Juliet after a moment.

"Does that mean it's time to leave New Orleans already?" Juliet clarified. Dax studied Juliet's face for another long moment before looking back up at the sky.

"I think so," Dax said. "Plus, you know, we need to get back to making money. Can't live off our savings forever."

"Definitely can't do that," Juliet murmured. She yawned again. "Alright, we'll find somewhere new to go in the morning. Somewhere with more jobs and more stars. Yeah?"

"Sounds good to me," Dax agreed. She helped Juliet down into the back of the van, piling her up with the pillows and blankets they had loaded up on the roof. Juliet buried her face in her arms, underneath the quilt half-laid over her head. Dax climbed in behind her, digging underneath the heap of covers to wrap her arms around

Juliet from behind.

"Did you like New Orleans?" Dax asked softly. Juliet turned her head enough that Dax could press her mouth to her cheek.

"Yes," Juliet said. She dropped her head back down so Dax could bury her face in the back of her neck. Dax exhaled steadily, breath warm on the knobs of Juliet's spine, and Juliet reached up to hold her hands against her waist.

"I'm glad," Dax said. She was silent. "Did you want to stay longer?"

Juliet felt the honesty in her question; that she would listen to whatever answer Juliet gave. She remembered what Dax had said to her, about finding a place she wanted to live forever, and a lifestyle she wanted to keep for the rest of her life. She recalled her own thoughts at the time, her own process of trying to find what it was she was looking for. With Dax wrapped around her, it felt almost right; it was New Orleans that felt wrong. No jobs tied them here; nothing felt stable in this shimmering city, filled with music Juliet loved to listen to, colors she craved to see, sunshine that she wanted to soak up, but no life that she wanted to live.

"No," Juliet answered. The last couple of weeks were stark in her memory, burnt and embossed around the edges, permanent. November was wearing thin; it felt wrong to not be in cold weather. She was ready to move on. "No, I think I'm ready to go. Are you?"

"I am," Dax replied. She pressed in closer, hands tightening their grip, one leg slung around Juliet's. She relaxed and let Juliet lead her into sleep.

Juliet woke up when the van hit a pothole and cracked unevenly back down onto the pavement. She shot up, flinching back when the sun hit her full in the face, and Dax laughed at her, eyes bright in the rearview mirror.

"Chill out, Nosferatu," Dax teased. She threw a paper bag into the back with Juliet. "I got you some treats."

Juliet dug through the bag, pulling out a lemon-lime sports drink, a new hormone prescription, and a cheap pair of sunglasses from the drugstore. She glanced up at Dax.

"We accidentally left our sunglasses on the roof," Dax explained. "They're gone now."

Juliet gave herself her injection before climbing up into the front seat, yawning and grabbing spearmint gum. Dax had a new pair of sunglasses perched on her long nose and two nicotine patches near the knob of her right wrist. "Gold is your color."

"Thanks, babe," Juliet said, and Dax shoved her, smiling. Juliet cranked her window down and let the wind smack at her cheeks to wake her up. "Where are we going?"

"Let's just let the road take us," Dax said. "I've just been driving. I saw a sign for Pascagoula a little while ago, though. What do you think?"

"Where the hell is Pascagoula?" Juliet asked. Dax shrugged. An Internet search revealed Pascagoula to be a resident of Mississippi, and the site of a prominent alien abduction. "Pascagoula it is."

"Pascagoula it is!" Dax shouted into the wind. Jazz started filtering through the radio speakers; Juliet reached out and flicked the station to neo soul. Pascagoula was only a couple of hours away from New Orleans by rickety van, so Juliet leaned back and let Dax chatter, making up stories based around the few very new facts she had learned about the abduction in Pascagoula. She was only partway through a story about how Juliet would be put in a separate cage than her in the space zoo, but that she would break out anyways just to sleep in the same hay stack as her, when Juliet interrupted.

"Hey, maybe we should stay in a hotel in Pascagoula," Juliet said, and Dax broke off to give her a confused look.

"Why would we stay in a hotel?" Dax asked.

"A motel?" Juliet suggested. Dax frowned.

"We have a perfectly good van," Dax told her. "Why would we stay in a hotel?"

"Motel."

"Holiday Inn." Dax turned to smile at her. "No, really, though. I'm good with the van. Are you good with the van?"

Dax's teeth were white; her one dimple was deep. Juliet nodded, "Yeah, that's fine with me. I just thought I'd offer."

"Offer appreciated and kindly declined, I'm good in the back," Dax replied. Pascagoula was only a few miles ahead of that conversation, and they coasted into town on old-school hip-hop and Dax's delighted half-correct karaoke. On Juliet's insistence, they spent the day job-hunting; finding themselves positions in Mississippi was a trick in itself, but Juliet was able to finagle herself a position as a front desk clerk in a motel by three in the afternoon. She followed Dax around for the rest of the day until she found a job as an administrative assistant in an office.

"So, what's your office do?" Juliet asked, while Dax found them a diner for them to eat dinner at. A shrug was barely an answer, but was characteristic of Dax, who soon after insisted on cherry pie for dinner, with corn for strength.

Their RV park was fifteen minutes outside of town; Dax got them a spot to park near the water. The two of them took a walk around the park as the sun set, shoes abandoned in the van; their bare feet crunched against the gritty ground. Juliet stuck to the grass, hand wound in Dax's, whose soles were more calloused, and so she walked with more bravery than Juliet could muster. After Dax made Juliet take a picture of her with a sign that said "Indian Point," they headed back towards the water.

"What do you think of Pascagoula?" Juliet asked. Dax was sprawled out across the hood of the van; Juliet's legs were dunked in the water up to her shins.

"It's fine," Dax said. Her hair hung down to the bumper. "Lots of water. Not nearly enough aliens."

"Do you miss New Orleans?" Juliet asked. Dax hummed as she thought about her answer.

"Nah," Dax said. "It was time to move on. Bigger and better things." She banged herself on the chest with her fist and burped. "*Jesus.* Nice."

"My queen," Juliet said dryly, turning back to the water. It shimmered against her thighs, the sunset glistening off the backs of her wet hands and the water droplets on her kneecaps. She glanced up; the water's reflection seemed to make the violet sky fluid. She was looking forward to starting her work at the motel, but her chest still twinged. "Pascagoula would probably be hard to settle down in."

"For us? Yeah, probably," Dax said. She turned her phone off and dropped it into the grass. "You wanna make out?"

"Sure," Juliet said, standing and shaking the water off her legs. She let Dax pull her up onto the roof of the van to pass the time until they fell asleep. No aliens showed up on the first night.

Working at a motel in Pascagoula, Mississippi left much to be desired. It was a fine place to be, but as Thanksgiving loomed ever-closer, it felt wrong for the temperature to be seventy-degrees and the sky to be shining with hot sunlight. Everything felt too warm all the time, and her body's natural calendar being janked up ruined the rest of her body's nature. She knew she was in a funk by the time Dax came to pick her up, fingers ink-stained from a long day at an office that she probably hated.

"We don't have to stay in Pascagoula," Juliet told her, the second Dax shoved the passenger-side door open from the inside. Dax frowned at her.

"We just got here," Dax said. "We haven't seen any aliens. Give it a couple days, kid. It's a good place to be."

Even though they had already broken the seal on loving each other, Dax still had the ability to get her heart pounding with the simplest of things. Today, it was how beautiful she looked in the driver's seat, one penny-tan hand wrapped around the steering wheel, hair falling tangled over her shoulders and down her chest, sunglasses shining on her handsome face. She reached out and took Dax's free hand in hers.

"We'll stay," Juliet said.

"For a little while longer." Dax took a smooth turn into the parking lot of the new diner she had found for them to try. "At least. Maybe we'll get abducted."

"Sometimes I wonder if I haven't already been abducted by aliens," Juliet said, and Dax laughed at her, taking her hand on the walk into the restaurant. Dax had a bold attitude and a sense of bravery unequaled in Pascagoula; she held tight to Juliet's hand and kissed her on the cheek while they waited for their Shirley Temples. Being gutsy to the point of openly kissing your girlfriend-of-color in a diner in Mississippi was borderline lionhearted.

"I think the guy in the booth behind you is staring at us," Juliet said quietly, keeping her eyes down on their shared basket of fries. Dax looked over her shoulder, plucky as ever, and scoffed.

"It's because we look so good," Dax told her, moments before she shoved a handful of fries into her mouth. Juliet hesitated, then reached out to brush a lock of hair behind Dax's ear. Dax let her head fall into the curve of Juliet's palm; when she smiled, Juliet could feel it in her fingertips. It's not like they were staying long anyways.

Day three in Pascagoula had the same emotional effect on Juliet as days one and two; day four was more of the same. Working at the motel during the day was less than thrilling, but spending her nights hand-in-hand with Dax, letting themselves slow down after the adrenaline-fueled fast-paced weeks in New Orleans, was joy beyond measure. On the fourth night, sitting hand-in-hand with Dax on the tiny shore next to their van, their pants rolled up to the knees and their ankles resting in the water, she let herself lean over and kiss Dax softly.

"Because I can," Juliet said, before Dax could ask what it was for. "I don't want to waste any more time."

Dax's smile was still enough to get Juliet's blood boiling. The sunset in Pascagoula seemed subpar after that.

Dating Dax was as easy as being her best friend; traveling with her as a girlfriend was about the same as traveling with her as a friend, or as the stranger she used to be. Crossing the country with her partner had added an extra layer to everything, made everything seem that much better. Adding Dax permanently to the equation seemed like it pushed her just that much closer to landing the life that she wanted, that Dax always talked about lately. Her whole life should have been perfect: she wasn't trapped in Big Bay, she was on the road discovering herself. She knew what she wanted to do for a job; she knew that she loved Dax, and she got to spend all of her time with her. She texted Dorian and Angelo as much; Angelo called her within minutes.

"What's up?" Juliet said, standing up and walking a ways away. Dax was half-asleep in the grass, fingertips trailing in the water.

"Hey, sis," Angelo said, voice crackling on the other end. "Mom and Dad say hi. Enzo says hey."

"Hi to everyone," Juliet said. "I miss you guys."

"We miss you, too." Angelo was quiet for a minute. "Jules, I think you're not happy-"

"I'm *happy*, Angel-"

"Let me finish, man. I think you're not happy because you're not at home."

Juliet stopped. She frowned. "What do you mean?"

"I mean. You don't *have* to come back to Big Bay. I mean, I'm leaving for school next year, so I'll be in Massachusetts in the fall. Enzo's tossed around the idea of coming with me. And we-"

"Alright, yeah, focus, what do you mean?" Juliet interrupted. Angelo huffed a laugh.

"I *mean* that you've always liked to be at home," Angelo explained. "You're a homebody. And that's not a bad thing! That's not at *all* a bad thing. You just aren't made to be away from home for

190

very long. Based on everything you said, man, I think you just want to be home. No matter where that home is. Or, you want to *make* a home, instead, I guess."

Juliet sat down in the grass by the little putt-putt golf station in the RV park. The shorn grass and dew prickled at her bare legs. Angelo was quiet, letting her think. Her brain rushed without coherence, thinking of more pictures and scenarios than it was saying words, before it settled to a stop.

"I think you're right," Juliet said softly. She could almost see Angelo nodding on the other side of the phone.

"So, I don't know." It sounded like he took a sip of something. "Ask her if she wants to get a place somewhere. Maybe she wants to settle down, too."

Juliet glanced back at Dax, who had sat up fully, waking up enough to start braiding plucked blades of grass into a crown. "I don't think she knows what she wants," she admitted. She heard a meow through the phone. "Hi, Lady Eloise."

"Say 'hi' to Aunt Juliet, baby girl," Angelo said happily, and Juliet let the conversation drift away towards less drastic topics, listening to Angelo play with his cat and talk about the new recipes he was trying for Thanksgiving in the next week. By the time the sun was fully set, Angelo was all talked out, and Juliet was curled up on her side in the grass, phone tucked between her shoulder and her ear.

"I'll text you tomorrow," Juliet promised. Angelo yawned for a long time before saying his goodnights and hanging up.

"What did Gio want?" Dax asked, settling one of her two grass crowns on Juliet's head carefully. Juliet picked up the other one and placed it on Dax's head.

"Just wanted to chat," Juliet said. "He let me talk to Lady Eloise."

"And how is our favorite cat?" Dax asked, and like that, they were back to normal, no edge to anything. Juliet's pulse slowed back to a reasonable pace. The doubt wriggled in the back of her mind, the sensation that she now knew meant that she wanted a *home*. She watched Dax as she picked up Juliet's hands and played with her fingers, running the pad of her thumb over the knobs of her knuckles. She exhaled shakily.

"You okay?" Dax asked. She stood, pulling Juliet with her.

"I just miss home," Juliet confessed. Dax reached up, letting her hand settle on the back of Juliet's head. Juliet allowed herself to be led into bending down enough for Dax to kiss her on the forehead.

"We'll visit soon," was all she said, before leading Juliet up to the roof of the van. Juliet shut her eyes soon after; waiting for aliens to come to Pascagoula held very minimal appeal for her that night.

"Hey," Juliet said, the next night after work, as they sat in the first diner for the third time. Dax looked up from her spaghetti, tomato sauce in the corner of her mouth. Juliet reached out and thumbed it away.

"Hey, kid," Dax said back. "What's on your mind? You've been quiet all day, you finally gonna spill your beans?"

Juliet pushed her fries around with her coffee spoon a little more. The salt dissolved against the lukewarm coffee remnants in the guts of the spoon. "I'm just worried."

"About what?"

Juliet watched Dax slurp up one noodle, then another. She grinned, scooping up a forkful of pasta and holding it out. Juliet smiled and leaned in to take it; the responding look of joy on Dax's face was enough to squash Juliet's fears for the time being.

"I'll get over it," Juliet said. Dax eyed her for a moment before pulling her plate back to her side and continuing to shovel spaghetti into her mouth. She caught Dax watching her at odd moments throughout the rest of the night, giving her the side-eye at the old movie they caught in town, throwing her a glance now and then as they drove back to the RV park and she thought Juliet wasn't looking.

"Why don't we do a lookout tonight?" Dax suggested, when Juliet was starting to doze off with her feet in the water, their new nightly ritual from the last week of Pascagoulan life. "I have a good feeling about it."

"You have a good feeling every night," Juliet said, but she could feel the edge that had returned to Dax; she wondered if she ought to call the motel now and let them know she would be heading out in a day or two. Dax's flighty nature was starting to settle like a block of ice in the pit of Juliet's chest, a cold weight that refused to melt away. Juliet let Dax pull her up to the roof and wrap her up in blankets and arms, nestling into her chest and relaxing. Juliet reclined to the best of her ability until she got exhausted enough to curl up on her side, one arm thrown across Dax's chest. Dax stroked her hair back from her face absently with tired fingers until she fell asleep.

"Jules," Dax whispered, somewhere in the drowsy haze, and Juliet blinked, squinted, and pushed her face into Dax's hair; she laughed. "*Juliet.*"

"*What*, Dax?" Juliet groaned, and Dax wriggled around to kiss her forehead.

"I saw them," Dax whispered. Juliet's heart did a jump-skip, her brain logging on so quickly that sleep instantly seemed like a long-forgotten pastime.

"Are we leaving Pascagoula tomorrow?" Juliet asked. Dax hesitated.

"Do you want to?" Dax asked in return. Juliet shrugged.

"No reason to stay if you saw them," Juliet said. "Pascagoula doesn't have much here. We're not even staying in town. Where do you want to go next? Maybe-"

"I looked it up," Dax interrupted. Juliet pulled back, propping herself up on her elbow. "There's a city called Madison three hours north of here, near Jackson."

"That's the capital," Juliet said.

"If you know one thing, it's your state capitals," Dax laughed. Juliet had to kiss her for it.

"Alright, we'll go to Madison," Juliet conceded. "What's in Madison?"

"For one thing, people," Dax answered. "For another, there's been sightings of disc-shaped UFOs. Nothing like getting back to the classics, am I right?"

"You're not wrong," Juliet said. Dax pressed a hard kiss to her forehead, her nose, her chin, the scar on her cheek. Juliet bowed under the attention and eventually fell back into sleep.

Saying her goodbyes to Pascagoula wasn't hard, not when there was nobody she felt attached to and the town itself had hardly even housed them. Driving up to Madison took four hours with the lunch break Dax insisted on taking in the middle of it, setting up a picnic outside a rest stop. Her avoidance of anything Juliet wanted to talk about was starting to grate, though; she wondered if maybe Dax had heard her talking to Angelo. She may not have needed to, though; in the almost-a-year since they had met, Dax and Juliet had gotten fairly adept at reading one another.

In any case, Dax had taken to skating around serious topics and only allowing lighthearted discussions to take place in any lengthy capacity. Most of her talking was rambling, telling stories and discussing nothing, just making noises for Juliet to half-listen to. Anytime Juliet had an expression that Dax's flighty soul must have deemed to be 'too much,' she skirted around the issue and hopped right back into a debate of which superheroes would be best placed on their heist team, Jules, what do *you* think? It itched under Juliet's skin after a while.

Madison was a beautiful Dixie city, filled with greens that probably never died in the eternal summer that was the southern United States. Everything seemed to be getting on Juliet's nerves, though, in the neat little town; the grass was *too* bright, the sky was *too* sunny, the people were *too* nice. Everything felt like a continuous dull razor that she couldn't shake off, and Dax's manic energy seemed to feed off of her frustration.

"Hey, maybe we could go for a walk, or catch a movie? Find a baseball, play a game?" Dax suggested, barely pausing for a response. The more irritable Juliet got, the more Dax seemed to talk.

"Dax, please, I just-" Juliet began, then stopped, dropping her head into her hands. "I just want to be home."

"You *are* home," Dax said softly. The campground they were parked in, just outside of Madison, was crisp around them in the nighttime. A cricket chirped in the distance; it frayed one of Juliet's last nerves.

"I think I'm gonna go to bed," Juliet said, hopping off the hood of the van and heading into the back. She bundled herself up in her blankets and turned her face towards the wall, trying not to cry. She *wanted* to be with Dax; she *wanted* to keep seeing her, kissing her, spending her days with her. She even wanted to keep traveling with her, someday. It was just, *today*, she wanted to put down roots. Angelo was right: she wanted to be at home, and home, for her, meant settling down. There was always more time to travel; she needed a base.

Once she got her feelings for Dax out in the open, Juliet had thought everything would be a thousand times better - and, in a way, it had been. Everything was more engaging, the world brighter, the sweetness stronger. Her life with Dax had only gotten better; her adventure on the road had gotten more fun. With it, though, the edge had gotten sharper, and the longing more acute. She had realized it was because she had gotten a taste of what she wanted - life with Dax - but not the whole thing. She only had half of what she wanted. Dax might have wanted something bigger than herself, but Juliet only wanted Dax and a home. It wasn't too much to want, she had thought.

Was settling down giving up? she thought. Had she come all this way just to give up? *No*, she thought. She had left Big Bay; she had traveled for nearly a year with someone who had been a stranger when it all started. She had trusted her gut, and she had found herself along the way, which was all that she had really wanted. She had found the happiness she had sought, as well as the person she had wanted to be *and* the person she wanted to be with. It was nearly perfect. She wanted-

She wanted to stop running, to take a breath, to put down roots, and, *God*, she wanted all that with Dax by her side. *Does Dax want me?*

"Hey," Dax murmured, startling Juliet out of her hazy thoughts. "Are you mad at me?"

"No, Daksha," Juliet whispered back. She stared hard at the dark window before turning onto her back in surrender. "Hey."

"Hey." Dax crawled forward, shutting the van doors behind her and flicking on the van light above their heads. "Hey, Jules."

"I want to stop," Juliet said, without hesitation. Dax froze in place, staring at her. "I want to stop driving. I want to stop- I don't know, looking for aliens, I mean, I guess. Maybe we can stay in Madison, maybe not? We can find somewhere. There's so many different places we'd be happy, Dax." She received no answer. "Well? Is that something you'd want? To stop?"

"Hell, no, of course not," Dax said, and Juliet sat up. Her chest felt hard, like the ice had expanded; she felt her own face shutter down. Dax frowned. "Don't you think that's a terrible idea? We've been doing *so* well, Jules. I don't want to fuck that up."

"Well, I-"

"I don't think we've found it yet," Dax said. "Something bigger. Remember when we talked about that? About something bigger?"

"Daksha," Juliet said softly. Dax's mouth clicked shut. "I can't keep doing this."

"What do you mean?" Dax said. Juliet's pulse throbbed in her throat, her wrists, her chest. She felt sick.

"I can't keep doing this," Juliet repeated. "I love you, but it's not enough. I just keep thinking about it. You *know* that I've been thinking about it."

Dax stared at her. Her face crumpled; she looked away. "Yeah. Yeah, I know you have been. I just thought… I thought if we kept going, you know, you'd keep having fun. You wouldn't think about it for that long."

"But I want it with *you*, Dax," Juliet said. Dax, her face still turned away, exhaled shakily. "I want to settle down with *you*. Don't you want that? We can get a nice place together, we can-"

"I'm not like you," Dax spat, and Juliet backed up on instinct. "I'm not- I can't just- My- I *don't*-"

"It's fine," Juliet said. She swallowed. It wasn't easy. "It's fine, Dax." She pulled out her phone and checked the time. "You know what?"

"What?" Dax asked, voice almost at a tremble. The way she held it back from reaching that breaking point was impressive, Juliet thought. She felt she was at a breaking point herself.

"I can't keep going," Juliet said. Her own voice was small. Dax squeezed her eyes shut; her face grew red, eyelashes wet. Juliet wrapped her arms around herself. "I can't. It's not fair. We haven't found anything-"

"It's not about the fucking aliens, Juliet," Dax cut her off. "It's not *about* that. It's about finding something bigger than us."

"I don't need something bigger than myself," Juliet said quietly. "The whole world is bigger than me. I've seen a lot of it. Maybe I'll see some more someday. But, right now, I found *me*. Do you know what I mean? I found *me* on this trip. And I found *you*. And I think… I think that's all I needed."

"Then why isn't it enough?" Dax whispered. Juliet hesitantly reached out, letting her hand soften to cup Dax's face. Dax pressed down into her palm, wetting her fingertips. Tears rolled down to Juliet's wrist.

"It's more than enough," Juliet said. "But part of me is that I want a home. And I don't think you know what that part of you wants yet."

"Can't we keep going until we find out?" Dax asked. Juliet wanted so badly to say yes.

"No," she said instead. "At least, I can't. It hurts too much, to know what I want to do and who I want to be and not to be that person. That's been the whole point of this, hasn't it?"

"I don't know what the whole point is anymore," Dax confessed. "I don't. I feel…" She exhaled harshly. "I don't know how I feel."

"Me, neither," Juliet admitted. "But I want to go home."

"To Big Bay?" Dax asked. Juliet hesitated, for a split second, but she shook her head.

"No, I don't…" She thought, for a moment. "I think I'll go to Vermont. I miss the winter. I want to make myself a home. I want to be *myself*, Dax. But you…"

"I love you," Dax hiccupped. Juliet stopped holding herself back and reached out, and Dax folded in against her, crying against her chest. Juliet stroked her fingers through her hair.

"I love you," Juliet whispered against the crown of her head. "I'm going to Vermont. You come find me when you're all done."

Dax shook her head, hard, and pulled back. "You can't go."

"I have to go."

"*No*," Dax said forcefully. "No, you *can't*. I finally- I can't-"

"I'm taking a page out of your book," Juliet said, "and I'm just going to do it. I'm going to- I'm going to Vermont."

"No," Dax said, softer this time. "Juliet, please."

"Come find me when you're all done," Juliet repeated. She drew Dax in and kissed her, getting a harsh kiss back in return, teeth on her lip, salt in her mouth. She realized she had started crying, as well. "I love you."

"I love you," Dax said. Juliet inched away from her. Dax sat in silence as Juliet packed as much as she could into two of her bags and kicked the back door of the van open. She felt regret heavy in her heart before she was even far enough away to have lost Dax's face in the darkness, but she knew the regret she would feel if she stayed would be far heavier, too much for her to bear. She wanted to have faith that Dax would run after her, maybe; she wanted to believe she would get to Vermont and Dax would be waiting for her. She wanted to think her life would turn out how she wanted. She wanted, she wanted, she wanted, but the puzzle pieces were scattered, of her own doing, and she cried the entire walk to the bus station.

Chapter Eighteen

Leaving Madison was a lot like leaving Big Bay had been. Abandoning the life she had known up until that point, those people that she loved, wrenched her heart as much the second time as it did the first; even more painful was the knowledge that those she left behind didn't want her to go, this time. As she sat on the bus to Memphis for three hours, rattling over a highway that felt empty without contemporary music blasting from a shitty radio and her best friend by her side, she only had time to think about what she had done. Her decision had not yet settled in her mind, and her breath felt watery inside of her; her face still burned hot, her eyes and nose prickling regularly. She kept her head down and her phone tucked away inside her bag.

Reaching Memphis was a hell in itself. She had chosen it on some sort of whim, and, when she picked up her phone and cleared her messages without looking at them before opening her Internet browser, she found out that Memphis had some reported UFO sightings. The same old shit that she had been dedicating her life to for nearly a year now, with the added bitter edge that she was doing it alone. She checked herself into the first cheap motel she could find, but the bed felt empty and hard instead of comfortable, like she had expected it to be; she found herself wanting the mattress in the back of the van instead, with a warm body against hers. She punched the pillows until they were almost shaped like Dax, and slept fitfully.

She roamed Memphis the next day like a ghost, barely talking to anyone, trying to rearrange her place in the world. One thing she and

Angelo had missed out on when painting the portrait of herself was that she hated being alone. Memphis had so much to offer someone who was willing to give it the time of day, but Juliet was completely unwilling. Traveling by herself had no spark to it. She talked to locals, hoping to find a connection to help her make it through the day. She had good conversations, but nothing that settled warm inside of her. She ended up at the train station before the sun had even set, her bags looped around her shoulders, scanning the schedule for a ride to Vermont.

While she waited for the train to Montpelier, she took up a bench outside, half-watching the clear night sky above the city. Someone nearby was playing a keyboard; the faint electronic sounds of it trickled through Juliet's head without settling. She realized, long after she had started doing it, that she was waiting for a UFO to show itself above Memphis, for an alien to abduct her. She realized even longer after that that there were never going to be aliens; it was always going to be Dax.

Juliet craved the pattern of their road trip, the stability of having a goal; it was something she had always needed. It was the reason she went to college, the reason she worked a job in almost every city she had been to, the reason she had wanted to keep Dax around in the first place, before she had actually started to like her. She wanted a goal, and she had one: *find herself.* Herself having been found, though, she had set her sights on the next goal: Dax. Once that was achieved, her next and final goal was to settle down. None of her goals had ever involved a UFO, or an alien, beyond the fact that that was what Dax had been looking for. It had never been about the aliens; no UFOs were coming to visit her, no abduction was happening. It was *Dax.*

It was Dax making the road trip matter, because she didn't want Juliet to leave. It was Dax who made up story after story about UFOs, because she wanted to give Juliet the road trip she thought she was craving. It was Dax who built their maps, Dax who drove them across the country, Dax who had loved her enough to create this adventure with her, Dax who trusted her enough to let her go when she said she was done. It was Dax that Juliet wanted to go back to, and it was Dax who she was missing right then. Juliet had no idea where Dax had gone; in fact, she barely had any idea where she, herself, was. She wanted to text Dax, or to call her, to tell her that she might understand what was happening, but Dax needed the same thing Juliet had had the privilege of obtaining: an understanding of herself, first.

If she wants to find me, Juliet thought to herself, as the Montpelier train rumbled into the station, *she will. I told her where I was going. She'll find me.*

Faith was a powerful thing, when it was faith in another person; Juliet's faith in Dax and in herself took her from Memphis to Montpelier, the majority of a day taken up by train travel and obsessive thinking. More than once she pulled out her phone, and more than once she put it away, fearing the very probable outcome in which she said the wrong thing and ruined things even further. She had lost her grip on what she was doing with Dax, and, in its absence, clung more tightly to what she knew she wanted for herself.

She arrived in Montpelier late in the evening, nearly at night, and found herself a bed-and-breakfast to stay at near the train station with the money she had stuffed in her bag. Another fitful night of sleep brought about another unsettled day, but Juliet felt almost at home in the snow that stacked up high in the capital city. She asked the innkeeper for a job, anything they had. Vermont was kind to her, as was the manager of the bed-and-breakfast, because she found herself working as a waitress in the little breakfast kitchen they kept. The days were busy; travelers and Vermonters alike kept the diner alive, bustling in and out at all hours for pancakes and eggs, giving her smiles and tips and, memorably, one hug from an elderly lady who insisted they both needed it.

The nights were less full; they gave Juliet too much time to think, to wonder if she should call Dax, to wonder why Dax had not called *her*, if maybe Dax wanted nothing to do with her. She had already called Angelo and told her family where she was; they were happy, if for no other reason than she was close to where her brothers would be in less than a year's time. She smiled and laughed for them and cried when she hung up the phone.

Spending each of her days without someone to pick her up, someone to have dinner with, someone to go to bed with was hard enough when she had had a taste of sharing her life with someone. When that someone was Dax, it left a specific hole in her life. She was aching from the empty space, from every moment she had turned to speak to Dax and instead wound up with words dying in her mouth. She felt her loneliness acutely; she felt the absence like an open wound. Her face ached; her chest was sore. She spent a great deal of time reaching up to touch her lion's head necklace, to remind herself that Dax had even existed at all.

Thanksgiving was quick to arrive, and the bed-and-breakfast stayed open that third Thursday in November. Juliet kept busy cleaning in the dishroom before one of her fellow waiters left due to illness and she got called out to work in the dining hall. She splashed her face in the sink before heading out; the innkeeper, who was kind to her, had the name Jane, and constantly lost her pencils, squeezed her arm before sending her to the floor.

Faces tended to blend together lately; she had served more than one table that seemed like it had the same families sitting at it. She was only halfway through her blurred shift when Jane beckoned for her to join her at the hosting stand.

"What can I do for you?" Juliet asked politely. Jane glanced over her shoulder, and Juliet frowned.

"There's a young lady outside just leaning against her van," Jane told her, and Juliet's heart leapt into her throat. "I don't mind terribly, but a couple people have been watching her and I don't want her to scare anyone off. Invite her in, won't you? Maybe she's hungry."

"Okay," Juliet said. She wondered, somewhere in the back of her mind, if maybe she was desperate for immediately assuming it would be Dax; that part of her quieted as soon as Juliet turned and found Dax outside the bed-and-breakfast, grinning away, sunglasses pushing her hair away from her face. Juliet kept her pace even through the tables and out the door, but once she was outside, she broke into a run. Dax pushed away from the van and opened her arms, and Juliet dropped into them, burying her face in Dax's shoulder.

"I've missed you so much," Juliet said in a rush. Dax squeezed her, holding her close, standing on her toes to better embrace her. Juliet was still bent over, but the crick in her spine meant nothing when compared to how happy she was and to the adrenaline coursing through her veins. The ice in her chest warmed and began to melt, loosening the tightness and weight that had been pressing against her ribs her since Pascagoula.

"I missed you," Dax murmured into Juliet's throat. Juliet

pulled back enough for Dax to grab her face and yank her in to kiss deeply. When they separated to breathe, Dax said, "I think I know what you meant."

"By what?" Juliet asked. Her breath was short. She stepped back six inches, and it still felt like too much.

"I stayed in Madison for another day," Dax told her, "before I left. But I had a lot of time to think, and I thought… I thought I've been looking for something bigger than myself. But what you said, that you were only looking for yourself, that got me thinking. I thought… that maybe I thought I was looking for something bigger than myself, but maybe I just thought that 'myself' wasn't big enough yet, you know? Does that make sense?"

"It does," Juliet said, "because it's you."

Dax smiled. "You get me."

"Forever, I hope," Juliet said back. Dax kissed her again.

"So, I left Madison," Dax continued. "And I drove here."

"How did you find me?" Juliet asked, and Dax laughed.

"Montpelier," Dax said. "It's the capital of Vermont. And it's a bed-and-breakfast, *right* next to the train station. I *know* you, Jules."

"You do," Juliet said, happy. Dax kissed her again.

"Anyways, I was driving, and I was thinking, I didn't feel like I should be putting down roots, because I've never really had a reason to, you know? But maybe… Jules, maybe you're all the reason I need." Dax looked down at her shoes; Juliet reached out and tipped her chin up. They made eye contact. "Maybe I've always been running from something without knowing what I was running to. And maybe I was running to *you* all along."

"Daksha, I fucking-" Juliet managed to get out before Dax was kissing her again, yanking her down to her height. Jane let Juliet off her shift, probably to ensure less tongue on her property, and it took only five minutes of debate for Juliet to convince Dax to stay in the bed-and-breakfast with her instead of in the van. Dax cleaned at the bed-and-breakfast freelance under Jane's watchful eye for a little while; only for a week or so, definitely less than two. Everything was a haze to Juliet, who had finally found what she had left Big Bay to find.

"You know," Dax said, in early December, "I heard that Bennington has had stories of a UFO sighting. Maybe we could go check that out." When Juliet glanced at her, a frown creasing the space between her eyes, Dax smiled. "There's also a nice house I thought we could check out while we were there."

Bennington settled inside of Juliet's bones like nowhere else had; not Big Bay, not Snowflake, not even McMinnville. The snow, the streets, the buildings - they all had an unerring sense of rightness to them that she held tight to. Juliet found herself a position at the bed-and-breakfast in town, working as an assistant manager; Dax found herself as a dance instructor downtown. Their house was small, but wonderfully so, and the van found its home in the garage next to two beat-up old motorcycles that Dax had started fixing up.

Dax brought Juliet outside when it was close to Christmas, when the snow had stopped falling and the sun was finally gone, to the flattest part of their roof to look up at the sky. She cleared the snow from their section of the roof and wrapped Juliet up in gloves and hats and blankets. The stars twinkled far above them.

"I think the aliens might abduct us from here," Dax told her.

"Yeah?" Juliet asked. She was on her phone, looking up places in Maine near the coast (since she had still never seen the ocean) that had reported alien sightings when Dax took the device from her and pocketed it.

"Focus, Alva. I'm spinning a yarn," Dax said. Juliet tucked her head under Dax's chin and listened, letting the cadences of Dax's voice carry her. She settled there, against Dax's chest, their hands wrapped up together, Vermont wrapped around them, the sky stretched above them. A star rocketed by, or perhaps a comet; Dax pointed it out to her.

"I see it," Juliet said. She craned her neck back. "I love you."

"I love you," Dax murmured, pressing a kiss to her forehead, her nose, the scar on her cheek, her chin. Her lips. Juliet sighed; heat-vapor came out of both of their mouths into the cold air. Dax fidgeted, only slightly, still restless in Bennington. Juliet wondered, deep in the back of her thoughts, how much further they still had to go.

NICOLE MELLO

ABOUT THE AUTHOR

Nicole Mello is a young woman living in Massachusetts. She has been writing since before her memory systems were functional, and reading even longer. She credits the influences of her family, her friends, and her favorite stories for pathing the way to her first novel. She likes space, history, movies, and dogs, and uses comedy as a form of defense. She looks forward to continuing to fill the world with her novels about women, minorities, queer people, space, or any combination of the four. She works as a writer with Backpack Digital and encourages both discovering yourself and adventuring throughout this wonderful world we all share. She would like you to know that it is never too early or too late to make yourself happy.